HEART

AND

HOME

ALVIN L.A. HORN

SHOUT OUTS FROM THE LITERAY WORLD

As the war winds down, Master Sergeant Sirletto Preer finds himself navigating through the shadows of a small French town. Although serving his country, as a black man in 1940, he finds himself having to move through the shadows. Not only is he facing the usual dangers of war, he's fighting the underlying horrors of racism and inequalities. Black men are banned from visiting the U.S. sanctioned brothels, but when MSG Preer meets an intriguing woman and falls in love, he faces battles he never imagined as he gives his all to protect his love. Armed with his intellect, leadership skills and his keen sense of morality, he's able to infiltrate and risk all for the woman of his dreams.

Alvin L. A. Horn has spun a masterful love story. He spins his characters richly, colorfully and sensually! HEART & HOME by Alvin L. A. Horn will take you on a journey that will excite you in unexpected ways. Awesome work, Mr. Horn!

B. Berry
Author of CLOTHESLINE BLUES

Thought provoking. Raw. Sheer poetry. Horn's writing will take up and down the Pacific Coast line and more. Heart-stopping, jaw dropping and definitely an author you need to look out for. Flawed characters, realistic situations and touching real-life moments, his books will definitely leave you thinking after you put them down.

Johnathan Royal
founder of Books, Beauty and Stuff

✤✤✤

Alvin L. Horn is a genius writer. His writings are poetry, a melody intro for a sensual, erotic thriller that leaves you wondering if you were there in the flesh—one of the characters. Alvin's poetry is just as poignant...tender, emotional, thoughtful, and erotic. I'm a true fan of this brother. I'd read anything he wrote. I'm looking forward to reading his works.

Bestselling Suzetta Perkins,
Author of Two Down: The Inconvenient Truth and Hollywood Skye.

✤✤✤

There is always anticipation when this author releases a new novel because there are no disappointments in his books. Strong energetic characters placed throughout multi-layered storylines are what you expect, and this writer delivers. Turning pages to this novel, I encountered a mix of characters of mental, physical variations. This novel is a must read!

Alvin L.A. Horn keeps you on the edge of what is going to happen with everything is tied situations laced in of deceit, realistic mayhem and secrets and social commentary through dealings and dialogues. I love the vengeance based on sentimental and moral justice. I highly recommend this book to those who love literature you learn and expand one's reasoning.

The writings in his novels are highly enjoyable and unexpected with descriptive narratives each time with absorbing smells, noise, and silence, makes one feel the potential despair or hopefulness. Alvin L.A. Horn's novels are on par with the best writers of our times with superbly written strengths, and human weaknesses.

Attorney Corey Minor Smith,
Canton City Council at Large Canton, OH

❦ ❦ ❦

"Alvin L.A. Horn transports the reader into the past through this intricate and well-written tale. Another unique and gripping storyline from this master novelist. Bravo, Sir."

Justina Wheelock,
Author of Knight Moves

Dear Reader,

A word from Romantic Blues Publishing:

What a pleasure to share with you, timeless characters, in this historical fiction. HEART & HOME is set during the World War II era, but not set to dates of factual engagements. This novel is an emotionally moving, tangled web of the mysterious unknowns while the characters try to hold on to unpredictable love, life, and liberty.

Within the pages of this novel you'll experience the timely music from the greats of that era – (Ray Charles, Cab Callaway, Muddy Waters, and Storefront Gospel.) You'll inhale the scents of campfire coffee, the sweat of fear, and the sweet perfume of Leena Horne. Travel back to the fashion time of the Dandridge Sisters, Italian cut hair styles, layers, and sensual dresses that expose shoulders yet come to the knees. Discover the dialect of that period. Become familiar with historical names and situations leading up to the 1940s.

HEART & HOME is a historical romance that shines bright on deep passionate love while giving hope for the future, as we peer back in history and often dreary narrations of our past. Between the covers, you become aware of the history of the American Black man and woman. Their joys and their pain. In this novel we go back and experience how our relatives before us lived through the triumphs and failures of that time. Known as Colored people and Negros, sometimes worse, they paved the way for us to thrive under most anything that we face today.

Heart& Home – inspirations for this novel:

Andrew Glasper, Veteran of World War Two – my grandfather, who told me about being in the service in France before integration in such a matter of fact way of speaking of, that was just the way it was.

James Alexander, Veteran of the Vietnam War – my uncle, who left for the war and came home to experience his personal world changed mentally, physically, and emotionally for life.

Robert Alexander, Veteran of the Army – my brother, who was stationed in Germany. While stationed, he received news from back home that he had to come home. No one should receive an ASAP message while away serving your country.

To every man and woman who faced any amount of racism – poor treatment because of their race in the Armed Services, I salute you.

As always, thanks to the supporters of the efforts of Romantic Blues Publishing. We strive to bring you fresh and ground-breaking stories that will help you escape reality when life seems overwhelming, or for when we just want to visit another time and place. We appreciate the love and dedication of our readers.

Previous works by Alvin L.A. Horn

The World That Fell Into My Dresser Drawer,
a book of poetry, 2001

BRUSH STROKES,
a novel, 2005,
a novel, published Romantic Blues Publishing

V

PERFECT CIRCLE,

a novel published by Zane and Simon and Schuster, 2012

ONE SAFE PLACE,

a novel published by Zane and Simon and Schuster, 2014

BRUSH STROKES,

the re-release, with an added short story, 2016

BAD BEFORE GOOD& THOSE IN BETWEEN,

a novel 2017

All are available in paperback and E-book

Alvin is also a contributing author in the anthologies: *Pillow Talk in The Heat of the Night*, and **The Soul of a Man** 2, as well as a **writer for the Inner City News**, and a feature writer for *Real Life Real Faith* Magazine, and essays written for several national newspapers and magazines.

Awarded by Flava News, the Unsung Peoples Poet Laureate

HEART & HOME

ALVIN L.A. HORN

Romantic Blues Publishing

www.alvinhorn.com

Seattle Washington

alah57@gmail.com

206 240m3468

ACKNOWLEDGMENTS

God, thank you for giving me the opportunity to write and to be read by many. You have blessed me with gifts that all your children are given for their own, and with my blessings and gifts, I thank you for allowing me to share, help, enrich, inspire, and bring peace. Many don't believe you laugh, but I assume you do, at the foolishness of men. I hope I made you laugh at some of the ill-advised things I have done acting as if I were in control. Through your grace, my aptitudes have been given a chance for all to see.

I give thanks to Big Mama - my grandmother - and to all the elder women who have taught me the value of the love of a woman, all in their own way. I'm blessed to have had all of you touch me in each of your individual ways. I write about women like you - the textured fabric of life I have been wrapped in.

I give honor to God for my aunts and uncles and cousins

I love my soul-sisters, as we know, blood doesn't always make someone your family no more than love itself. I have been blessed with women who just made it possible to be friends to share life as sisters and this brother from different mothers and fathers.

To the men who helped shape me in the mode of whom I am without ever knowing the impact you have had on me. Whether you were my bloodline or a mentor, I have watched you for what is right or wrong - allowing me to choose which is best for me as a man. I love the old soul I am in how I dress, talk, and enjoy the music I do, because of my elders creating the Renaissance man I am, so I pen you in layers of storylines.

To those who loved me when it was easy, I'm a good man, but not a perfect man. I walk humbly knowing the mistakes I have made, and the good things in life I have been able to do. All my writings, I pen to bring awareness to the struggles that this world places as burdens on you and me. Every woman and man handles the weight of mankind differently, that creates narratives, and I'm going to write them.

The friends and family very dear to me, the song says, "We go a long way back." Even if it's not true... dealing with me, I'm sure it can feel like it. Thank you. Each one of you somewhere along the way has loved me in your special way, helping me to stay on course or to get back to where I needed to be, and I thank you for that.

I lost some loved ones, as time waits for no one, along the way of writing HEART & HOME. It hurts like hell they are not here to see this book come to print, but I'll be sure to write those feelings I felt and feel for them in every novel to come. Rest in Love, Cyn Sprague and Juanita Spinks, and Dobbie Reese Noris.

My editor on the project: Mrs. Editor - Lorraine Elzia, you are my friend and a real pro. Besides editing, you make me laugh and feel good about how and what I write. Lorraine Elzia, Senior Editor at, aVeeda Literary Services. Award Winning Author & Ghost Writer. www.LorraineElzia.com, and Award-Winning Author.

Thanks to the other eyes-

John Huguley of https://www.johnhuguley.com – offers - editing & Proofreading, and freelance writing.

La Tanya Green – proofreading services

Alexandria Cornet – proofreading services

IX

＊＊＊

My Seattle family of friends HEART & HOME is you and me in the 206, 425, and 253. I'm writing for the rest of the world to know just how we do it. We are multi-ethnic often in our bloodlines, and diverse in our friendships. We are rain, and the bluest skies, the fresh ocean air, and snow-topped mountains that can, and do blow up, and we are rivers and streams in the middle of our neighborhoods, fresh fish, crab, and shrimp.

We are the posse on Broadway, Beacon Hill, Rainier Valley, and in the CD Renton, Skyway. We are the posse living in Mountlake, Capitol Hill, Mount Baker, Leschi, Madrona, West Seattle, South Park, White Center, Kent, and further south. We are the posse strolling around Seward Park, Alki, Coulon Beach, Lake Washington, Green Lake, the University District Avenue, Lake City, the Fremont District, and Queen Anne Hill. We are the posse rolling across floating bridges to the Eastside.

We are the posse living in, or near Rainier Beach, Duwamish-Tukwila, Burien,   Kent, and Federal Way. We are the posse rolling down to T-town - the 253.

We are Jimi Hendrix, Bruce Lee, Quincy Jones, Bill Russell, Marshawn Lynch – Breast Mode and many more. We are rain, sun, mountains and oceans. We are Vikings, Quakers, Bulldogs, and Eagles. We are the Seattle Super Sonics forever!

Alvin L.A. Horn

Shine down on me

Let me shine for you

Warm the path

I'll walk in your direction

Hold my head, cradle my thought

I'll embrace you until time stops

Alvin L. A. Horn

HEART AND HOME

Episode 1

"Found another two dead."

"Where?"

"Up in the road on the east hill."

"Where?"

"In a wooded area off a small trail road."

"Who discovered the girl way out there, to have come across another dead one?"

"White patrol – they told one of the MPs, who told me to tell you they found an abandoned camp."

"Pretty girls?"

"Yep, Italian."

"Skins slashed?"

A fire rose to the sky. Rain fell into a burn barrel, causing smoke and fumes to coat our darken faces and highlight musky skies of gloom. The burn barrel is our psychiatrist couch, our church, and our place to brag of our sins with women, or the times we outsmarted the *man*. The barrel is our place to cry and act as though the smoke is the cause. Hot flames rising, it is our place to light dreams of wanting to be somewhere else.

As we are gathered, we also use the time for somber remembrances. All too often, while we try to survive on foreign soil, we have received a letter of news of someone passing away back home. We pray we will see our grandmothers, grandfathers, and other family members again. We are young men, who some are not as spiritually connected as other men, but all pray in their own way of hopes of returning home to see our mothers and fathers.

We all dread our families don't receive a knock on the door from a man wearing a uniform bearing the bad news of they will never see us again. It means, not even our dead bodies will come home, at best, a dog tag will drop into a mother or father's hand with a thank you letter for the sacrifice of your son. A dusky glow lifts to the faraway sounds of death by way of bombs dropping from the sky. We are well away from battle zones, but the sound of explosions, hundreds of miles away, weighs heavily around us. My fellow dark-skinned soldiers shiver as we battle burning – watery eyes. Our green and black camouflage helmets keep some of the downpours off our uncombed heads. Our Army fatigues shield little, if next to nothing, of protection from the elements. Ice–cold rain pops and sizzles against the red – hot barrel.

Little Roy shared information with me while the rest of the men carried on in different conversations.

"Nah. The skins, I guess, were left alone this time instead of flat. How many you have now?"

"A lot."

"You know I want one, right?"

"You have told me more than a few times. I have heard you." I watched icicle cold rain pour off both sides of his broad nose as dual rain gutters. "I've got you covered man, as well as those MPs. When I retrieve all these dead, or left for dead, motorcycles and ship back to the States, this French town will be a lost memory. Once I'm back on American dirt, I'll put these two-wheeled angels back on the road."

As I spoke to Little Roy, I understood more than anything I needed off this foreign soil. We're stationed in the French countryside fighting for freedoms when we Colored soldiers come from very little emancipations.

Exhaled under the French skies, we speak of historical hate for us Colored men hovering like black smoke ever since we landed thousands of miles away from our kinfolk. The scent of a Jim Crow foulness has followed us. It is hard on the souls of Colored men. We despise a system of acceptance of death as winning. Death transports the birth of heartbreaks like a million shards of glass piercing psyches longing for repair as civilizations become cold. We Colored boys – we are born with hostiles chasing us like circling vultures from the lack of humanity. I look around and see men standing in the murk of mud while holding cold steel rifles. We should always be on guard, ready to shoot hot led into warm-blooded bodies – we call the enemy, but coffee, cigarettes, and laughter are what we live for when not fighting to survive. These men are trained to be to machines with a kill-to-survive skill. Some of these men can kill with no remorse. Having feelings about taking a live-in war could get you killed from a delayed response. War is a job we have to separate duty from the mindset of unwillingly wanting to play a hand in death.

War can cause dreadful mental demises, as we endure war's nasty existence. The spoils of this war, hopefully, I hope these carnage-filled grounds leave us to find some balance. We Pray. We hope. Before we die, we recognize nothing can erase the struggle. We must learn to accept the emotional wounding of our eyes and ears while we breathe in the stench permeating around our souls. Living with the scorn for our Colored skin, we often hurdle fears with false bravados in hopes of avoiding a haunting for the rest of our lives. No amount of money, love, or a lifetime of nights alone with Leena Horne or the Dandridge sisters will erase being in this war. We fight to contain misery to a limit. The wretchedness of battles always results in evil in our souls rising up to celebrate the killing of other men, instead of the morning of one of us being dead. Oddly, death cannot keep us from smiling, laughing, joking, thinking, and talking about sex, gambling, and drinking, while planning our future with more sex, gambling, and drinking, as we stand around a fire barrel. I have a plan – God willing, I'm speaking of rebuilding motorcycles left by dead men, or men who ran away to save their lives.

"Little Roy, you say the tires still have air in them so I can roll them out of the woods."

"Yes, sir, the skins are still decent. I'll help ya if you want me to."

"Just give me the compass settings."

"Right here."

Boom...boom...boom.

Heads jerk, but quickly, they act as if they heard nothing. I watch eyes slowly close – I assume souls are praying. Emotional ground sends tremors to souls, and some act brave – some show fear for their lives. Fear comes as chills of anxieties, masked in heroic speech and body language as I watch chests expand under wet uniforms gradually deflate as rain drips off our helmets.

Although we have cleared the Germans out of this area, hundreds of miles away we think we hear ten-ton bombs penetrating structures of man-made buildings turning human bones to *ashes to ashes, and dust to dust* as Nazis all fall down. Our bombers create earthquakes of fear in the name of being on the right side.

The Germans ran from this region but left booby traps of arsenals and landmines to kill long after we have killed them. We must always stay on high alert or chance our bodies will become fertilizer for French gardens as unmarked graves. The best your kinfolk can expect is dog tags.

Moments later, the ground tremors shake us again, the same as Count Basie's horn section makes a dance floor come alive. On the roads and the nearby grounds, from 100 to 200 miles away, crews explode landmines marching toward Germany. Bodies shift as if little boys might have to urinate. Many of the men can't hide their discomfort. We have long since stopped teasing each other.

Evil must ride shotgun to help summon up the backbone to kill other men. These men understand, when you make a deal with the devil, he then wants out of the bottle like a genie. No doubt, some soldiers will go home with the mental taste of blood, with much like a mad dog, they will slaughter friends, foes, lovers, and even family members.

"Man – look at that girl, she needs some ass. She's so skinny I can't tell if I'm looking at the back of her neck or her ankles." Lanky Slim talks with his eyebrows rose. He does so by trying to be funny as one of the regular guys. Coming out of his mouth, the subject never sounded natural. Even when someone is not funny, we laugh out of the general practice of comradery.

"Her little ass can't keep a worm warm at night," one of the soldiers says as he walks by.

Chuckles and shakes of heads meet other movements as we keep our hands moving in our pockets, trying to fight a biting chill from stiffening our fingers. Sometimes, holding your dick is the warmest, along with best feeling one can have. Squeezing your dick often reminds one you are alive.

One thing for sure, we all recognize for sure, don't let them **White** boys catch us gawking at the women who look remotely close to what looks like the woman from the Wizard of Oz. We do look, though. Any virile young man will desire, at least through their eyes feeding lustful daydreams.

Sad to say, but the ugly truth is boys turned into soldiers have not lived long enough to turn into decent men as of yet. Colored soldiers learned while being civilians to scan from the corners of their eyes, cataloging a woman's visual assets. Men who have learned the values and virtues of a woman, but many are boys experiencing for the first time, knowledge about women beyond their mama's love is beyond what they can only see in a woman's appearance. French women, along with Romani Gypsies, walk in the nearby fields. I'm sure lustful minds paint those women in sexy garments when they are not.

We are Negros in another country in the Army under the rule of Uncle Sam, which means we are under the *man's* boot, as if still on American soil. We are chained in a sense by law – we can't fight, eat, or sleep alongside White soldiers even though we are all Americans fighting for America. We have to act as if we are Negros from Mississippi, we know better than to look at the non-Colored women. I'm not from the South. I've lived close by in Gary, Indiana, and then we moved to Detroit, Michigan, afterwards, we made it to Seattle. No matter where a Colored man is born, we identify when, where, and how we learn to act around the *man* who manipulate their hate-filled racist ego against us.

I experienced a few encounters with French women, who seem like fragile glass, detached from reality – maybe the war has shattered or cracked their souls. I guess war piling up dead men in mass graves might have something to do with lips pressed tight and eyes open, but refusing to see.

"Lanky Slim, you just like them ham hock, thick thigh, Louisiana Bayou sun-kissed Colored gals," Little Roy mocked, with his meaty face and an immense smile. As we try to make the best out of ugly times, we keep wiping the rain off all the hues of our brown cheeks. We share jokes in the mud, but at the other end of the camp they sit around in large dry tents with kerosene heaters. Some of those tents, Colored soldiers erected them, and we Colored boys sleep in pup tents making us crawl in on our bellies.

Little Roy is a short-stout Negro with a built-in smile between his chubby cheeks, and even when he's angry, he smiles. He laughs at his statement, then turns his head away from the circle of soldiers and spits on the ground. He faces us again, there is drool slithering off his jaw as he speaks.

"Man, oh man...them White boys, they like them skin and bone French fillies, but I can't do no woman lessen she some thick-thighed with some extra behind. I may live in Chicago, but I want me a Texas-size woman."

Lanky Slim taunted with his Cajun drawl and proclaimed; "Now you know you would dive into those French dips if you could fit all your meat into her tight stuff."

Roy is well known for his manly girth. Modesty is nonexistence when you live and fight in the fields for months.

The men slip off behind tents or near wooded areas with a girly magazine appreciably passed around. They'll take some whale oil or some Glovers Mane, which is a sulfur and pine tar combo in mineral oil for some lubricant. They do it to help satisfy and relieve the tension of the war. It is a temporary reduction of the pressure a young man has from a hard-on from even the wind blowing something from a womanly-sweet daydream. Some of the guys will holler out for who has the nude girly magazine twice a day. We don't even tease each other. What is human nature is our nature raising it beyond an understanding of simple lustfulness. Our desire for sex, it is an internal physical demand – a young man has little control of his blood hardening his manhood.

Certain men let their physical manhood size, or the number of times they need to relive one's self, as a bragging right to be a man. You can't prove you're a ladies' man out here when you're a man fighting to live. To live another day, it is your partial stud degree. If you live to see and tell an American woman your name when you make it back to American soil, you might have lifted to the heavens. Men brag and claim to be God's gift to women before boot camp...legends in their head.

Another soldier chimes in, "Just because dem gurls be skinny, don't be meanin' it's tight, especially after all dem White boys done parked dar gas-soaked peckers in it one afer enother."

"I know that's right," I say.

I am Sirletto Preer, the highest-ranking Negro amongst the Colored soldiers here. I have no rank over any White soldiers at any time. Thus, they rarely address me with respect, as they should, but they call me Preer. On my dog tags, my name is Master Sergeant Sirletto Preer, but the Negro soldiers closer to me when off official business, they call me Sir-Sir.

"As I keep reminding you guys, this may not be Mississippi, but with most of them boys over there being rednecks..." I point to the other side of the base nearly a football field away, "...when it comes to the women over here, we might as well be down South. Don't be stupid, don't slip up, laughing it up, or smiling at, and for sure, feeling it up with these French gals. Show respect, even if you don't feel respected!"

Most of the men nod, recognizing I am on point. We all fear the accusation of Colored men crimes of so-called immoral deeds with an Olive Oyl that can lead to us being lynched or shot with no judge nor jury. A jury system is a farce for a Negro. Immoral exploitation of truth leads to punishment against us for sexual crimes that they love to say Negros commit. I keep a watchful eye on my men for many reasons, but I'd like to think maybe at least in my platoon, we Colored soldiers have some common sense – we avoid any hint of Judy Garland to Mae West looking like women and all in between them when it comes to (sexual transgressions trouble.) The women we look at, she better look like she had a slave heritage.

"Well, those girls, they're nothing. Even those Gypsy women all look old and dumpy, and they hate us, and then on top of that, some of them are darker than some of us yellow Negros. Besides, I don't want one of them Gypsies to put a spell on me. They might poke pins in a doll, and keep my dick from ever working again." Tony Tiny Taps spoke with his New York-Puerto Rican accent. We nod our heads in agreement.

Tony Tiny Taps speaks up to all of us, literally. The man stands at the legal minimum weight and height limit, which led to his nickname Tony Tiny Taps. His real name is Tony Tapia. Tony is a boxer, formally ranked the number-one New York City welterweight, and number five in the world, in line for a world title shot. Some low-level gangsters pinched him into a corner on a set-up. They tricked him into believing he had fallen for the sexual love of a mob boss's daughter, and those Italian mobsters were known for killing Puerto Ricans if they found out about race-mixing sex with their women. The woman actually made a living as a hooker, and they used her to set him up. These were whiskey barstool wanna-be mob boys who threatened Tony that he had to throw a fight, or they would snitch to their Italian mob boss about Tony dipping his Puerto Rican sausage between the thighs of the boss's daughter. Well, they scared Tony. He could beat a man one on one with his fist, but not the mob...he thought about his family being in danger and felt pinched into no choice. Tony threw the fight to a guy who hit like falling snowflakes.

A warped sense of irony fell upon Tony. The hooker fell in love with Tony, and she told him the truth after he threw the fight. The low-level mob boys had her living in fear if she had told him the truth before the match. A furious Tony, seeing a lifetime opportunity slip away...he found a connection to the mob boss, and told the head mob boss that his boys used his name in a shakedown, and those boys stole the mob bosses cut of the prize money made on the fight.

The mob boss arranged for Tony to beat the men unmercifully in an alley in front of the mob boss's eyes. The mob boss and his trusted cronies took bets on how long it would take each man to be knocked out. Several of the men outweighed Tony by 50 to 100 pounds, and he knocked out each one in less than thirty seconds, except for the ringleader of the scam. Tony beat him for a three-minute round against an alley wall and never letting the man fall. The man is now brain dead from the beating. The mob boss is the one who gave Tony the nickname Tiny Taps. The mob boss arranged for Tony to earn a legitimate title shot, but the draft board gave orders for Tony to fight a war first. We all think of Tony Tiny Taps as the uncrowned champ.

No one in the Army ever talks crazy to Tony despite his size. One time, a captured German, well over 200 pounds, called Tony a winzig schwarz monkey—*a little black monkey*. Tony invited the German to put his hands up. We all formed a human boxing ring made of **White** and Negro soldiers. We were all smiling, getting ready to appreciate the pain of a beat-down coming to someone who deservingly did not know what kind of shit he talked his Hitler-loving ass into. The German took off his jacket, unbuttoned his shirt, and then he spat on the ground and smiled toward Tiny Taps. He acted tough, but our little Puerto Rican champ walked right up to the German, and hit him with a left to the gut. The Nazi grunted and farted in the key of, *oh-F*, and not the musical key. The German doubled over, and Tony followed with a right hand to the temple. The sound detonated like an oak tree snapping from a lightning strike, and the German fell like a sack of coal. Now, not even those Texas - Oklahoma cowboy soldiers will look at Tony Tiny Taps in the eyes with a dare.

Nicknames – most of us bore one from something we did, lived with a history of doing, or earned. We often chop to pieces another man's name and make something new as a way of not connecting too much to one another if one of us dies. When a dead soldier is referred to by his real name, we would be able to tell ourselves, *I didn't know him well.*

Feet are walking in place to keep warm, making slushing sounds in the mud where we stand. Sparks lift and swirl from the fire in the barrel. Moments ago, someone threw pieces of broken chairs and the straw from the back of the chairs into the barrel.

"Well, me...I'm not looking at them thin French derrières, they don't have any backsides for me either. I'm like Little Roy – I like me some meat on the bone."

Handsome N-Booty, a Clark Gable look-alike as a Colored man, stands 6'3" and might weigh 150 pounds if dipped in solidified bacon grease. Neflow Bonds is his real name, but with us, he is N-Booty. He is so thin, it looks as if from his neck, back, and down to his legs, there is no behind – hence the nickname, N-Booty. We joke, "The man is so thin he turns sideways and disappears." He is also our hawkeyed-sharpshooter. With one shot, he can pick off a Nazi running at full speed across a field 100 yards away. N-Booty is also a loyal friend away from all the Army theatrics and protocols. With thoughts of his skinny body, coupled with him speaking of thin derrières and no backsides, we tease, and he laughs with us. Laughing helps while shivering in the pouring rain.

"I can tell you what to do," another soldier, Clement, spoke as if he devised a master plan, but Little Roy cut him off for the moment.

"Boy, let it wait, I gotta take a dump."

"If you wouldn't take so long, I'd wait, but you're heading for the field to crap instead of the outhouses."

"You all know I don't take a dump near them stank` shit holes, so hurry up and say what you got to say then."

"Well fellas, all you have to do is...when you are doing it from the backside, you know, doggie – doggie, when you spank em' on the ass, der' behind will start to grow. I've been doing dem' New York chocolate satin dolls, and they like it. They be all skinny from dancing all night long, like thin, long, black licorice ropes, so, I be spankin' dem' good and plenty. But make sure you kiss them on the rump when you're done spankin', so they let you keep on spankin', so der' behind keep growing."

Total silence met with side glances and whispered words slipped under some soldier's breath. Even the pops from the burn barrel seem to take a deep breath, with only the sound of the rain sizzling as it hit the hot metal. No one responded. Eyes connected and seemly carried on conversations of, "What did you say, boy?" None of the men knew what to say, or whether to laugh. If any of the men partaken in what they heard someone said aloud, they would deny it. Men have this thing about another man – he doesn't want others to assume what they may do in private with a woman. My men, they sure weren't going to be the one to say so in support of Clement's statement.

I said, "Boy, you mean to tell us you been kissing ass?"

Laughter roared up to the overcast sky. Some laugh so hard they have to pee, and others wipe tears from their face instead of rain. We're laughing at

Clement. With him, we knew most everything he said held no truth. He lied so much. We all knew if he said he will die one day, none of us would believe him.

Clement, he is one of those men who acts as if, he is better looking than all the rest, yet he's an odd-looking fellow. When he smiles, he frowns at the same time. Reason being, at some time in his life, he received a deep knife cut on his cheek, and oddly enough, when he smiles with his horse size buckteeth and the healed cut on the side of his face, it resembles a frown.

We are a tight-knit group of men who watch out for each other, but Private Clement is the subject of jokes behind his back and verbal scorn from his fellow soldiers. We nicknamed him, Two-Faced.

He's far from being my favorite soldier. He's a bit of a thorn in my side. He often appears to be sticking his nose up in the White soldier's asses, or he kisses their asses, trying to gain favor. They despise him too, and mock his cooning Black Sambo foolishness. There's nothing worse than trying to keep a man alive when you know he'll sell his testicles away to take your place.

Clement is from Hobbs, New Mexico, and I doubt he's been anywhere near New York City. His hometown, boot camp, and now being on French shores, is as far as his life ventured. I'm sure of it. I'm his platoon leader – I've read the records of all the men under my command. He is a tough son of a bitch. Hobbs, New Mexico is a black cowboy town, and Clement broke wild horses and rode bulls in the rodeo.

I boxed from an early age until I went off to college, and I knew if I ever had to fight Clement, I knew to stay on my feet and move. An exceptionally powerfully built man, he gives me a reason to pause. I imagine the cut on his face came about in a bar fight, and a switchblade left its mark. He said his woman came home and found him in bed with her sister, and his woman cut him with a razor. *Truth?* Doubtful. A woman wanting to be near him, I'm trying not to visualize. I think he would have to pay her well, but two women wanting him, I think it would be a stretch.

I need him to follow orders, and nothing less. A **White** Master Sergeant who disrespects me as often as he can, Master Sergeant Jude, spoke rudely to me one day concerning Two-Faced Clement.

He said, "I admire your watermelon eatin' Private Coon', he's always trying to lick my boots."

A redneck with a military rank the same as mine or over mine and a not so slick private cooning for attention are equal to fire and gasoline. I have my hands full keeping the matches put away while wishing I could light both their asses up. I can supervise a company of one hundred men of any race if allowed, but I led a platoon of Negros. Nothing wrong with having Negro soldiers as my brothers in arms. We are some fightin' grunts. We killed plenty of Hitler's boys.

I'm in charge because of my educational skills. I have a college degree in mechanical engineering and a minor in music from Morehouse University. Before the war, I lead a team of Negro, Japanese, and **White** mechanics as the HNIC (Head Negro in charge) of the Seattle Police Motorcycle Pool before being drafted. I have a street degree of knowing backrooms and back-alley meeting rooms.

My education and supervisory skills qualified me for a bit more consideration in earning my sergeant stripes. What the Army brass saw in me, and what they don't see, I worked anyone in the way of my wellbeing or future, like a poor but pretty, sexually stimulating woman can work a rich ugly man.

I proved myself on the battlefield too. I've commanded my men into several areas and cleared out the Germans – I have not lost a soldier yet. I even saved a **White** superior.

Some of the **White** soldiers respect me, but they don't address me as an equal. I'm sure some would treat my rank respectfully if the Jim Crow good ole boys club would let them. Whizzing bullets and the sound of planes dropping bombs in front of any man regardless of race keeps the Jim Crow segregation rules to non–fighting times. In a foxhole – a potential grave – a man overlooks what race he is in a hellhole with.

If you need protecting or cover to reach safety, and a man of another race is there to provide it, you absolutely don't think if a man likes you or hates you. However, when the fighting stops, we filter back into being Negro – second class – citizens from America on the shores of another country. We Negro's, we are standing in the rain, and most of the **White** soldiers are in wide tent barracks with kerosene heaters.

My superiors direct me to lead my Colored boys out front more often than not. We saw Hitler's guns first and dead Nazis shortly thereafter. We kicked ass, as drilled into us in boot camp by the Colored drill sergeants. They understood for us to survive we had to be unrepentant warriors to kill or be killed. We are drilled in winning. We fought with more aggression – it put fear in the Nazis in battle times with the Colored boys.

We have a fire inside us when we are fighting. When we have a gun and a clear and present enemy we can legally fight, we kill. My men know how to get the job done. When we don't have to fight another war, meaning the mental influences concerning being lynched or feel that judge's gravel might come down to sentencing our life to a chain gang, we win battles as if we were born for this. For the first time, against white looking skin, we have swallowed the power to get even as if, to take justice – make justice. We Colored boys know committing crimes in America is something we try to avoid as we're falsely accused enough. Fighting Nazis, we celebrate by pulling the trigger.

Many of my fellow Colored soldiers volunteered for the service to earn their first paycheck. Most of any money in their pockets before this war came from the sweat of hard back-breaking work as in picking cotton and sharecropping. Present day, we have the pleasure of serving Uncle Sam instead of being served Jim Crow back home. Now we are being paid to shoot at Nazi's who look like the men who lynch our people back in America.

We know when we return back home, we'll buy homes with the aid of the government VA money along with going to school free. Most of the Colored boys, they don't believe it to be valid until our government gives us what is pledged to us. We hope it's not another false 40 acres and a mule promise.

Sadly, Uncle Sam pays us in cash, and some gamble it away before ideas of a plan take hold. The paymaster has not made it to us to pay us in cash as of this month...yet. I made it clear to all the Negro soldiers before we left from American soil to have their money sent to a trusted relative, or wait till we returned home on American soil and collect a lump sum of money, as they will not need money while fighting for their lives.

Episode 2

There's a certain romance of fighting on foreign soil. We Colored folks have seen the Saturday matinees of the American armed forces always coming out on top and hailed as heroes. When we see The Brown Bomber – Joe Louis – in a military uniform, he is a hero we can identify with, but now we Colored boys could be like him and knock Germans out. Many of us like me walked before a draft board. There are a few of us whom a judge gave us little option in the matter. Being a Colored boy, falsely accused of stealing a stick of gum could lead to a five-year sentence of hard labor on the chain gang, or the choice of joining the Army.

Maybe we're helping to change things. Then again, a tripped land mine makes no difference when your body rockets through the air, and wherever you land, you don't feel that missing limb. However, eyesight brings into focus your limb lying across from you. One's right hand might be able to shake hands with a torn-off left hand. No matter, you want to live to see another day – whether it is here abroad, or in America as a Negro. In battle, our hearts, minds, and guts, dig deep within our souls as if we are already six-feet down in the ground and we are digging out to live.

I look at our tattered coats with worn thread patches from cigarette burn holes or tree branch rips, or from crawling on the ground, which now, if ever barely holding enough warmth, it's better than no coat at all. It's almost New Year's 1945, and a year and months after we have landed here in France. We

American armed forces have pushed the Germans out of France. Many of these Southern French towns lie in ruins, and we come through and fix them up for different uses. After we Colored and White Army units have kicked butts, we Colored boys swing hammers, haul trash, and bury French bodies. We burn dead German soldiers in large fire pits. It's a horrible stench and comes with the added grief as we yank dog tags off of Nazis so someone back in Germany will know their son or husband ain't coming home. It's humanity in the middle of the madness.

Maddening insanity is when captured German soldiers sit in prisoner camp tents, and we Colored soldiers assembled them, and then we watch Nazi's treated well by White soldiers. The play cards and share cigarettes with German prisoners of war, while many won't eat with us Colored boys. The Germans slaughtered the Jews and the Gypsies, and beat the French down to the ground, and yet I'm still a second-class citizen to captured German soldiers. In this war, nothing shocks me, knowing Nazi's sleep well at night under our watchful American eyes. Logical no, but we follow orders.

We came into France from North France through Normandy, but made our way down to southwest France in the Gironde. We removed most of any Germans from this region. We have been here a year and will be in this little town for some time to come. Supplies move through here and transfer in and out. There is a shipping terminal within thirty miles away. We do repairs of equipment, and small squads of men work in adjoining towns.

The French people are kind to us as we Colored boys make life bearable once again for them. We clean up and pretty up, but the command keeps us away from the ordinary French people as much as possible.

The detail we're working on is not for the French people. We are fixing up a long row of houses near the outskirts of town where women live in, and make money on, their backs or knees. We are repairing brothels. American GI's come into town on leave from many miles away to relieve the stress of sexual desires. We restore whorehouses to arise from the ashes of Nazi-controlled hell. Whores from parts of France, Spain, Portugal, and other war-torn places work in these houses.

The Germans pimped the girls when they overran France, and here we are doing it in houses of pure sinful pleasure for hundreds of American men. Part of the work we do is to make and maintain a wash and shower area for the White soldiers. They clean up their foul bodies if they want to dip themselves in these whores. Most of the soldiers use a leave pass to come to town for less than a five-minute rump in the sack.

We Colored boys are amused. We watch them line up for the hedonism of being inside the same women hundreds of others before them have been in. Funny though, their behavior...they act as if a New York steak is waiting for them to eat. With stupid smiles on their faces, they're all so eager to buy a piece of what the last man fell through. Humorous as it is, we know most of them end up stroking themselves in front of one of the women to release pent-up semen onto the breast of the women.

They hand out rubbers to them—the fools, but we know some don't use them. Shit, I imagine most ejaculate as quick as they went through the door from just being near a naked woman.

After we Colored soldiers built the clean-up area, the White soldiers' line up to dip their naked asses in barrels of high-octane purple gas before they run upstairs to meet with a whore. When they come out of a whorehouse, they take another dip in the barrel of high octane gas. The barrel has a mix of rubbing alcohol, and then they shower with lye soap and cold water. It helps from catching the clap, so they say. On the other side of town, there is a medic unit for men groaning from burning pee.

I guess if you ask a man to put his life in front of a bullet, bombs, and maybe crapping in a hole in the ground next to a dead man, you cannot tell him a case of syphilis or gonorrhea is all merciless pain. What I find funny...these men will dip their naked asses in high-octane purple gas to feel a piece of ass, despite gas burns even more severe as the clap. If you have been on the march trenching through mud and forests, fighting for weeks, you don't know when you'll ever feel a hot bath. You wear the same clothes, and maybe an occasion arises to rinse out and dry your socks...maybe. You can have cuts, rashes, foot rot, crotch itchiness, and you're gonna scratch and make it worse. If you have been out in the field for weeks, you have not bathed, and your body will have problems. Most of the Colored soldiers come from much harder lives than others, and we find ways to stay as clean as possible. Hell, even bathing in muddy water while we sing a Muddy Waters' blues tune is far better than not bathing at all.

Imagine pouring pure rubbing alcohol in your eyes...that's how some men describe the burn of dipping their foul asses in barrels of high-octane purple gas before they meet some female for some sexual fun.

Those men jump out of a cold shower, then they towel off and then bite down on a towel to muffle their agonizing groans when they lower themselves in the gas. These men scream as if someone stabbed them in the back when the gas enters into cuts or scratched privates...oh well.

I once helped my Uncle Sonny kidnap a musician. The musician beat a woman in my Uncle's juke joint – she rejected him when he didn't have enough money to pay her for sex. We took the woman-beating musician to my dad's auto chop shop. My uncle took me along to learn about street justice.

Justice is not always about courts, juries, and jails. We Negros have no business being judged by people who have never been *just* in treating us with equal arms of the law. Often crimes amongst Negros – they go unpunished as the White police don't care, and many times we know they are the criminal.

My uncle tied the man to a chair and placed the man's trumpet mouthpiece against the side of the man's lips. My uncle used a blowtorch and heated the mouthpiece to red-hot metal. With a rag stuffed in the man's mouth, my uncle pressed the burning mouthpiece against each side of the man's face. The musician gained the nickname Hot Lips. The muffled screams reverberated much like these men who dip their bodies in purple gas. These soldiers must love the pain, as they come back for more of the same.

Episode 3

My mother raised me with a civilized amount of decency. Her morals instilled compassion in me for people who have been used or abused by people who don't have any decency, or who don't have any personal conflict with doing wrong. I learned how to deal with those people of shortcomings from my father and uncle, and the slick men they encountered in the streets of Detroit and Seattle.

I am two people. On one side, I can speak the King's English and outthink most of my teachers from high school and college. I learned from my mom good diction, and I learned from my dad and uncle the language of the streets. My dad and uncle encouraged me to know what lies before me out in the streets, and they taught me to have the edge over the cons, crooks, and liars who defraud their way through life.

My uncle loan sharks and runs small street ventures, and sometimes he promotes his juke joint. My dad is a master of many trades who runs an automotive repair shop – a stolen car chop shop. Quite often, if someone owed my uncle money, my dad and uncle would confiscate the debtor's vehicle, or even the relatives of the person might lose their wheels.

My mom knows what my dad and uncle do, and she, from time to time, played Robin Hood and has asked them to furnish a car to someone in need. My part in all, I counted the money at an early age and moved on up to be a forger – making fake car registrations for the new owner of a car. Once, my dad and uncle confiscated a debtor's car, stripped out the brown interior, and replaced it with another color from another seized car. They painted the car a different color and sold it to the next-door neighbor of the person who used to own the confiscated vehicle.

While in high school, I started collecting money owed to my uncle, and I rarely ran into problems. I drove one of his many Cadillacs or clean Buicks around town by the age of fourteen.

Unlike most criminal activities, my family devised legitimate businesses, and we kept all out of sight out of mind. We always paid the right people, which included the cops. Knowing and understanding people's nature is what keeps you out of jail and keeps you alive.

One must recognize who your friends are, and who can hurt you the most, and one must be willing to change directions. Other streetwise knowledge, I understood, an unarmed man is like a bird that can't fly. In knowing so, we all stand a chance someone will serve you up on a platter if you turn blind, dumb, and deaf. You are your own best protector.

Growing up in a home with no shortage of anything, I still saw the other side of town – meaning, life down South. I knew the life of the deprived poor of a segregated life of the South. When I was a child, my parents moved from Clarksdale, Mississippi to Detroit, Michigan. By the time of my junior high years, we moved to Seattle, Washington.

I inherited my work ethic and know-how from my dad and mom. Dad could fix anything from a tractor motor to a car engine or whatever needed a screw turned. Mom owned a musical instrument repair shop. Initially, she taught music, but she repaired and restored the instruments of her students.

One day, she stopped teaching band instruments, and only taught voice lessons, and opened a musical instrument repair shop and rented and sold musical instruments. Some of those instruments came by way of musicians who owed gambling debts to my uncle or dad. Many respectable musicians came to town with an exquisite horn and left with nothing in hand to play on the next stage. Mom also rented out practice space to students and other music teachers. Both of my parents possess a musical sense. My dad plays sax, and mom can sing opera or the blues while playing the piano. I inherited their musicality.

Around the burn barrel, or even out on patrol and around a campfire with the guys, if we are out of harm's way at night, I provide music for my guys. I play the harmonica, or when I can come up with a guitar, I sing and play the blues. On Sunday mornings, I sing church hymns. Some White soldiers will sit close by and listen to me sing or play. Some nights, I sing romantic blues kind of songs of a man missing his woman. Most of us understood missing a woman kind of blues, whether a woman is waiting for you back at home or not. The blues touches the soul when missing love on a lonely night. We could dream with our eyes wide open and see what I'm singing about and picture a woman in our arms.

"Oh, my babeeeeee
please hold onto my love
hold onto my soul
I'm comin' – comin' back to you
oh, I just wanna love ya forever and forever more."

Through the low clouds and dim light of day, I see women in the distance from our camp all day. At times, we see them stop, and it appears they look at us. Some of the men will wildly brag that pretty women are looking at them and not the rest of us. I know some of the men have never been with a woman, and maybe never have even kissed a girl, except for their mama's cheek.

Some men in this war are teenagers. Most have only held conversations in daydreams wishing he could tell his thoughts to a woman. For sure, if you ever spoke to a woman and had a crush on her – you can hear her voice even thousands of miles away. I have conversations in my head, wanting to express my feelings to a woman. I'm hoping for a chance...again.

When I close my eyes, and think of a woman's touch, it is the one joy nothing can change in the middle of this war. At night, most men rollover from their backs or onto their sides, or stomach to hide a constant, hard-on. It just can't be helped, and your body wants what God made, and made exceptionally well – a woman. Self–gratification love is no relief.

All one can do is think of the last woman, or any woman from the past, and the next time possible when one will feel her body or her emotional love, and for me, it is both.

On the battlefield, you worry – will you ever have a chance to feel a woman's touch? No matter if it's cold and rainy in the dark of a warring night, I have heard bombs in the distant, and I still fantasized about the feeling of hearing whispered desires and inhaling the scent of love.

I have my parents' emotional and artistic souls, and I express myself through writing in my journal. Sometimes, it's a poem or just my thoughts. I often lie on my sides with an oil lamp or candle and write things like:

Imagining her, her lips
Imagining her hips

I visualize her thighs curled into my hip socket
I'm reaching and squeezing, caressing her as I kiss the back of her neck
With each breath, I exhale slowly near her ear
She sighs
She makes sounds of desiring feelings
I roll over onto my back, and I see her body rise above me
She stares down and sees my desire rising
I'm wanting to meet her heat
Liquid excitements
We both have rivers flowing
She lets me enter her yearning
I feel her heat
Her lowering her body and taking me in
I hear her unrestrained pleasure
I can't help myself and make sounds of a hound howling in the wind
I feel her heat from deep inside her ecstasy
She is sweet to my tongue as she kisses me
I am breathing deeply in my sleep
I don't want to wake
I don't want to miss a moment
Of being inside her and her intimately in my dreams

All we have are dreams of staying alive to feel the warmth of a woman. They draft us anywhere from eighteen years of age to twenty-nine years old, and the world has us sitting in foxholes thinking of sex and how to kill the enemy in alternating thoughts.

Love and war hardly ever work out. The women left behind on the shores of our homeland – some have the seed of man growing in them. Their man is fighting over here, and many of these men will never come home to be a husband or father. I know of men who have died on the battlefield who were fathers-to-be.

Criminal carnal abuse – this war gives way to violent assaults against women. The Nazis, we hear, they have and do some horrible, disgusting things to women, yet they do not walk alone in leaving a foul stench.

We have traveled through French towns after the Germans have pillaged the women. Then here comes the Americans repeating wicked, nasty deeds against foreign women. American history since the time of slave ships and plantations...the abuse of women has lived on and thrived in homes, bars, churches, workplaces, and street corners. In the life of all levels and sorts, sick bastards have kill the spirit in young girls and young boys, and the devil in some men drive in spears of immoral rage and creates mutilations in wombs and souls.

We are liberators for freedom, but we create the worse, with the best, in order to do the job as is needed and wanted. After this war, there will be European children fathered by American men...and not out of love. Some Europeans will hate us Americans forever as much as they hate the Germans for the same criminal carnal attitudes.

We Colored men share our stories of crime back home. Most often, our sins have been to attain food or shelter, and crimes for prosperity. Crimes for wealth are much like one country invades another country for achieving what it has, or to get more of what they selfishly already have. In the end, one side justifies, and the other side pays with wounds that never go away.

Most of us Colored soldiers have suffered under the rule of thumb of being treated less than human, yet here we are fighting for the cause of freedom. Back home, Negros work in physically dangerous labor, which often leads to death or maiming. So, the thought of doing something dangerous is a standard way of life.

Episode 4

The White soldiers most don't treat me with respect – it's as if being an asshole is a right. Acting with contempt toward us Negros is a way of life, as if God planned it, but no, He did not. The *man* has never known me. None have ever tried to understand me as an equal man. It is ignorant, for anyone to feel they're better than me, or above me. A select few treat me as a friend until their asshole comrades tell them to knock it off.

Captain Castellani is the first White man to asks, how I am doing politely, and I detected no sarcasm behind his inquiries. He's in charge of our base. I think of him as a silver dollar as his hair shines. He is second-generation Sicilian as his skin appears tanned. Often with his gray eyes, he asks for my opinions. A few of his men call him Captain White Sambo behind his back because he's not ill-mannered toward the Colored soldiers.

We all have a role to play. I am a black chess piece. I change to another treasured piece when needed. If I needed to slide diagonally or jump over to a place to see, or hear, or take action...I did what I did with the thought of being two moves ahead. Captain Castellani has used my help to keep us all safe and win victories. He has asked for my opinion on a few subjects in front of my Colored soldiers. I believe the Captain wants them to respect me. More importantly, he does not condone the White soldiers openly disrespect my men.

I saved a White staff sergeant in battle. The man I saved meant quite a lot to the captain, but the righteous deed I did, it left me emotionally scarred.

⁂

Months ago, we were advancing on a small Nazi-occupied town at night. We watched the Germans from afar for two days, and we planned an attack to run them out. Captain Castellani set up the offense from different flanks. My men would come in from the south as a frontal attack, and another part of the company would protect the west to avoid the Germans escaping. In a delayed attack, the last platoon would come in from the north to kill or capture the Germans who were trying to escape.

My men were coming in from the front to distract the Germans so that they would retreat into the rear. I knew the frontal attack order did not come down from Captain Castellani. Several times in the past, he designed the attacks for my men to come in from the back or side, and would let the White platoons lead the offense, which would have put them in more of harm's way, but he'd receive orders to place the Negros in more dangerous positions.

So far, no matter which way, or who went first, my men did their job without losing a man, with just a few injuries, but all were alive and walking for the most part. I have lost a few men to maiming injuries, and they're home healing. I pray they heal and learn to deal with the new life in front of them.

⁂

When the attack started, we were pushing the Germans back as planned. They were retreating into the trap, but something went wrong. The troops in the middle fell into a firefight and delayed advancing and squeezing the German withdrawal.

The captain followed the orders from his commanders, and placed the Negro soldiers in the front, but he did not place enough men – the White soldiers on the west side flank. He staged most of them near the back of town who were having problems moving forward. The side flank soldiers were pinned, losing lives, and taking on many injuries.

I decided to divide my guys and help the side flank. All hell from all the planets in the universe seemed to lower its fury on all. It was a moment of kill or feel the hot lead of evil as death songs whistled and whizzed by our bodies with each second we breathed. We started to run low on ammo, as did the Germans. Knives, bricks, and guts became the weapons of survival. Hearing screams and grunts of pain made you aware you weren't dead...yet. Cursing in English and what sounded like German, met ears at the same time as fists and knives landed against and penetrated the flesh. Enemy warrior eyes locked on ours for the length of time it took for spit and blood, or for teeth to hit the ground. I killed a German with the bayonet end of my rifle.

How could there be any human compassion for evil people who are murdering thousands of Jews, and would kill a Colored man all the same? We held anger that many White soldiers might not possess.

We felt White soldiers fought with a sense of, I am an America fighting for, we must be right because we are Americans.

We Negro soldiers feel more in tune with, we are fighting for our freedoms in hopes to achieve equal rights because we fight for America.

Why – our country, in many ways, allowed the killing of Indians and Negros for control over us. I have Jews in my neighborhood, and I grew up with them. They own stores and gave credit to people who didn't have much. I made grocery deliveries for them as a kid. I'm defending and fighting for people I went to school with, and with whom I shared my neighborhood. With my gun and military uniform, I might as well have been Joe Louis defeating Hitler's best.

Bullets and hand grenades met blood and limbs. Dark evil fought with our dark and White American skin in the streets and buildings with no lights. Above me, on a three-story building, a sniper kept our backs against a wall. His bullets put Americans in line for death. I sent men up, and we fired shots up there to distract him.

What felt like an hour in time, but in five minutes, a body fell off the building onto a brick walkway. A Nazi landed just raindrops away from my feet. I see a bullet hole in one cheek, and it came out the other. I kicked him to make sure his death arrived. He still had a heartbeat, so my bayonet pierced his lungs. I heard his last breath wheeze as if a car tire sprung a leak.

I looked up from where the German fell, and I saw Two-Faced Clement standing on the rooftop smiling with his crooked frown-shaped mouth. I wondered if he shoved the Nazi off the roof with the intent of death landing on me. I needed to stay alert while shooting, stabbing, and killing, to survive from all possible attacks.

Squatting low and near the end of a building, I needed to make my way through to the alley. I peeked around the corner. In the dark, a tank mortar explosion nearby highlighted a German soldier dragging a White American GI by one leg. The German fired two shots from a pistol. The bullets hit the side of the building, and brick fragments blistered my face. I felt instant moisture run down my cheek. The rubble wasn't as hot as a bullet would have been. I'm breathing hard, proving I'm not dead. I tasted my blood slithering into the corner of my mouth. I wiped the blood away, but my chapped lips stung from the abrasions of brick particles pricking my skin.

I thought of the mineral oil my mother used to rub onto my lips as a child, and here I am a grown man fighting to stay alive, and thinking of my mother's pampering. In the dark violence of this war, I felt like a child. I wanted my mother's lap to curl upon and feel safe. I wished I were five years old in my mother's hold, protecting me from the danger, but I'm near thirty, trying to hang on to my life as my own man. I knew God held the rights to my life, and my faith faced many tests with all the death around me.

My momma said as I shipped off, "God will carry you home." Right now, I'm not sure what she meant. Home could be heaven or coming back home to American soil.

Momma and dad caught the train with me, and we spent our last moments on the railway on my way to New York City. They watched me board a ship with the thought they may never see me again. Momma held her head up high with a stiff chin, showing pride and strength, but her eyes did not hide pain drenched with fear, and her forehead worry lines disappeared into her hair. Dad – the emotional one, his anger showed. Dad helped me to be a man, and Uncle Sam wanted me to kill other men for a country who made life hell for men who looked like him. Dad's wrathful – pedestal didn't matter now as the devil is dressed in a Nazi uniform.

I took another quick peek down the alley, watching the Nazis dragging the American GI through a doorway, and slam the door behind him. I went running down toward the door in a zigzag stop and go sprint. I hoped darkness cloaked me from a bullseye. I spotted three doors side by side. Which door did they disappear behind? I insanely recited a nasty nursery rhyme, as killing to live does take some measure of lacking rational thought.

I lay on the ground between two of the three doors. My service revolver held six shots. I pointed my gun muzzle skyward as if to pray my bullet will crucify Lucifer and send him back to hell. I prayed for some sign of where I should shoot. I shouted the nursery rhyme we learned to say in combat, "Eenie,

32

Meenie, Mighty Moe...catch a Nazi by his balls and make him say hi Hitler up your ass in fucking hell!"

Wood splintered from a door. Bullets whizzed well above my head and to the right of me...the third door. Men with guns, when under pressure, can lack smarts – he gave away his position. I rolled in front of the door and shot back through the wood at mid-height. I heard a grunt and the fall of dead weight against the door. I ran and rammed the door with full impact. The door came off the hinges, and it fell over the top of human flesh. A dead Nazi lay under the door, and the other soldier inside—an American, lay wounded and sprawled out in the corner. Maybe the Nazi thought he apprehended a ranking officer he could trade for his freedom.

The White soldier suffered from a bullet hole in his hand, and two bullets wounds in his leg, shattering a bone. I ripped the clothing off the Nazi and used it to wrap tight my compatriot's wounds and drug him to safety. The fighting died down, and my troop wound-up on the better side of the battle.

The rear flank and the side sustained significant losses. My Colored boys survived with minor flesh wounds, except one Colored soldier. He lost an arm from a grenade. The soldier I rescued, he held value if captured. The captain's son–in–law, a staff sergeant, set out to prove his bravery, which can cause your death, or you get someone else killed. The captain's son–in–law had been ordered to stay close to the backlines. Now he is a wounded man looking as if he was brave. *What kind of man did it make me?*

Episode 5

Now months later, I'm still in the rain and mud of war. This burn barrel keeps us gathered for warmth and brotherly love. Hot cocoa or coffee and chocolate bars are the only sweet things I have. Life is sweet for the captain's son–in– law. He went home as a war hero for surviving. His hand will be okay, he'll walk with a limp as a badge of honor, and he's at home just in time to see the birth of a son. What a blessing to live and see the delivery of your child.

The captain is happy his new grandchild will have a father, and his daughter will have a husband. I'm looking around at men who hope to see their children again, or who want to be able to make a baby. Saving the captain's son–in–law is an emotional scar for me as it scabs over, but won't heal as he's with his child, and I cannot be with mine.

I made a baby with my high school sweetheart, Kathy Brown, eight years ago. At the time I landed on the shores of France, she moved in with another man, putting my child under his roof.

She stated her threat almost daily, that if I went off to war, she would leave me for another man. She always threatened to leave me, and had left me for short periods of time, but we would repeatedly break–up and then make–up. She kept her threat this time, and there is no turning back. I will not take her back anymore. The United States of America drafted me, but she acted as if I controlled the United States of America. I tried to marry her before I left, but she would not hear of it.

She said, "I don't want to be a war hero's widower, and I don't need to put flowers on a man's grave and still have his last name."

Ten years ago, Kathy Brown wanted to marry me right after we graduated from high school, but I headed to college. I sought to make a living to ensure a bright financial future without hustling in the years to come, so I could take care of her and any child we might have. The future came before I graduated from college.

My son's name is Baritone, named after the saxophone my dad plays the sax, and my mom loved to hear. Dad also plays the tenor, and he loves it as well, but he loves to please my mom more.

Something changed in Kathy right after my son entered this mad world. She didn't want marriage anymore. She wanted to live with me, but not marry me. I said no. Maybe I should have listened to her. Perhaps I did the right thing. I knew it would upset my mother and father, and I felt in some ways I failed my parents and God when I helped create a child before marriage. I sought to rise above the negative thinking. My son is a gift, but I wanted to be married to her and have a family. I told Kathy how I felt, but she always laughed it off.

My mother and father for over twenty–nine years stayed married, and out of respect for them, I chose not to live with a woman under the same roof without being married. I paid for a lovely apartment for Kathy and my son. I helped her earn her degree in music by coming over in the day or evenings and taking care of my son while she went to school, and I paid for her tuition.

Kathy always wanted to be a music teacher, and I met her as her voice seemed to touch the rain clouds in Seattle and part them. My mother taught Kathy voice lessons, and vibrant and sultry and sassy came through her lips much like Dinah Washington. Kathy stole my heart within four notes. With the first look at her stunning beauty, and hearing her songbird voice singing next to my mother, I might have fallen in love as she looked over at me.

I think she loved me, but she never fell *in love* with me. She loved the fact that I made money, and I used my skills to treat her to the best things, and later on, my son reaped the benefits of my love and lifestyle. As I look back, she eyeballed bad boys. Although there is a side of me that is wild and dangerous, I might have come across as a choirboy. In Kathy's words, "My bookworm annoyed her at times."

I stand here in this rain, hoping this war does not take away the possibilities of me ever seeing my son again, but I have stopped missing Kathy. She stopped letting my parents see my son when I shipped off, and it's breaking their hearts. When I return home, I'm going to fight for my son. For my son, I have hope that I'm in the last generation of having to have an extra side hustle to have a little more in life. I plan for him to know what hard work is, but he will use his mind to earn above the board money.

I spend as much time with my son as his mother allowed. I picked him up at school, and he hung out with me at my place until she came by to pick him up, and often she would stay over, or I would stay with her. I bought her a car and gave her, I feel, the best of me.

With me leaving to ship out for the war, I went by to tell her the date of my departure. She didn't answer the door. I figured she would bring my son down to see me off, although she said she no longer wanted to be my lover, my woman, or to be in my life. I left her notes. Each time I went to her door, I called her on the phone in the hallway of her apartment complex, and she never called me. I left notes on her door. I needed her to let me hold my son before my departure. Finally, she met me outside of her apartment and made it known she had another man, and she did not welcome me into her place anymore where I paid the rent. I quickly put some people on it to find out who would be around my son. I think of myself as a man of knowing what is going on, but that wasn't the case when it came to the fact that she had a man hanging in the wings. I stayed faithful to her when we were together. Whenever she took one of her breaks from me, I saw other women. I assumed she did the same during those times we were apart. I never believed I owned her or controlled her. I never thought she would move another man in with her and my son.

I received an education when she turned me away from me and my son for the last time. She gave me a diploma in having a painful frame of mind. She tossed my heart out like garbage, leaving me as useless as rotten meat a dog wouldn't eat.

I am standing here at a burn barrel in another country reflecting on saving another man's life, and he is now with his child. I need saving. Inside my head, there is mental maiming, ripping at my heart. I can and must overcome the hurt of losing my son, and up until now, I've been killing Nazis as my pain reliever. At times, I have thought I wanted to take a wounding bullet to send me home and chase the enemy away from my child. But then again, a bullet in me would only add another insult to my wounded heart. The enemy didn't steal her, she invited him in, and I received my walking papers.

I received a letter from Kathy months ago. She wrote that, *she and her man were moving to California. Leave her alone and her man and my son alone.* Being a harshly worded letter, I knew her well enough to know she didn't talk so absolute and dramatic. I assumed the man might have forced the issue for his own insecurities. Her new man is now my enemy.

That letter...

The day after I read her letter, I killed a Nazi in battle. I ended the life of other Nazis, but this one, I shot him ten times when I knew the first bullet put a through and through hole in his head. We were on a night patrol, and that letter had me distracted. I leaned against a tree having a nightmare with my eyes wide open, seeing each word on the paper as burning words. My nightmare – the dark forest became a movie screen. I could see another man making love to my woman, and my son slept in the other room. I saw myself standing in the doorway of her bedroom watching him touch her and penetrate her, and then, my son walked right past me and up to the bed to where he and I watch the naked man thrust into his mother.

My son asked, "Daddy, why did you leave me?"

Footsteps in the dark awoke me. A German soldier, as he stood in front of me all by himself in the forest. He walked right into my path. He pointed his rifle at my heart. I could see his finger pulling the trigger. *Click!* Nothing! I wasn't dead! I felt my stomach drop into my testicles. He pulled the trigger again and the same effect. Nothing. The Nazi's rifle jammed. I should have been dead. He tried to unjam his gun as I felt frozen while caught in between my nightmare and the reality of death aimed at me. He stood ten feet away, and life and death finally made me lift my rifle. I shot into the bridge of his nose. I rushed forward to his fallen body. I pointed my weapon downward and shot through his heart. Then I aimed at his crotch and fired bullet after bullet. I slaughtered any manhood he had. I repeatedly pulled the trigger so fast the barrel of my gun sizzled and popped as if hot grease and cold water hit a frying pan. The dead Nazi's blood popped like popcorn off my searing gun muzzle. Other Nazis could have run up on me and killed me, but my fellow soldiers surrounded me and removed my gun and patted me on the back as if I hit the winning home run in a baseball game.

I miss my child. I may never see him again. I sometimes cry when it rains. My son and I loved to play in the rain, and now...mist hides my tears.

Episode 6

Some of the White soldiers started to offer some form of positive acknowledgment after I terrorized the devil one hundred times, overly killing that Nazi. They might have thought, "Damn, this Negro is crazy," or just a killing machine for the cause.

I don't think I'm crazy for using a Nazi as a punching bag of bullets to help rid myself of the stress of losing love. It didn't help, but for a moment, I stood as a winner of a bad situation. I'm on another shore, and Kathy walked a gangplank headed to another man's land. I'm irritated – I guess for not feeling in control. In some ways, men can think as countries do in trying to control another country for the reasons they create as a reason justifiably or not.

Captain Castellani asked me what he could do for me after I saved his son–in–law. How do you repay someone for a life saved? His son–in–law was headed home to a safe environment, and I'm still here treading mud in a war zone. The man I saved – he'll be able to see his child, and I cannot. I took full advantage of the captain's offer. I came upon a Spanish classical guitar in a nearly burnt-down farmhouse to the south of town while fixing a radio tower transmitter. I wanted to keep it safe – put it in a place where I could retrieve it and play it. The captain kept it with him and trusted me to go into his tent to retrieve the guitar anytime I wanted to put it away for safekeeping to take back home one day. His MPs were told to make sure of my access with no racist games. I enjoyed mad faces as I passed by.

Afterward, I made a box from old planks of wood, and I modified it to hold the guitar, and I padded the guitar by using dead Nazi's coat sleeves and patches. I then kept the guitar in my tent. I also collect booty of German Luger pistols and anything one can call priceless, and I tucked it away in the guitar case. The guitar is my baby, and the box is a holding cell for valuables. I killed a ranking German soldier, and I claimed his British Walther PPK. He might have killed a British soldier to attain the gun. I intend to take it home...if I live.

I requested to set up significant endeavor. I wanted a way to ship motorcycle parts from all the German, Swedish, and Italian motorcycles the Germans left behind. To my men, they are known as pretty girls. It taunted me to see all these motorcycles lying around. I could strip one down into parts in a matter of twenty minutes.

Large tents house the mechanical work repair shop area where the service and repair unit work is done when we aren't fighting or cleaning up. I supervise repairs of anything from guns to trucks. I make parts and tools when needed. My crew sharpens knives and makes crutches for wounded soldiers. I soldered broken wire-rimmed glasses for those in need. I learned, in my mother's instrument repair shop, the knowledge of small-item repair, and combined my dad's passed-down expertise of mechanics work for anything else. And, no doubt, having a degree in Mechanical Engineering helped me do many things.

The captain used his connections to set up shipping of torn apart motorcycles in wood crates headed back to the States. I have an idea of what I will do with them when the war is over. Containers leave from our camp daily on trucks and make it onto ships. The captain made it look like an Army assignment, and nobody knows it's all for me.

I made two more requests of the captain, and he never even flinched when I asked. I did save his daughter's husband from peril. I wanted any soldier under my rank or equal to me in rank, to address me with the level of respect anyone of my class deserved around my men. Me being a non-commissioned officer, they could not salute me, but they could verbally address me with respect for now on. He elevated me to the rank of First Sergeant, and some Medal of Volar award that come along with some medals. It's the same rank, but comes with more pay, authority, and respect. I'm a fightin' man and a thinking man.

My last request, "Captain, I want a place for my men to let off some steam. There is an inn at the end of town, they serve beer and wine, but the inn sits empty of anyone drinking or eating most of the time."

"Master Sergeant Preer, if I agree to this, it can be only for your Colored men."

"Captain, I want it to be for only the Colored soldiers on Friday and Saturday nights."

"There can be no drunkards or fights. I can't have any race-mixing with the town women. I have others above me who will feel loathing of any interactions."

"Captain, I'll do you one better. My men will not escort any women in, and no race mixing will happen outside of the inn. Women will be free to come in on their own, but for sure, they will not walk with a Colored man outside the inn."

"I want White MPs at each end of a one-hundred feet limit. I approve of a trial run."

I wanted a place for the Colored boys to have a place to drink a bit and to blow off some steam. The captain sat in charge of overseeing row houses of brothels for the White boys, and a courtyard tent for drinking. The Negro soldiers deserved their watering hole.

Episode 7

I sleep in the mechanics' tent at night. At daybreak, I walk out into the freshening of the morning fog. I make it to our Colored soldier encampment before dawn most mornings to make sure I have an accounting for all my men. Some men snore like tank motors revving. Little Roy...his snore is louder than a train, so he sleeps at least four tents away from all the rest.

I make some small talk with a few men and see all is in place, and I make it back to the mechanic's tent. I'm tearing down motorcycles and constructing shipping crates for the parts. This war gives a man so little of private time, and I need and love my privacy.

A few other men who have sleep problems are drinking coffee around the burn barrel. Other men rise earlier than the first call just so they can hit the outhouses, or something a little freer and cleaner, the open fields of tall grass. I dug my hole and relieved myself at first light. Most of the southern boys lived in rural places and were new to a flushing a toilet when they came to boot camp.

My visits down South taught me the lesson of the better things in life. But, living in cities, I grew up in a house with an indoor flushing toilet and running hot water. A hot water shower in our house is all I knew as the norm in our home as my dad proudly installed a homemade system. I would love a hot water bath or shower to wash off the French dirt. From a boiling pot of water, I have been able to wash myself down. I have a setup in my tent, using a welding torch or a kerosene heater and iron pots to boil water. I am a solitary individual, and I only let my most trusted men know of some of my perks and hand-built advances, and I let them use my setup occasionally. Everybody else uses cold water, but I built a cold-water shower for the men in my area by pumping water from a low-lying aquafer in the adjacent wooded area behind the tents. We have knives sharpened for shaving. We Colored soldiers like to look clean even if we're not. We cut each other's hair and even shave another man's face.

As I'm walking into the work tent, my alarm goes off. I have a warning system if someone is approaching. When we beat the Germans down and out of this region, they left behind many things, one of them is dogs, and now, inside the tent, sits a German Sheppard – my buddy, Jerri.

From the nearby mountains, we heard howling all night long for weeks when we moved into this camp. Some soldiers wanted to hunt and kill, figuring the Nazi's left the dog behind, and the howling kept them up all night. The captain would not allow the men to hunt and shoot a dog, and he made it clear with the threat of solitary confinement for not following his orders. Germans had control of this area before we ran them out. There were remote sightings and captures of Germans that happened when soldiers were separated from their retreating troops.

I snuck out and went into the forest looking for the dog. I found the dog with cut paws and barely being able to walk. The dog never growled at me or even barked when I picked the animal up and carried the limp body back to camp. I nursed my new pet back to health and let no one pet or feed my new friend. Now, I have a four-legged warning system with keen senses, even if a rat is near. Two low-volume barks and my four-legged alarm gave me warring of any humans nearby. Jerri, my dog, walks out of the mechanic's tent with me, and we meet Little Roy coming my way.

His expression on his face matches his joy. Oh boy, I'm looking forward to tonight. We can dance our way into town and have a beer, and maybe some thick looking hind–quarter ole` French gal might come through the door."

I forced an agreeing smile and nod to mask my thoughts of the chances of a woman picking Little Roy as her choice for the night. I could see women in his past, as he might have emptied his wallet more often than not.

"Man, what the hell are you doing up so early?" It's drizzling and turning into a downpour, so I signaled for him to move over to under a tree. "The only thing you're ever early for is food."

He chuckled and pulled out a cigarette, but didn't light up. The guys in my troop knew I hated the way cigarettes made my eyes water.

Little Roy is from Chicago and could be a scary Negro if he lost his temper. His temper...I figured it rose out of fear of being embarrassed. I always stayed in my space when around him, but out here on the battlefield, we try to connect as you never know who might save you. It may be fear. In this war, we all dealt with many worries.

Fear ... you're lost behind enemy lines with no food or water and low on ammo.

Fear ... looking down at your leg and the other leg has just been blown off.

Fear ... all mental and physical pain, real or anticipated, could be the last fear you feel as you are dying.

Fear ... even the slightest cough could turn to be the beginning of a death call.

Fear ... it calls your name before you close your eyes, and fear says hello at dawn.

Fear ... is what people felt when they encountered Little Roy's violent side.

He is a guy with some insecurity issues when it comes to women wanting him, which often makes him replace his lack of confidence with arrogant conceit. He has an evil twin. The evil in him is uncontrolled physical anger. I protected him from laying pain on anyone who might end up on his wrong side. Except for the first time when I failed.

❧ ❧ ❧

Back during boot camp, on one Saturday night leave, a bunch of us Colored soldiers made it to our side of town to throw back some beers and tear the sweet meat off some ribs. A civilian who thought his, at least 6'4" and 250 pounds of ignorant arrogance were enough for him to talk crazy, made comments by saying what Little Roy's family must look like in foul ways. The man mocked my fellow soldier over a woman showing more interest in Little Roy instead of him. Little Roy spent a lot of money buying drinks for her at the bar, trying to act richer than poorer with a near empty wallet, and he and this woman were nowhere near leaving as a couple for the night.

Little Roy is not an attractive man, nor a smooth talker. Although he tells stories of his conquests of women, you always knew the truth ran far away with him. His telltale sign appeared in a nervous tick of his soup cooler bottom lip quivered when his lies outraced the truth, and a fair amount of excitement exited his mouth in the form of wetness. You kept your face out of the way of his jokes or rage. The truth: his main outlet was passed around dirty magazines, but generally, he's a nice guy unless provoked. The loudmouth civilian with foul jokes caused the woman to move away from Little Roy.

Little Roy smoldered on his barstool after the verbal insults, and after a possible date walked away. Pulsating veins in his neck, and a visual throb in his forehead, were telltale signs that his heart pumped rage in his soul. One could see his dark brown skin turn to reddish-purple on his broad nose, and his lips became tighter and thicker with a whitish ash line which had formed around his lips. He boiled on his bar stool. He was becoming hot as a pot of grits bubbled in a pot on a stove. Little Roy's anger was fire-poker red when he followed the civilian as he went to the bathroom.

Little Roy followed with a beer bottle in hand. I grabbed his forearm, it's larger than most men's thighs, and for sure, it felt as hard as the oak bar where he had sat. He jerked, and my hand released quicker than a rattlesnake bite. His pull reminded me of my grandfather's mules' team, ripping caked hard dirt. All I could do was follow the destruction coming and try to keep it from turning into a murder charge.

The arrogant fool stood urinating and laughing when Little Roy stood behind him. In a sarcastic tone, the civilian spoke over his shoulder. "Little man, what–cha– n–here– fer? You wanna shake my thang off?"

Oh shit, Little Roy is broader than the man is tall, and yet the man has the nerve to call him a little man. Often, civilian men tested soldiers – knowing soldiers' codes of conduct and behavior which meant they would put themselves in jeopardy if they attacked a civilian. However, each man has his breaking point.

While still urinating, the foolish fool turned and peed on top of Little Roy's boot. His boots were polished brighter than any others in camp. Little Roy put meticulous care and pride in his shine.

Mocking a man and then peeing on a man's pride...how could a man insult another man twice in a matter of seconds, and not expect the worse to happen? Little Roy swung the beer bottle like a whip across the tip of the man's penis. The man's face twisted like a pinwheel as if his foreskin peeled off and stuck to a wall. At the same time, he exposed his jaw. A left hook from Little Roy turned into an uppercut. The great heavyweight Jack Johnson wished he'd thrown that punch and knocked out his lesser foe instead of throwing a fight when he gave away his championship title. The blow from Little Roy landed on the man's chin, sending the civilian flying back in time to Africa before a slave ship arrived. Blood, so much blood, sprayed upwards to the ceiling as the man landed in the urinal trough. The trough cradled the sucker as if he were a newborn baby. Little Roy then broke the beer bottle against the man's head. I'd been a fool to try to stop him, as no man would be wise to step in—between Little Roy's rage and the pleasure of handing out the pain the civilian felt.

With the broken beer bottle – drinking end, Little Roy stuffed it in the man's mouth. I'm almost ashamed to say what he did next, as my skin crawls when I close my eyes and relive what he did. Little Roy pulled out his penis and peed into the broken beer bottle. A funnel of urine went down the throat of the beaten man as if he swallowed a tall glass of root beer. I thought it might be okay to pull Little Roy away right about then.

The story made its rounds, and even Master Sergeant Jude avoided saying anything foul to Little Roy, which meant he acknowledged the destruction one man could bring. When a Redneck with power shows you respect, it's usually fear as the reason.

❀❀❀

Coming out of that memory, Little Roy calls my name. "Sir—Sir, I don't know if you heard, but one of the prostitutes down in house seven...she either killed herself or maybe somebody did her in."

I felt fear flowing in my blood like chilling instant ice, if there ever was such an invented thing.

"Little Roy...what? Tonight, is the first night for us Colored boys to party at the inn."

"Yep, and I know what you're thinking...the captain might shut down our party."

"Little Roy, tell me what you know."

"Sir-Sir, oh, I overheard a White soldier saying he thought one of the prostitutes killed herself or somebody took her life."

"This is the third dead prostitute in four weeks, Little Roy."

Episode 8

A suicide, although it appeared strange to be self-inflicted. Another prostitute is dead. I'm wondering what the hell might be happening. *Why?* Death, by any means to a non-Colored woman, is a threat of death to Colored men anywhere near. Supposedly, one of the Gypsy housekeepers found another prostitute hanging in the same fashion. Us Colored men being downwind of this problem is a direct path to trouble.

I repaired motorcycles for the MPs with parts I had to make sometimes. In doing so, I attained some White associates. The guys in the military police, they were decent people, and one is from northern California, and one from Seattle. My relationship with some White soldiers is good. When a man is more in tune with being a man, he also knows trying to use his race to control other men is leading a low self-esteem existence. There a few men from the other side of the camp that will tell the rednecks to go away when I'm around. It allows me into conversations about what is going-on around the base.

But now, Little Roy was told about something he should not know about. It makes no sense that someone told him about these deaths.

When the first girl came up dead, the MPs told me something didn't look right if she had killed herself — it didn't seem possible in the fashion her life ended. It would be my opinion...these women in this sector of war can't love their experiences. With strange men touching them by the hundreds, they must die inside with each encounter. How does the mind wipe clean each time, as each man, in a few sheer minutes, spills their insides in you or upon you?

What inner spiritual life dies with each encounter? It might be out-of-body experiences having repeated sex with brutish men, or boys – I can hardly call them men because seventeen or eighteen-year olds are popping pimples and having sex for the first time.

Alternate thinking – these women might be mentally tougher than any men who can kill an enemy gunner. Whether someone approves or disagrees, I admire the mental fortitude of a prostitute. The oldest business on the Earth, and if a woman chooses to sell her body, it must be the hardest thing one can do unless you're completely numb.

Early morning drizzle landed with the news of human death into my coffee like spoiled cream. My mind is overloading with questions.

"Little Roy, I'll be back. Make your way back to camp. I want to account for our men right away. It may not be a problem, but with the death of a woman – a prostitute, and with Color men nearby...we have to make sure we're all in the clear." I'm moving toward my tent workshop.

"Sir–Sir, don't you think you may be overreacting. Ain't none of us would ever be bothered with this kind of mess." He speaks to my back, and I turned to let him finish talking. "We don't do shit like kill non-Colored gals in the middle of a bunch of White men around." He's looking at me as if I'm crazy.

I walk a few feet back toward his direction. "You need to understand one thing, even as giant as your ass is, the Army will not think twice when it comes to hanging you, or lining you up for a firing squad to help you take your last breath. They have no problem sending home a letter telling your people you have been court-martialed and executed. Pinning a murder on a Negro, instead of the right killer...*shit!*"

Staring at him, we both watch raindrops hit out noses and run into our mouths. "Hear me and hear me well. Little Roy, condemning any one of us is something they'll do and sleep well. If murder is the case, they'll look at us first. Just one of our men in the wrong place at the wrong time is something I need to know and clear up quickly. I'm not overly cautious or paranoid. This is always the life we live."

He nodded – I think he now saw the gators in the shallows. That is an old saying we said when we Colored men knew trouble could be near.

I washed my hands of grease and cleaned my stress lines on my face. I could have torn down a whole motorcycle by now and almost finished crating up the parts, but instead, I needed to deal with the situation at hand. I hate when anything separates me of my joy. I had my mindset, I would have all day to concentrate on the motorcycles, and later I would have liked to have caught a nap in the back of the tent. I devised a hidden second inner layer of tent material to hide a room. I have a little private four–foot–wide by eight–foot–long room with a soft cot and a nightstand. A troop–carrying truck without a motor in the engine bay, and a few crates and barrels hide my private world entrance. If anyone came into the mechanic's tent that is full of tools and equipment, no one would know when I appeared from the rear of the troop–carrying truck. I kept tools back there just in case.

I head back to where my men slept. I cut back through by the outhouses, and scanned the area. My corporals need to take full written accounting of all my soldiers. I need to know when they went to bed. I want to know who they slept next to. If need be, I wanted to see where each man took a shit, or peed, or smoked a cigarette in the middle of the night. I want my men to be in the clear of any suspicion. I want stories straight.

I walk in this mud of a tent city of men. It's damn cold in France, but it will turn fire red hot around here if these girls died by the hands of a Negro, or if one is suspected.

Army investigators snaking through a locked–down camp could stop my motorcycle transport business. Worse yet, if a Negro soldier kills anyone other than a Negro or a Nazi, my command will end. Then my men will face a wave of aggression from the command.

Shit! Master Sergeant Jude is standing in front of where we Colored men line–up. I see my men crawling out of the tents. Jude and I are on the same level, except for the fact that his main concern is supposed to be the White soldiers instead of the Colored. He's always looking for a reason to make me and my men look bad in the eyes of the captain. His presence before reveille dictates that I move my butt down there to intervene, but I make like I'm trotting as if I'm working out instead of being in a full dash. This man Jude is a hound dog sniffing for trouble. I don't want to track in the smell of fear, or act like there might be something wrong when there *is* something wrong.

Low–lying fog leaves a brisk, but refreshing, mist on my skin as the rain has lifted a bit. A fresh shave has my pores open. I wipe my eyes a few times as I trot, bringing things into focus. Life here is in gray tones. The landscape, the buildings, the damages of war, and most people you deal with—life is in shades of gray. White is not a color, but when mixed with hate, whatever the color of hell is that is what I see in front of me. I see hate ahead of me, and it is clear.

I turn on my professional soldier demeanor. I talk to my guys first as I would any other time. "Fall in men."

I turn to Master Sergeant Jude and give him my usual, almost condescending expression of speech, "Morning, how are you, Master Sergeant Jude? What brings you to this part of the camp, if I may ask?"

"Do you know what has taken place?" He has the face of a young male with pockmarked skin, making him look old. His blonde eyelashes harbor flakes of dead skin as his blonde peach fuzz confuses you from assessing his age. I know he is thirty, as we share the same birth month and year. We will never share a drink and the good times of friendship. I am a threat to him. I am taller and built as if I'm Joe Louis, the heavyweight champion, and he has the build of a middleweight with a sunken-in chest. His mean mouth affixes hate to his evil filled stare, and his rank and race is his only defense – otherwise, I would knock his yellow scum-covered teeth out of his mouth.

"Preer, do you know where all your men are? Do you know where they all slept last night? And Preer...where were you?"

I smile as if I'm happy to see him, but someone is approaching our Negro or meeting.

"Good morning, sir," I say, talking to Captain Castellani. Jude slowly turns to face the captain. Then Jude turns back to me, glaring as if I've gotten away with something. I stare back at Jude in hopes he can read my mind, and I am saying, *kiss my ass.*

Jude proved he's stupid, again...it's not the first time for him moving too fast in trying to know who, what, when, and where while attempting to work his bullshit into the mix. I know his hate-filled heart dislikes the fact that the captain respects me. He also hates that I saved the captain's son. Jude can never match my competence when he lacks my capability. The captain and I keep our business to ourselves. He knows like I know, we all have people around us who would pee on our graves after they have shot us in the back. Once a man does some dirt, it involves someone else no matter what. Behind the back deals and setups, there are many possible ways of blackmail, and the captain and I know this. We have discussed the *what ifs*.

❧❧❧❧

I, a Negro, became the head of the Seattle Police. Why? I'm damn good at what I do in attaining knowledge of someone's dirty deeds. An assistant deputy chief of police-involved himself in a sexual tryst, and he paid the price.

Every week, I delivered the cash payoffs for police protection for my dad and uncle's street businesses to an assistant deputy police chief. On one such delivery, the assistant chief asked if I knew of any male cross-dressers, declaring he knew of someone with a lot of money who partook in such a fetish. Of course, he made a point of deploring such sexual immorality. I read into his horseshit and of his want to satisfy his freakish desires. I assumed he asked me instead of my uncle because, at the time of my young age, he might have thought I appeared not savvy enough to know he chased male booty with his police badge.

He knew my uncle Sonny's schemes to supply whatever anyone asked. There is no surprise in this world concerning the high demand for male prostitutes who crossed dress for rich and powerful men who live in a house with gates and estate names, and request such treats.

This assistant deputy police chief with a sweet tooth for loving a male butt behind closed doors automatically blackmailed himself into a corner from the supplier. How awful it would be to have your wife, children, or colleagues see pictures, on the front page of a newspaper, of a Negro man dressed in skimpy women's clothing, hugging, and kissing on you, or possibly a lot more. Corruption would be funny if it weren't as evil as being the same people coming down hard on a Colored man's throat. Powerful people living *castles made of sand*, they are just as criminal, but they throw Colored men in jail or do worse to us.

I arranged for the cross-dresser and the assistant deputy police chief's *friend* to meet at a hotel. A two-way mirror and a camera captured the sodomizing deputy at his worse, as he like giving in and taking it. It all worked out in my favor as the assistant deputy police chief wanted to satisfy his deviation, and I used it against him and I became the HNIC (Head Negro in Charge) of the Seattle Police Motorcycle Pool. It all adds up to a lesson of *be careful of who you do business with*.

※ ※ ※

The rain is picking up speed as men scurry into formation. I stare at Master Sergeant Jude with a smile of, "I got you again."

"Why...captain, good morning." Master Sergeant Jude made a feeble attempt to lick his ranking officer's boots. "I came down here to inspect the troops this morning.

The captain cocked his head and cut his eyes hard at Jude as the fool kept babbling. "We need to keep the Negros ready to fight if need be." Nervously, he spoke as if he knew his ass stood in the wrong place. In the background, I could hear my men clearing their throats and spitting on the ground.

The captain turned to me and instructed me to dismiss my men, and I did. Then he addressed both Jude and me. "Gentlemen," Jude's face reddened, and I know he despises the thought of me being categorized as his equal–even though I am—as the captain addressed us both. "We might have somewhat of a problem."

Master Sergeant Jude shot his mouth off, trying to gain favor again, and he might as well put his ass in a skillet of hot lard. "Sir, I came here in advance to round the Negros up to make an account of their whereabouts so we can..."

The captain cut him off. "Under whose direction did you do anything, soldier? Master Sergeant Jude, there is no *we*. For you to make decisions is premature, and it's leading you to make foolish engagements." Captain Castellani's gray wolf eyes narrowed and seemly ripped the hair from Jude's once puffed–out chest as he stood deflated, and I enjoyed it.

The captain continued. "Let me start over. Last night, or early this morning, another death of a woman who worked in the brothels occurred. It's strange for two women to lose their lives in this fashion. From the first reports I have received from our MPs, and the reports from the base doctor, its self–inflicted strangulation suicide by her own hands, and both women appear to have slashed their throats as the cause of death."

I'm listening, and I take it to mean it's uncomplicated when it comes to justice issues and with Colored men in the area of crime scenes. I see so much going on in this little French town that we Americans are occupying. We are doing wrong. The war left from this area some months ago, and here we are...the American Army is running a prostitution ring. We are pimping to keep our soldiers happy under the guise we need this area for shipping.

The Army is stealing American GIs' money. They give a drop in the bucket to the brothel owners, and then the whores receive the trickledown effect of hardly enough money to survive.

Maybe it is suicide taking their lives. Most pimps convince their prey they love them and want to take care of them. The reality is they pretend to care just enough to let a trick dream of a better life. In America, we pimp with twisted thinking of an enhanced experience of life is coming as we give our minds and bodies up for a roof over our heads, a decent meal, and maybe some pretty things.

I stand here listening to the captain with one ear, and trying to add up how all of this helps me or hurts me.

Jude does not know when to stop with the mistaken points running out his mouth. "Ah, captain...we should cancel the Colored soldier's party for tonight as a safety precaution of keeping track of them."

"Master Sergeant Jude, you're dismissed." The captain also gave Jude a dismissive glare as he almost barked at him, "I have no more to say to you."

Jude stands looking confused when I know he's not. A bullet–filled with his hate could tip the rock of knowledge upon his head, and his self-righteous stupidity would still have him dumbfounded in hate.

Jude turned away and silently cursed the ground. I'm sure I am the ground in his mind. It is me who is not stepping into his bullshit.

The captain barked an order, "Jude, return to me right now."

Jude turned with his face flush and his eyes filled with hostility. I watched a heavy splat of rain hit his helmet, and it made a thudding sound.

"Master Sergeant Jude," the captain's voice seems to dig a hole under him. "Understand what I'm saying, it is a fucking order you are to obey to the fullest. You are not to engage any of the Negro soldiers with any orders, or give directions from here on out unless I direct you to do so. Am I fucking clear?"

The captain allows Jude to nod instead of replying.

"You're dismissed."

A memory reminded me – when my cousins and I were young, and we almost got our little behinds tore up for something we did, or at least one of us did which got us all in trouble. But when Jude turned away this time, his eyes did not curse me. Apparently, he felt the sting of embarrassment. Then I noticed the captain's eyes were on me, and the fire sent in the direction of Jude had died out from his gray wolf eyes.

We stood in silence. The rain became loud, and my men were now in the distance from the both of us. I collectively could hear their boots stomping in the mud. A battle brewed, but where? I fought with my heart to let me slowly think about how to avoid war and conflicts.

My men are heading over to the mess tent to eat. The White soldiers are leaving from the food line. I can tell the captain has more to say to me as we turn and watch Jude in the distance. It looks like I'll miss the morning meal.

"Sergeant Preer..."

"Yes, sir,"

"We...I need you to look into all of this. I need you to look around every corner possible to find information, but we must maintain as much confidentiality in our doings as possible. Don't draw attention to you as you are seeking and searching. We need this problem to go away. The girl this morning did not kill herself."

"Did the other girl take her life?" I knew the answer, but he expected me to ask...or, so I assumed.

The captain shook his head while he looked behind him and toward the mountains but not at me when he spoke. "Come to my tent at noon, and I'll give you more information to work with." He stopped talking suddenly. His lips pressed tight as if someone might hear us talking, but we were thirty feet away from anyone else. His eyes still didn't engage me as he finally, with a low voice, said, "If you find out any of *your men...*"

The captain's wolf eyes scan from left to right, still avoiding eye contact with me. I can tell he does not want to say, Colored men, as if it would offend our relationship.

"Captain, if I may be frank?"

"You may."

"Captain, if you want me to look into this, I will. We both have a stake in keeping this area off the radar of higher-ups. A soldier of any race can blow apart our interests. We must stop harm from coming to those women. We all have mothers, sisters, daughters, or lovers."

The captain finally connected his eyes to mine. He understood his connection to women.

"Wherever this leads to, we have to stop it silently. I know of a man in a White unit – he can help if you can arrange for him to work near the brothels, sir. He can help me help us. I'll send him to you."

The captain nodded, I gave him a salute, and he walked away. I knew his balls were in a vice. His commanders, the other thieves in the den, are counting on him to keep soldiers buying sex from the women.

Hitler gases his unwanted, and the Americans rescue those unwanted and pimp them. *What is the right side of morality? What is the lesser of two evils?* I wonder did Cain kill Abel before women started the world's oldest profession.

We can never know all of the reasons Cain killed his brother. Maybe a woman of the night caused his anger to rise to the point of murder.

The temperature is dropping, and my skin feels more than the usual chill. I look up in the sky. The gray is turning darker and moving. There is a storm rolling in, I hope it is not snow. The French say this time of year, a snowstorm can drop up to four feet, and it makes me feel more pressure to find out what's going on as quickly as possible.

If the captain is feeling pressure, I'll assume I'm not the only one he asked to be on a search mission for information. When some people feel stress, they tend to walk on strained sensitive grounds, causing an earthquake of negative responses. Unknowingly, they add more pressure and can cause panic and help things to fall apart.

I turn and face the oncoming trotting in the mud footsteps. "Master Sergeant Preer."

"Yes, corporal."

"I accounted for everyone. I know where all slept last night and I have confirmed each soldier's story with another soldier verifying." Lanky Slim is one of my corporals, and he relayed to me what I wanted to hear. His Cajun accent attached some joy to the news. Well, only one person could not account for his whereabouts and what they were doing last night.

Episode 9

I'm that person.

I slept in the mechanics' tent all last night with my German Sheperd—Jerri, and with my lover—Valentina.

She and I were making love until just before the early morning dawn. Soldiers see her in the distance and believe her to be Romanian, or a gypsy, and she is not. They view her moving slowly around town, dressed ragged and semi bent over, much like a middle-aged lady, and she is not. She appears to be feeble, and for sure, her body is feminine, shapely, and sensually alluring hidden behind her tattered clothes. She wears a shabby, woolen throw-over as part of her disguise. It looks as if she's a monk in a monastery hiding her womanly figure and the actual woman she is. Many of the common folk in and around this area dress in whatever the war has left them. I come to know some women dress as unattractive as they can for many reasons, but mainly for self-preservation.

Her name full name is Valentina Zadar, and she is the most attractive Colored woman I have ever known. How she has hidden from being exposed could be called magic.

One night I went into the forests to find the howling dog, in hopes of fetching him in order to keep the other soldiers from killing the dog. I encountered her for the first time in the forest mountain range overlooking the French town the base is near. We have survived this war, but if heaven is above the ugliness of this hell, for now in my life, she is a blue ocean and blue skies.

I rescued the dog, and Valentina saved me. The dog howled in the forest for weeks, and soldiers were going stir-crazy in trying to get to sleep. A hunting reward of cartons of smokes, chocolate, black licorice, and other things waited for the killer of the dog. Before a non–commissioned hunting party snuck out to kill the dog, I set out to save the dog if I could. My corporals covered for me so that I could head out in the mid-afternoon. It's not uncommon for me to be in the work tent, repairing items. I demanded my secluded time, and I delegated duties and kept order while I did my work in the mechanic's tent.

The captain resisted letting a hunting party go out to look for the dog for fear of running into Nazis. The last sightings of the enemy trying to escape back to Germany were months ago, but I prepared myself just in case.

I did not want the dog to pick up my scent and get scared away, so I trekked along a back ridge, which made my hike into the forest hours longer. It is coal black in the woods, and turns colder in the hills, so I moved as fast I could to stay in the last of the daylight. A half-moon acted as the sun peeking through tall trees, helping with lighting my way a bit. The barking we heard for weeks always started to the north of us, but sometimes it moved around. The dog had to be high up on the mountain ridge, and his howling echoed down on us.

Before it became dark, I made it to the top of the back ridge. At the top, I found a well–worn, narrow path through low–lying branches. With light dwindling, I spotted blood on the ground; some dried, but a lot of it was fresh.

The brush became thicker, and the path tighter and the light disappeared. I took time to stare into the dark, and my eyes adjusted.

I made my way with less than three feet of space in front of me at a time before I had to stop to move the thicket out of my face, but a worn trail under my feet allowed me to keep going. It became harsh on my back and legs after making the long hike up the ridge and then having to bend low. I moved slowly to hear and smell while not announcing my presence. The dog may have already moved away, sensing a human near him. I thought that because I listened for barking or howling as the dog usually did at this time of the day. I decided to sit still, rest, and monitor. I slumped down, leaned against a large boulder to close my eyes, and just listened to the forest breathing. Fatigued, I fell asleep.

I awoke to see the moon leaning to the south. Moments later, the town bell gave notice of midnight. I slept for a while. What woke me, but did not startle me, was a brownish German Sheppard who sat between my legs. An awful smell permeated off the dog. The dog sat non-threatening and calm, but whimpering. With the dog inches away from my face, I reached my hand out to let the dog smell my scent. I did a long, low-volume whistle hoping it traveled through the woods. The dog cocked his head. I started singing to the dog and rubbed the chest area gently, and the dog laid down.

I stroked the top of the dog's head. The hair felt matted and caked with dirt, and the dog smelled dead. This condition of the dog made me feel awful, and the strength of the stench had my stomach tossing and turning. Along the way, I dropped dried beef and sat by the rock to let the dog find me.

I reached in my bag and pulled out some dried beef. The dog slowly licked and then removed the food from my hand, but all the while eyeing me. I lifted myself to one knee, and I reached and felt the dog's legs. With bone-thin legs, and fresh and old blood under the paws, I knew I would have to carry the dog out. I pulled out some rags and salve. The dog hesitated from pain, but let me wrap its wounded paws. In the process, I discovered what I thought would be a boy dog, but she's a girl in need of love. I poured water into my tin cup and tried to feed the dog some water the same way you would give water to a human, but it did not work too well. She licked water out of my cupped hands instead.

I walked away a bit to see if she would follow me, and she did, but she limped hard in trying. Her body shook with pain. I'd have to pack her out, and I lifted the dog to carry her as if she were a child. I took deep breaths to encourage my body and back for the trek back down. I hoisted her over my shoulders. She let out a feeble yelp, but she surrendered control. I made it back to the top of the ridge and started to work my way down. The half-moon reflected a shadow as a hunchback man. I kept my eyes down on the dark trail, and I walked into a long barrel of a rifle with a bayonet. I felt it pierce my coat and prick me. I looked into the face of pale broken skin that showed fear in a dangerous man. The dog began to growl and I felt the dog's body vibrating on my shoulders.

The pale skin enemy said, "Geben Sie mir ihre Nahrung und Wasser Darkie oder ich werde Sie bleiben." I understood three of the words the Nazi said: food, water, and Darkie.

He pushed the bayonet tip into my skin. I felt the stings of the piercing, and I let out a low grunt from the pain. The blade stopped when it hit my breastplate bone. I felt warm blood spreading on my chest. I slumped down to one knee – a sixty-pound dog on my shoulders weighed me down, and now with a chest wound and anxiety, I lost a little strength.

I pushed my side bag forward to give to the German, but he didn't take it. I looked up from the ground, and I could see a Nazi in lousy shape, and maybe he smelled worse than the dog. A frayed and filthy uniform hung loosely from a once healthy body. His bearded face did little to hide the sullenness produced by hunger. His comrades must have deserted him when they evacuated the area. I would assume he tried to escape back to Nazi land but ran into American troops at the end of every road and trail. I guess he hid in the forest as his only option, but he understood hopes of a future were slim as death loomed with each human heartbeat that came near him.

I tossed my bag behind him, and he didn't turn to retrieve it. The Nazi depicted being frozen and not looking at me, but staring over me. The dog rumbled on my shoulders attempting to growl, but it was feeble. A deafen gun blast from behind me made the dog jerk and yelp. The detonation lighted the area around me as if a lightning strike had hit just a few yards away. The German started to fall back when another gun blast from some distance away echoed. Now his body spun and dropped. The dog kept yelping, and she shook with terror.

I knew where the distant blast came from, and why the German spun like a top. From a distance, a sniper hit him bullseye. N–Booty, my Hawkeye sharpshooter, trailed me as my extra precaution or protection if needed. He kept 50 to 100 yards behind me all along the way.

The first shooter spoke to the back of my kneeling body. "Are you alright?" A soft, English–speaking voice entered my ears. A woman with an unfamiliar accent stood directly behind me. I struggled to lift the dog off me as the dog's heart pumped hard with laboring weakness.

"Let me help you."

I felt the weight of the helpless dog lift off my shoulders. The dog would have let buzzards pick her bones while alive. I stood and finally took some labored breaths. Before I turned to face the first shooter of the German soldier, I did a long, low–volume whistle as I did before to tell N–Booty, my sharpshooter, to stay in place and not come...yet.

I turned and faced a woman in a tattered woolen throw-over. She held the dog in her arms and made a gesture to hand her back to me. At her feet lay a German rifle.

I said, "She's cold and scared. She's going to die unless I can help heal her at my camp. But first, I need for you and me to move around the ridge. My shooter, who is somewhere on the other ridge, he might think you are a danger to me. You are not a danger to me, right?"

"Soldier, are you a danger to me?" a soft, but stern voice parted from her lips.

Before I could answer, she turned and walked around the ridge, and I followed. My whistle to N–Booty would keep him from approaching. Once around the hill, she faced me and stared, then stroked the dog.

"The Germans left her. I brought her food, hoping she would not howl and your soldiers would leave her alone, but I not have much. I see you did not come to harm the dog," she said.

I'd seen her near the town in those same clothes. I never saw much of her face as a draped hood always covered it, and she wandered around acting a bit feeble, and as if she were one of the Romani gypsies...at least I thought. The woman removed the hood from her face. The half-moon light cleared up any notion of an old lady. She was hardly that, instead, she showed me otherwise. She looked to be maybe in her mid-twenties, perhaps a bit older.

Her light-skin, as in sandalwood, I guessed her heritage to be Spanish or Northern Italian. The incline of the slope made her look taller than I am, but on level ground, the top of her head height met my eyes.

I put the dog down and squatted to her level. I stared up at the woman. We stared at each other and kept silent while I tended to my injury by making a mudpack and pressing rags against my wound. I would survive with a nasty scar and some pain for a while. I kept looking at her while tending to myself and re-buttoning my coat.

I finally spoke. "What are you doing here, and who are you?" I said in a slightly more aggressive tone – still not knowing whom, what, and where she came from. She held a rifle. She wasn't aiming at me, but still.

Again, I heard her unfamiliar accent and I tried to make out her background. She said, "Please care for the dog. I will make contact with you soon." I could sense her concerned emotions for the dog's emotions.

I believed in fate, but how in the hell is a woman out here on this ridge helping to kill a German who would have killed me. I have no idea what she thought while looking at me.

She pleaded with me. "Please take the dog now and care for her."

She helped place the dog back over my shoulders, and as she did, I saw with her hood off, she had a silver streak of hair a couple of inches wide to the left of the center of her dark hair. She's deceptive as she layered her silver hair to hang out of her hood as she walked around town to look much older.

"What is your name?"

"Valentina."

Before I could ask another question, the one I wanted to ask next, she answered.

"I am of Spanish African descent – some call me a moor. Now, leave please."

I headed down the hillside with an almost dead dog on my shoulders, and I walked away from a woman in the hills of France who could pass for a woman whose parents produced a light-skinned Colored girl from Detroit's Black Bottom neighborhood. Her lips were full, and her eyes were almond-shaped, and she held her head with the pride of a queen.

*** *** ***

At the bottom of the mountain, and near first light, N–Booty and I met up at our arranged meeting spot. We could never be to close on the trek, or we might risk detection by anyone.

He always smiles when he talks, and he asked, "What the hell? Are there gypsy people, along with Nazis, out here? It's a good thing I came along. I could not tell...what if a man or woman shot the Nazi up there on the ridge. I could not see well enough from my vantage point. You blocked my sight, then you went around the ridge. The best I could do is to make sure the German in my sights went down for good. I just prayed you could handle whoever. I hope the sound of the shots did not bring alarm to the camp."

I'm not sure why I felt like I did, but I felt relieved to hear N–Booty did not have a clear view of the woman on the ridge.

"Yeah man, a gypsy came out of nowhere right at the right time, and the both of you shot the Nazi." I placed my hand on my wound as seeping blood stained my shirt to almost full red dampness.

"You okay?"

"The Nazi sliced me in my chest area, but I'll live."

"Well, seeing the dog on your shoulders on the ridge, I'm glad you knelt, it gave me a clear shot at the German, but I couldn't see well enough behind you. It's a good thing I heard your whistle letting me know you found the dog and then the second time you whistled letting me know you were okay after the German went down. I'm glad I did not have to drag your body down the hill.

I nursed the dog back to health while tending to my wound. I named the dog Jerri. I grew up with a male collie with the name Jerry. My new dog...I gave her the female version of the same name. A couple of tasty meals and some warmth, and she quickly adopted me. Jerri did not venture far away from the work tent, and she hid unless I came inside. One day, Jerri came from behind a barrel barring teeth and growling at one of the guys who went inside the tent. She didn't bite his skin, but she ripped his pants leg and kept him pinned in a corner until I came. Quickly, the word got around to make sure I was inside the work tent before anyone entered.

Episode 10

I saw Valentina in her full dressing as an older woman, and bent over to hide her true self on the road across from the Negro part of the camp. She and a few other Gypsies and town folks walked near the field, headed to the river. Her silver streak of hair flowed out from under her hood. I couldn't see her face, but I knew who lived and breathed the saving of my life. She stopped and faced my way from across the field. It seems she lifted her hand to wave, but she quickly put her hand over her eyes and looked away.

After a long day of marching and field exercises that we had to do once a week to stay in fight shape, I retired to the work tent. I couldn't sleep, so I worked. The rain pelted the tent-like baseballs thrown by Satchel Paige, but in a rhythm, and the storm hit as fast as Cab Calloway sang Hi−De−Ho−Ho from the song Minnie the Moocher. I jitterbugged, and injected tempo into my walk as if the dirt floor inside my work tent represented a slick ballroom dance floor.

My dog, Jerri, sat on the floor as I glided around her while carrying parts over to a shipping crate. I laughed aloud thinking, *I don't want one of the guys to come into the tent and catch me acting silly.* I didn't have to worry with my dog in her new home alerting me to anyone's presence.

Jerri looked at me, cocking her head as I relived nights of partying in the nightclubs with pretty women. Jerri slowly rose and started walking in a circle, and then walked to the entrance of the tent. I pulled back the heavy tent curtain for her to exit. I figured she went to go potty. While bent over in a crate arranging heavy parts, I heard Jerri pawing at the curtain, coming back in by weaving her way through.

"You saved the dog." I heard the same accent from the mountain ridge, speaking to the back of me. I slowly lifted my head out of the crate and faced Valentina. I felt almost in a hypnotic state of shock. I stood frozen. Her two-inch full silver mane of hair highlighted what some might call a mirage of beauty. She stood in front of me, and I stood mesmerized. Jerri sat at her feet.

She ran her hands through her silver mane of hair in the core of the rest of her black hair. She rolled her lips in and blew air out in front of her words. "The town people say your soldiers wanted to kill the dog as a sport to silence her. I thank you for not harming her."

"Enough death has come from the hands of men who should only kill to save," I answered.

How did she get this close to danger? It's midnight, and there are soldiers assigned to night patrol in the area. Others are active at night as sleep escapes some and only an hour or two of rest and some men were awake. I hope she walked in undetected. My dog sat calm and relaxed.

"I have questions of you," I asked, and she nodded.

Our eyes connected, as I wished I had answers to questions without asking. Valentina asked for something warm to drink. I nodded as I wondered if she is someone I should be this close to. Maybe I should ask her to leave for the safety of both of us.

A few minutes later, my brass percolator bubbled tea up to the glass dome as it heated on top of my kerosene heater. The scent of steeping tea made from black licorice and hard peppermint candies helped to override the smell of diesel and gas, and made for a much better setting. The aroma calmed my nervousness, that I felt and maybe for both of us. I placed a wood crate near her to sit on as the tea brewed. The kerosene heater spread hot heat in a large circle, so we both sat at a distance from the heat, but it moved us close to each other.

"Do you want to remove your woolen throw–over and let it dry by the heat?"

She pulled it over her head and placed it near the heater. She wore a men's plaid shirt, and her pants were tweed. She stood tall for a woman, and her figure resembled a Negro–colored version of a Lana Turner from the silver screen. Looking at Valentina, it made me have hopes of one day watching Colored women who looked like her in the movies, and not just playing maids. Her walking around town, bent over as an old gypsy woman, also hid her grapefruit breasts, but they did not overly protrude.

The absence of being near a woman in this war heightens a man's sensitivity. I missed the nuances of a woman. I thought it to be odd to see her stand and sit in an almost elegant manner. She moved like those girls who carried books on their head. Her posture was much like a painted perfection. She must have hard time walking around bent over as she does to hide her real physical persona. I poured her and me some tea in old fruit cans.

"Mr. soldier..."

"Sirletto – my name is Sirletto Preer. Master Sergeant Sirletto Preer is my Army rank and name."

Back home, in the streets, I might see a pretty woman and instinctively try to turn the heat up to see where it might go. Although, after having my heart broken, I'm sure my approach will change, and maybe I won't try as I used to do. I have reread a letter my dad wrote to me after my woman ran off with my son. I know hurt and angry feelings as well as I know my name. My father's words, I don't know if I can live by them. "When you meet women in this world, she can be made out of dreams come true, but dreams never tell the whole story because we wake up all too often before the vision is complete."

I wrote back to my dad, "I have been fighting a war with hopes of seeing an end to my heartbreak. Will I let another feel my heart because she's pretty? Well, I have awakened from dreams as I have tossed my heart back into reality. I don't see another woman in my future anytime soon, even when I make it back home."

His return letter: "Son, there is no part of life you should give up. What you do is, rearrange or move to a better time or place inside you."

❦ ❦ ❦

I stood amazed at her presence in the middle of what some might call hell. What the hell should I think or dream of in the middle of a war-ruined town in the south of France? There is an attractive cream in her coffee. Her light brown skin, I'm used to seeing at church, a downtown street, or a nightclub. She could be the woman around the corner. She has to be a dream, and I'm trying not to wake.

I poured more tea, and then she talked. "I hid from the Germans in the hills when they were here. They sent the dog to root out the enemy, but I formed a bond with the dog while the Germans occupied the area. I went uncaptured as the dog friended me and would warn me. The town people hid me and fed me.

"I am of African royalty. My great grandfather in history lived to be the last recorded Damel – a ruler – a king of the Wolof kingdom in a part of West Africa. Some now call the region, Senegal."

"Well, I'm honored to have you in my tent, but are you sure no one saw you?"

"You Americans are not aware of what is around you when you focus on what the enemy must look like, so you turn your attention on how to create harm in your efforts to seek and destroy, and you put less effort in how not to be harmed. You Americans don't gas humans, but you do take what is not yours."

"Yeah, you're right on all points. I am interested in your history. Please tell me more." I started to make more tea.

"My great-grandfather in the mid-1800s around the time of slavery in America, he died in battle fighting the French. The French captured our territory and tried to make sure there would not be an uprising in the future by bringing the young sons of my grandfather's royal family to France to educate them. At least one of the sons would go back as a puppet ruler, hoping it would keep the people happy. In reality, he would never rule, not even his own life."

"America has notably left the world spinning in a bad direction," I said. Valentina lowered her head in a slow nod as I told the truth that I believed.

"But I believe one day, people will rise from the depths of despair and take back stolen life and lands."

She lifted her eye to the canvas tent ceiling as if she could see the nighttime stars. I wanted her to see me in a better light than most Americans.

I heard the hopelessness in her voice. "Then more people will die for what they claim is theirs. Is there any good being right or wrong if we fight to the death?" her voice carried dejection in my path of thought.

She made me realize I'm a part of fighting to liberate a country with a history of enslaving other countries in the name of kings or queens and generals to gain, and keep control of land and resources.

"One of the sons of my great–grandfather went to the best schools, and even went to England for more education. He is my grandfather. The other brothers...no one ever heard from them again. After a while, the French figured they did not need puppet kings, and he did not want to go back. He traveled to America, and now lives in a city called New York. My father entered this world of some privilege as before grandfather migrated to America. He married an English woman and my father, he too, went to the best schools in France and England and had the excesses in life spoiled upon him as he was handsome and well educated.

"My father branded himself as if he were a king with a harem of French and Spanish women. My mother is of Spanish–Moorish people. She took care of the rich, and worked in the brothels on the Spanish coast from royalty down to the harsh men, and that's how I am here.

"I'm often mistaken for being an East Indian, or gypsy, which put me in danger with the Nazis having the same hate for darker skins as they have hatred for the Jew. I have a brother from the same mother, but we have different fathers. He is a little darker than I am, and looks as if he is Senegalese. We both hid as our skin tones as well as we could when the Nazis occupied the area.

"I assumed the Nazis would send us to some horrible fate because of our heritage. Bastard children, we often have no documents. I have no papers. The only other place I travel to is the seaport town of my birth in Spain. I've done a terrible deed to survive, for which it has brought me here. My mother died, saving me from a man who did awful... he did...I have a hard time telling you, but he hurt her and me as a young girl. My little brother played in the next room most times when the man harmed my mother or me. Then one day, my mother took a knife at the man, but he grabbed the knife from her and stabbed her. I rushed to her aid and pulled the knife out of her. Ramming the knife into his heart, I stared deep into his soul and felt the power of life and death as I felt his life draining. I pushed the blade with all my force. I stomped on the handle as he lay on the floor until it poked through his chest and it came out of his back.

"My mom died and the town prostitutes raised my brother and me. The women moved me over the mountains, and here I am. When the war came, they hid me again while the Germans occupied the town."

"What became of your father?

"A kind man I could call him. At times he showed love toward me, but he never accepted my mother on his perceived stature. He died from the fever of too many women in Senegal. His pride and vanity kept from using his education from great schools to stay clean."

"Where is your brother?"

"I lost contact with my brother years ago. He grew up as a spoiled rotten child, and he stayed a child in a man's body when he became of age. I did my best to keep him hidden from the Nazis, but I finally stop interceding on his selfish dangerous behavior. Rumors say the Nazis took him away."

"I am sorry."

I am not sorry. In this world, sometimes you are better off releasing the burdens of others to save your own life."

"What became of your brother's father?

"He's the man I killed!" Her voice stabbed the air as I asked no more questions

Listening to her while oil lamp flickers light off her cheeks, and reflecting on the strands of her silver hair, I'm in full allure of her. She spoke in clear English with a mixture of accent. Then her mouth, I got lost between how her lips moved. When her lips parted, her African heritage bore through in the fullness of her lips. Even when she sat quietly, her lips stayed slightly parted as if she were going to whistle.

She left with the promise of returning soon. Soon came the next night. She started to visit often, and stayed until almost morning light, and then she would slip away. I even started to miss her and worry when she did not show up on some nights.

During those nightly visits and sipping black licorice mixed with peppermint candy tea, Valentina and I shared our history. I received history lessons and learned world history never written in the books I read. Something I always understood, a history teacher in college told us, "History is written by who has the most guns."

Listening to a woman with knowledge, I know many men are fearful of feeling less than a man through some ugly train of thought passed down by insecure men. *Insecurity is a killer of growth*, my uncle would say. I always thought to hear a woman speak of things I knew nothing of, it presented a mentally striking opportunity to grow. The intelligence of a woman brought desires out of me.

However, the time called for me to show restraint for my wants. I needed to respect. I could not take advantage of her femininity. Acting like a man on a lust-fulling hunt from the spoils of war is Godless spoils.

I saw her as a woman through a completely different light when it came to being in a war zone. I wondered why we couldn't stop all the wars for at least as long as it took to remove all of the women and children. I guess I felt too idealistic if someone is gassing humans as if it were a sport.

One day I sat out to another town to fix up the local wells. I found, in an abandoned farmhouse, nice woman's clothes, and I brought them back for Valentina. I directed her to my hidden sleeping area to change. When she re-emerged, she exposed calm, or maybe felt embarrassed to look so womanly. She smiled, and then bit her full bottom lip as if embarrassed from being in more delicate clothing.

As usual, we sat by the stove in the tent, talked, and sat for long moments of no conversation. One night, she rubbed her nails when in our silent moments. I don't think nervousness controlled her. The heater made her comfortable enough to remove her shoes. Her bare feet slid slightly back and forth in the dirt.

I wanted for her, the woman inside her, to feel on the outside her shine. "Valentina, may I have your hands and your feet. Please trust me."

Her eyes looked up from her lowered face and she nodded.

I used some fine sandpaper, some whale oil, and Glovers Mane to polish her nails. We used the items to clean and shine electrical contacts from corrosion. We Colored boys – we used it on our scalps to help with dryness. I took her over to my workbench. Without saying a word, I began to sand gentle the ends of her nail tips, and then I polished them. The women back home would be jealous of the job I did. I acted as if holding her hands did not affect me. I couldn't fool myself. I felt a partial healing to the wounds of my lonely soul. I felt secluded in my own thoughts about me and so few other thoughts, but when I touched her, I sensed a feeling of wanting and wanting to give.

I finished with her hands, and then I soaked her feet in hot water in a washbasin. After some time, I massaged her feet and trimmed her nails. Her toes were pretty toes, but the lack of proper footwear left scars. The whole time I took care of her hands and feet, we never said a word, but our eyes connected and stayed on each other.

We sat sit in the open of the tent as usual. We always kept our voices down low. I made it difficult for anyone to slip through the tent canvas by overlapping canvas tent material. I did this before knowing Valentina. I like to control my world as much as possible.

Someone approached the tent once when we were enjoying a late-night meal and conversation. Clement called my name, knowing the dog presented a danger to him. He came to the work tent at 11:00 p.m. I slipped up. I promised him I would reattach his burl wood handle grip on his rifle. I told him I would deliver. I should have made it clear I did not want him near my tent at night while I worked in private and quiet.

Jerri growled the whole time at Clement, no matter how much I tried to hush her. I didn't want to silence her. I wanted her to bury her teeth in his coon ass. Dogs know. But then again, her mouth deserved better asses to bite.

The warning from Jerri barking, and without a moment of wasted movement, Valentina crawled into an open engine bay of a truck and pulled the hood down. Her instincts on where to hide shocked me. I'm sure hiding quickly had been a way of life during war times.

We kept our late-night friendship going for weeks, but I started to feel that maybe I ought to end whatever we were doing. Whatever we were doing, no name could be attached. I mustered the courage to talk to her, hoping I would not hurt her feelings. "Valentina, I'm a man on foreign soil. One day, orders will come for me to ship out. The end can come with each sunrise, and our friendship will blend into memories."

"Are you leaving now?" she asked. "What are you saying? Are you saying you wish for me not to come back?"

It felt like a break-up with my girlfriend, and my stomach churned, but she wasn't my beloved. "Valentina, our bond of two people stuck in the middle of a world war, and the uncertainty...it has made me miss you in advance of being away from you. I want you here with me, but this war when it ends, I'll be going back to American shores.

Her expression soured my stomach. "You have so much to go back to." her voice trailed off.

Several times before I told her of how much I missed my mother, father, uncle, and most of all...my son, whom I needed to find and then fight to keep.

Her lowered head spoke to the ground. "Me, being nobody, anyone claims when you Americans leave – we go back to almost being nomadic people. We have to start all over. Some people around here feel lucky to be living. Some others, like me, feel no luck. The German cut and scarred he cut me for life."

"You are the light of my world to have you as my friend, Valentina, and what are you speaking of when you say the German cut you?"

"Sirletto, I have buried females of all ages; it's like peeling skin in my dreams, and I can't help but pick at the wounds of the past. But I try. Wounds of my heart are sick nightmares of worrying I'll die here, and no one will remember if I meant anything to anyone."

I heard her blues, and it traumatized me with fear for her future. Inside me, I wondered will my son remember me, and will I mean anything to him if I can't find him.

"Valentina, I am not going to mislead you and say maybe I'll come back and visit you here in France. This war in this country, it does not leave a romantic impression on me. I want the hell out of here, and the thought of coming back here, I don't know if doing so will remind me of too much death."

The moment I finished speaking, I knew I dropped a bomb of unkindness for me to say what I said. I spoke aloud to myself, but she heard my words. I felt I did wrong, talking so openly about my feelings of wanting to leave.

She saved my life up there on the mountain, and I'd have to leave one day on a ship going to the land of my birth and will die one day. Maybe in the future, if they ever allow Colored folk to fly to wherever and whenever, with no segregation, I'll come back here. Negros can hardly ride a bus across the country without trouble, much less flying in a plane sitting alongside White people. They tried to court-martial Lieutenant Jackie Robinson, who refused to move to the back of the bus, but he fought it and won, but most Negros have not been so lucky.

"Sirletto, I understand living is living, and you will go back to live a life waiting for you. I also understand dying is dying, and we all will die someday."

We both rose from our seats with our eyes on each. She reached for my hand and kissed my fingers, each one of them, and then placed my hand against my lips and she walked away.

My hand seemed to be glued to my lips. I wanted to hold onto to Valentina's touch. I sat back down, and my dog Jerri came and sat at my feet. Candlelight in the darkened tent entombed my blues. I hummed songs while tasting my salty blues.

A work detail came for me to fix a radio tower out on a high peak some fifty miles away. For a week, I suffered each night wishing I could see her, be near her at any cost. I never kissed her, and I never tried. I manicured her hands and feet, but I didn't hold them as a lover would. I did not know what her embrace felt like, but I wanted her near. I could not love her and then leave her. Valentina risked her life to save mine on that mountaintop.

I wrote in my journal.

Come Near

I watched her eyes penetrating me

I imagined she thought as I was hoping

Sending a clear but soft message

Welcome to my body

Come near my soul

I feel her warm exhale into my inhale

I take it deep within me – it dizzies my balance

I gather myself to lift her into my firm embrace

I carry her to horizontal entanglements of motions and emotions

Like in the millions of years before us

A man and woman have always danced

But in this time and space

We share

I hear you – I see you, and I feel you saying

Sending a clear but soft directive

Touch me

Your eyes beg me to

Touch me

Touch me there

Yes, even touch me there

I watched her eyes penetrate into me

As I penetrate your heavenly universe

I hear you,

I see you,

I feel you saying,

Welcome to my body

Come near my soul

Episode 11

Love entered my soul. I felt love rising in me for Valentina. I realized she saw something in me from the first moment she encountered me. My encounter had gone long past amassment in meeting her. I knew I wanted her.

Being away from Valentina, my temperament began to fluctuate, and my men thought there were pissing me off and making me mad when I cut them no slack on work ethics. I cursed a White, equally ranking sergeant from another base. His equal rank, much like Jude's means he had status over me. Their skin color makes them out rank me even if we share the same amount of stripes. He gave me some attitude – I gave it right back. He threatened to have me reprimanded, and I didn't care. I think my anger frightened him, and he left me alone.

The first night back at camp, I sat inside the tent waiting for her to show – she did not come. The second night, I found myself breathing hard with fear thinking she left the area to avoid saying goodbye.

Night three, and a full moon haunted me into notions of running into the hillside calling out her name. I paced in the work tent thinking, *what if she shows up – what will I tell her? How do I tell her how I feel*, and also thinking that one day the Army will move on from here. I'll leave from here on a ship headed back to the States.

My dog, Jerri, paced with me everywhere I went. He became somewhat of a camp favorite. It became acceptable to see my dog trekking alongside me as if she's a dog soldier, but the men kept their distance. Maybe Jerri missed her too.

I paced as I tried to work at night. I attempted to work the last two nights, and the only thing I did was more pacing. I went into my hidden sleeping quarters and tried to sleep. My sleep came quickly from a lack of sleep, and I dreamed of her.

⁘ ⁘ ⁘

"Sirletto," her voice landed on my face with peppermint scented breath. I wanted to kiss my dream, but I lay wide awake with her inhales and exhales which gave me life. Her presence opened a window into my soul. Her voice stroked my wants and desires, and although I'm awake, I keep my eyes closed and feel her presence surround me. I didn't want to open my eyes and find her not there when I know she is.

When I did open my eyes, I saw my dream. Valentina sat on the floor next to my cot, whispering my name. She said my name as if singing a love song. I reached out and touched her hair. She stood up, and I stood with her. With no hesitation, I kissed her with love flowing in my hidden room, enclosed with layers of embraced hidden desire. I could light an oil lamp without casting a shadow outside due to the layers of the canvas tent. I struck a match and held it for a long moment. I watched the light flicker in the darkness of her eyes, and then I lit the oil lamp.

85

She removed her top. My chest expanded, and my heart must have stopped for a moment. Her hair with the silver mane fell between her breasts. With a quick jerk of her head, her hair flew back. The lamp light highlighted a healed-over jagged scar. From below her left nipple to down past her waistline. Man had tried to change her beauty, but he failed.

I sat down, and she removed all the rest of the clothing she wore and stood naked before me. A scar trailed from her hip and through her pubic hair. Although her body compared to a woman of a Nile River Goddess, Valentina's healed wound captured all my attention. She knew where my eyes focused.

As she said before, she said again, "The German cut me. The one up on the mountain captured me. The same knife the evil man cut you with... he did evil to my body."

I flinched hearing her sharing her painful memory.

I don't know why, but afterward, as the Nazi lay dead from two-gun blasts, I had removed the bayonet. It is under my bed. I shivered. Should I toss the double-edged short sword? I felt the tightness of the healed wound on my chest. With me now sitting on my bed, I slowly placed my hand on her belly, and lay my cheek on her scar. She put her hands on my head. I rested against her scarred flesh. Her softness led my feelings to want more of her.

I kissed her just below her breast. I turned my head slightly and moved down to kiss her scar. Slowly, my lips trickled to the jagged trail of previous terror. My tongue floated in a butterfly motion while edging near her pubic hair. I stopped to take in the perfection of her womanly aroma, and it taunted my animalistic senses. Deep breaths of her scent, and I knew my lungs would never be the same—always in the future. I'll be seeking her imprints on my senses. I placed my hands on her hips and slid them around to the firmness of her backside. Her sad soul dropped tears on my forehead, and they trickled near my eyes. I removed my lips from her scar and looked up into an alluring face. I reached up and wiped her damp cheeks.

"I show you my scar. I show you what he did. I show you what he took from me. I show you I have no shame in showing you, as you have been a man who has not taken from me, but only gave me a place for my soul to rest. Sirletto, please take me as I am. Just love me for as long as you can. Another man may never want to touch me as I am marked. I am damaged inside and on my body. But please take me. Please."

I took full view of her from the floor on up to the silver streak of her hair. I didn't see one flaw. Her scar is a byproduct of a man trying to destroy God's creature, and like most things in life, man is just not strong enough to change what God has created.

I stood and wrapped my arms around her and pressed her head against my chest. She tilted her head away and began to unbutton my shirt. I shivered, but it was not from the cold, but from the velvet warmth of her fingers. In this war, no man could expect to feel a woman who wanted him and made him feel needed. Before this moment, I did not know I needed. I knew I missed the sensation of a woman as any man would. Valentina in where we were, and at this time, I had to marvel at how a beautiful woman could be here with me.

I stood, and she kissed my navel methodically, but with heated passion as if she wanted to connect to my lifeline. She tugged for me to come down onto my bed with her. I removed her arms, but held her hands and stared at my dream and reality. She turned her body away and lay on her side in the fetal position, but she turned her head as much as she could, and kept her eyes on me. If her eyes could call my name, I felt her calling me. I removed my pants, and I curled in behind her. I pulled a blanket over us.

With my arm wrapped tightly around her on her scar, my mouth sucked on her shoulder. I wanted her taste to remain when I removed my lips. Valentina trembled even though it felt hot under the blankets and the kerosene heater almost made it too warm in my little space.

"I cannot have children," she tried to sound firm in her declaration. I understood her bravery as she kept telling me her story. "The Nazi put things in me – he hurt my insides."

I felt her heart race through her back and against my chest. "And I bled. I became sick. He left me in the woods to die. I almost died. The dog found me and kept me warm, and I gained enough strength to make it back to town. The madam and the mid-wife, they looked inside my body. They say I'm part of a woman now – no children can I have.

"After three full moons, I healed, and I set out to kill him. I hunted him. I needed to end his life even before you encountered the bastard." Her feet bounced on top of mine, and she shuddered. I placed my finger across her lips.

I felt her need to be held through her pain. I wrapped my arms around to help her through her hurt and to feel safe. My internal wounds from thousands of miles away is an ugly realism that sends pain waves after each reading of that letter telling me I lost my woman and lost my child, and never to look for her or my son. I understood too the pain of losing something dear, although Valentina's pain – I could never feel what she felt. The best I could do for both of us is give comfort as she wanted

My body wanted her, yet, I'd let her decide what she needed emotionally and physically from me. She said she wanted me, but I would like her to direct our love of me kissing her, touching her, and me inside her. We drifted off to sleep with her body pressed skin tight to mine. I think I slept soundly for the first time since I landed on the French shores.

Valentina woke me hours later with her gentle sounding deep breathing musical score. I placed my lips on her skin lightly. She pushed her backside into my hips, and then she pulled back the blankets. The beauty of her stood up above me on my homemade bed. The oil lamp flickered, and my eyes captured the sight of her sensuality, and my body reacted hard and fast.

Valentina eased down on my rise, and I felt the warmth of her insides on the tip of my hardness. She held still, and I felt her desires liquefied. With the past cruelty of a man mutilating a part of her, I'm sure it made her hesitant, but her body came for me. I felt her juices flow down my shaft of hardness as she eased more of me inside her. I tried to push upwards inside her. An incredible feeling took my breath away from how she felt. A loud sound escaped past my lips. I worried for a moment, but I remembered Jerri, my dog, would warn me if anyone were near. Valentina's breathing became louder, and she began gasping. She almost took all of me inside her. She used her hands on my chest to brace herself. I wanted to move, but I waited for her.

She leaned forward, and I felt her body relax as she placed her lips on my face and kissed my eyes, nose, and lips. She took my bottom lip into her mouth and treated me like a spoonful of molasses. She started to move her hips, and I joined in.

Our lovemaking danced with no music. We worked ourselves around so I could look down into Valentina's eyes while she spread her legs wide and I stroked in and out of her wetness. I felt her finger vibrating on her – near my hardness. Something foreign to me I watched for the first time a woman self-pleasuring herself as I stroked in and out of her. Our eyes mated. I felt her body become rigid and then trembled and shook and jerked, and then she went limp. I held still inside her letting her enjoy her moment

I started a slow grind inside her as we enjoyed ourselves until she looked at me and put her hand up for me to stop.

I lifted and she turned and placed herself on all fours with her hips up high. Her artfully curved hips had me slide in behind her as I put my hands on her waist and met her hips. She did not hesitate with lighting fast strokes, she pushed back and took me in and rode my hardness, letting me be still and take her loving motion of taking me in and out and feeling her hot, tight, wetness.

I drove myself to the point of releasing in Valentina. She slowed her movement and let me ride. I wanted to release badly, but I did not want to give in so easily. I kept driving deep, hard, repeatedly. Sweat dripped on her back from my forehead. With each stroke, she sucked air, and I exhaled hard in exertion until I let out a sound maybe a bit too loud.

She relaxed her body flat and stretched out. I rested on her back while still inside her as my hardness remained unyielding as we drifted off to sleep again.

Episode 12

Valentina is now my lover, which is causing a battle in the middle of this war, which is nowhere an ideal place for love.

If she were in the States, I'd take her out on dates. We would go for long walks of holding hands and do almost anything we want to do. Then we would also spend time in silence feeling love flow in our veins. In my mind, I paint pictures of how we would dress, and her choices of dress shops and how the dress would be made to fit her. I speak of the kind of cars I would drive her in on our dates. I would love to hear her opinions when we visited parks, zoos, and the movies we would see, and restaurants where we would dine.

All I have is her being in my little hidden room. But if I could, I'd show her how to dance, as if we were in the clubs or dance halls, and I would take her to twirl her heels off. Then, I think maybe she has never worn heels. I dream of her wearing those stockings with the little black line going up from her heel and onto her hidden curves and secrets.

I have shared spiritual ideas of the church we would go to, and if she wanted to find another, there are many we would visit. I made it known to her my love of God, and she has the same passion, knowing God has saved her life many times. She has a mixture of history of Christian and Islamic views, and I listen and learn. I speak of my mom and dad, and they would love her.

I talk, and she listens. She speaks, and I never want her to stop whispering in my ear. I love her, but she and I know one day we will have to part and then I feel regretful after we talk.

We then make love, and it seems right for the moment. Being in her presence is the most reassuring thing I know. Then outside my tent, the world is cold, and death is always hovering like the clouds of rain.

We can't date – we can't be man or wife, but if I could, I would take her to the altar, and I would show her off to the world. I thank God for her, and I pray for her. I would marry her and have children with her if we could. My love will never end, but our affair will.

⁂

While I have been making love in the wee hours, someone has been killing the prostitutes in the whorehouses. My enterprises, the welfare of my men, and the lives of innocent women are all on the line. And, whatever is happening, it affects Valentina. She could be a mark. The killer is targeting what I assume is forgettable women. With Valentina identified as a Gypsy – a person not thought of as valuable, if the killer is left to do what he wants to do, he could move on to other women some might think of as invisible.

The women killed as of late are in other nearby towns in smaller brothels.

Incoming work has picked up, so I make sure the mechanic's tent is clear of Valentina and my love for her, as work has started earlier and gone on later. I devised trip wire noisemakers in the field behind the tent 200 feet away, to alert me of anyone coming; they shouldn't, but if they do, I will know. I dug an escape tunnel for Valentina to come in and out. I used empty barrels in the ground to keep the dirt around it in place, so there is no fear of dirt trapping her. Of course, my dog Jerri is the best alarm.

Sadly, I'll have to leave my dog behind one day too.

Whom do I trust? I believe in no one when it comes to the knowledge of Valentina. I confide in only me. I am closer to a few men than others: N–Booty, Little Roy, Tiny Taps, and Lanky Slim...and know them, but if any of them found out about Valentina, obviously it puts them in danger of being blackmailed. Any secret can be used to trap someone from saying or doing what they need to do to save their ass.

Valentina is one of the Romanian Gypsy-looking housekeepers in appearance in her old woman persona who cleans the whorehouses. I can't tell her to stop working and not have food or some income in a place where there is no money. We paid for all work and deeds to the French people with American currency, and our money is worth more money now than any European funds. Ironically, America is stepping out of the depression from building war machinery. I have thought often about this war which has brought death to millions – could it be a part of a master plan for a growing economy in America?

I need to stop this killer before the day comes when I must leave. I can't go home and leave her in danger. I hear many of these American soldiers speak of staying here in France or some other parts of Europe. Depending on where a Negro lives, this place is paradise as far as how people treat you. The French people don't seem to care if you're a Negro. Then again, after men from the neighboring country—Germany controlled your country with such brutality, you would look at people differently too.

I can't stay. I must go back as I have parents and a son. I loathe the thought of them passing away with me being on distant shores.

It is a problem trying to find information on a killer, and trying to figure out who you can talk to as a Colored Man. I can't walk around the White parts of the Army camp and ask too many questions, or even look and see if anything stands out. Street-life back home has made me aware of underground life. Who's watching whom is a matter of survival. My dad and uncle dealt with all kinds of people. They did not look down on anyone for the life they led if they brought something to the table. The only people my dad and uncle would harm were a thief of their property or money, or a rapist or murderer of women and children. They also taught me to listen while observing. Often, a person up to no good looks out of place trying to not look out of place.

Episode 13

Lanky Slim the Cajun, who can pass for White, has a White boyfriend. I had taken notice of his lack of comfort around the guys when they bragged of their sexual conquests. Uncomfortably, he'd try to join in on guy talk about women and sex, but I could tell he felt awkward. It might have been religious influencing outward responses as some men let the church be their guide to sexual needs and subject. Nonetheless, even most Bible-thumping men when around other men, they act as if the Lord gives them the all-mighty sexual rights to brag as long as they don't cuss. Often, holy-roller men pose and primp, portraying the Bible authorized a special pass for them to have concubines – meaning in today's world, it's okay to have side women and wives.

With Lanky Slim, I could tell as my Grandmamma would say, "There's sugar inside that man," or she would say "There's a woman inside him and maybe more than one." Lanky Slim didn't pamper like some of the queer men back home, but he's soft in a way I had seen before that I identified on the streets. I could care less of who he wanted in his bed, or whom he wanted to share company. Nevertheless, I do need to know all dealings and situations that could lead to circumstances of good and what can be paralyzing when it came to the men placed under my charge. On the streets, one hopes to gain and keep what you have whether it is physical or a mental advantage. It is an advantage to know the lay of the land.

Lanky Slim's double life came to light when we first settled this camp into two different sections: the Colored side and the White side. Some men need freedom from being close to anyone for private thoughts with no disruptions. Some want privacy with a girly magazine. Some want to go somewhere to cry alone because maybe they lost a friend, or they miss home. I went out in the woods to pray in the wilderness. I ventured out to keep rereading the letter from Kathy stating I was never gonna' see my son again.

I noticed Lanky Slim would slip out in the remote woods to almost a half-mile from the edge of the camp. He went a long way for private time, and much farther than I authorized my men to venture. So, I followed him one day.

I observed him one day watching all of the other men from the corners of his eyes. Me watching him, I'm far better at shrouding my visual probe of all things going on. Near nightfall, he appeared nervous. Lanky Slim wandered some distance and then stood at the edge of the woods. He backed into the woods and disappeared. I made my way to near where he entered the wooded area, and made my way in moving slowly with limited daylight. Twenty minutes later, and over a mile deep into the forest, I figured I might have lost him. Suddenly, a match flashed in the distance. I weaved through the trees. A man is entitled to privacy, but I need to protect myself with knowledge of what people did or would do. Anyone going remotely far, I knew this was more than a private session with a girly magazine or to have all to yourself some stolen brandy from a farmhouse.

The forest is never silent. The noises of nature – of non-people, it has its own nightclub of life going on. The tree underbrush made it challenging to move without making a sound. Low branches swatted my face and slowed my movement even more. Just after I spit some pines needles from my mouth, I heard voices filtering through in the darkness. Lanky Slim's Cajun accent and another voice sounded muffled. Maybe a lost Nazi held Lanky Slim at gunpoint.

The lack of light made me feel my way around. A burning ember of a drawn cigarette burned bright in the darkness and helped my eyes hone in. I peered through the thickets, and I saw why my fellow soldier wanted his privacy. Lovers were kissing and sharing a smoke. Two almost naked men stood grinding. Lanky Slim leaned his head back on a man's shoulder as the man's face, his lips, and his tongue slid in and out of Lanky Slim's ear as he held the cigarette up to Lanky Slim's lips.

A Colored man and White male...homosexuality, it is one of the worst kinds of crimes the Army will never stand for. These two men, a Negro, and a White man, found love in each other in the French countryside amid the worlds' worst conflict. Someone might consider it romantic if you're willing to suffer one of the worst humiliations and possible executions, which is what the Army would shell out through a gun muzzle. I guess one might consider the romance of dying with your lover or for your lover.

I also thought this could hurt me or help me. If I had an inside man on the other side of the camp, it's another tool. But, for now, I decided to let them be and head back to camp. I would figure out what to do later, or whether I should do anything at all. I slowed my exit to a creeping worm's pace, but my boot shoelace snagged on a branch, and it snapped. Silence shed light on trouble as I heard no voices. I tried to hush my racing heart with the comfort of my PPK Walter with a bullet in the chamber ready. I stood tall, hidden behind a tree, but then decided to act as if I was peeing, and while facing the tree, I held my gun as if I were holding my penis.

"Don't move," a southern voice, so thick with Mississippi drawl said, and it sounded as if the voice said, "Da–mvooh." A rifle barrel inched toward the side of my face.

"No, you don't move," I said. "I have a gun aimed at your balls." I turned slowly and faced Lanky Slim's lover with my gun pointing at the man's balls.

Lanky Slim stood behind his lover. "Sir-Sir...sir, we...ahm...we were...James, lower your rifle, it's my Master Sergeant."

Lanky Slim reached over and pushed his lover's rifle down.

I held my gun aimed at his manhood without taking my eyes off of the two of them. I didn't need an excuse for what I knew, so I stopped any attempt as they both tried explaining.

"You both know the dangers of what you two are doing. You know what the Army will do. They might tar and feather you first and then blindfolds you and blows your heart in half. If I spotted you, others can. If discovered, you're better off to go AWOL and hide, and never return to the states."

They looked at each other and knew I spoke life or death.

Private Francis W. Cutter sounded like a Mississippi boy, but he hailed from the Florida panhandle. I didn't ask, but I sure wondered how they found each other and became lovers? Is it a look they see in each other? Is it an emotional map that connects likewise relations? How can a Colored man and a White southerner in the Army, be in a forbidden love with each other, but they can't eat at the same table for multiple reasons? How – why, these two men could be in the Army, but they can't fall in love openly with women of the other race if they wanted. Their love is faith in something I did not understand in so much of the danger it presented. However, their love is meaningful to them and not to be minimized by my lack of understanding or judged by me. My worry though, a soldier under my direct command and his secrets could cause my dishonorable discharge or worse.

They both let me know they understood the importance of concealment of their want for each other. The next day, Lanky Slim told me he and his lover wanted to show their appreciation by telling me useful information. Their male-male love affair gave me a way of gaining knowledge of what went on behind the scenes on the other side of the camp. I need to be careful of this knowledge, and they need to be extremely careful. A White soldier betraying his fellow White soldiers with a Negro is considered an evil with intent to harm his people. It's no different than a Colored man hiding under a Klan hood at a Klan meeting.

Most of the things Private Francis W. Cutter found out were pranks, except for the time some food intended for the Colored soldiers came up missing. Through his inside connections, we were able to recover food intended for the Colored soldiers. I knew White soldiers threw curve balls, but I hit them for base hits and then stole home.

When I told Captain Castellani I knew a man I could trust, I put Lanky Slim's lover working close to the brothels since no Negro soldier could wander near the area. The captain did want to know, *how* and *why* I knew of a White soldier who I would trust. I told him I encountered many of his soldiers who were not hateful of Colored soldiers.

Episode 14

I needed an up-close look inside the brothels to take notes on the layouts of entrances and exits. I arranged a work detail of plumbing and other detail work, and it just so happens, Private Francis W. Cutter, is now elevated to the status of MP. He is going to be my escort into where the murders took place.

Valentina did her housecleaning during the afternoons, and those houses are closer to the base. She and I began spending most nights in my arms. *Out of harm's way?* Who knows? Valentina's rebellious in always saying, "I can take care of myself." I respected her defiance, as she showed purpose with an unruffled demeanor – after all, she had shot and killed a Nazi right in front of me.

After I met with Captain Castellani to arrange my work detail into the brothels, it coincided with the first Saturday night party for my guys. I thought the captain might play it cautiously and cancel the Colored soldier's party at the inn, but he did not. I kept my part of the agreement and setup all the security arrangements. Some of the Colored soldiers did not want anything to do with what some call the devil's work.

Numerous Colored soldiers could be extremely religious in their faith. Some preferred hearing me sing and play gospel music on Sundays as they were in tune with their spiritual side. With some men, this war helped them find God even when not so steeped in religion, as they saw the horrors of war could turn them toward spiritual hopes out of fear they felt.

Apart from that, I didn't want to have fun with the guys at the inn. I could spend the time with Valentina, but my guys needed this. She said she'd be waiting for me whatever time I returned.

Many of the Colored boys washed their uniforms and ironed them with a piece of metal heated in the burn barrel. I repaired a short–wave radio and enhanced it to play loudly. The radio picked up jazz band music from Paris, which from the news sources we learned that we Americans had liberated the city for some time now as we were kicking the German's asses, and running Germans back into Germany.

The music made a few men play around as if they were dancing with each other and acting silly after a few beers. We were loud, and most drunk too much within the first hour of party time at the inn. The sober men escorted the drunks back to camp sooner than much later.

I set up tabs for each man's drinks. The money would come out of their pay. The captain pocketed his fair share as he did with the White boys to allow them to buy five minutes with a girl in the brothels. I set it up, so I retained a small fee from each man. Everything in life is a hustle.

The night went fine, and I'm back in my hidden room with Valentina sleeping in my arms, but at a point, I needed to relieve myself. I kept a can in my private area to pee in, but would not pee with Valentina in the room.

"Hey, sweetheart, I'll be right back."

"Yes."

I love her sensual voice.

I'm stepping out from my hidden room, and the security pressure switches trip. With Valentina coming around more often, I had stepped up my security to removed pressure switches from disarmed land mines. I buried them on the incoming roads and the nearby field to send a small current to a low volume bell in the tent to go off, and Jerri lets out a signifying bark. Jerri might even growl if he felt threatened and if someone approached within thirty feet of the mechanic tent, I would jump to attention in seconds.

Jerri is barking and growling. I'm in full concentration in response.

"Preer, hold the dog. I'm coming in. Hold your dog or I'll have to shoot to kill anything moving."

It's Master Sergeant Jude.

"Come in. I'm holding the dog."

I'm sitting at my workbench with an oil lamp fixing a riflescope with a magnifying glass in my hand, and holding the dog on the other side. I'm under control when Jude weaves his way through the overlapping canvas. He's with two MPs, and both are friendly with me as I have done repairs on their motorcycles in the past. I'm sure Jude is unaware of that fact, or else he wouldn't have brought them with him.

"Why do you have the opening set up like this? What are you hiding?"

"I'm working in the cold on our machinery, and it helps if I can keep some heat inside. I have glues for the Woodstock of guns and rifle butts, and it must be kept warm to cure properly, Master Sergeant Jude." I give him some tone. I want him to know what I do is essential to all. I also know, and he knows, the captain has told him to fuck off when it comes to me. Whether Jude likes my ass or not, I know I have an ace in the hole with the captain.

"Have you been here all night?"

I intend to take my time responding to him. I want to treat any of his questions as being silly. I turned the oil lamp up to shine brighter and lit another. I saw the hate in his eyes.

"You know where I have been. I accounted for each man, and I turned in the check-off list at the guard post. I know you know."

"Are you giving me some attitude, Negro Sergeant Preer?"

"Actually, Master Sergeant Jude, you are addressing a high-ranking non–commissioned officer. I'm the First Sergeant of this company. Maybe you have not been informed of...oh wait, I did hear the captain tell you so." I knew the MPs where aware.

"My equal? The hell you are, Nigger." Spittle from his mouth reached several feet, but well short of touching me. It is clear he is staying over there away from me. He is asshole, but not that stupid. I would whoop his ass so bad, his Viking ancestor would not accept back into the cavemen village of idiotic fools. He knows I'll accept a court-martial and hard time to putting a hurting on his. His spit land on me, and I will hurt his ass so bad, he will never walks again, or be able to feed himself, or be able to wipe his ass of shit.

"You can call me Nigger, but nothing from your body better touch me!" I stood and glared – sending signal I will kill you if I have too.

❈ ❈ ❈

There are three kinds of Niggers to a White man as told to me by my dad. One, is you're only a Nigger after you leave the room, but you were Colored or a Negro when you were in front of them. The second kind of Nigger is when a White man will call you a Nigger as if you were *his* Nigger – as in, his *Nigger friend*, in that event, the White man doesn't think he is offending you much, and you're there to do his bidding as *his* Nigger. The third level Nigger is when they call you a Nigger with all he can spew, with a, "I hate you, and I will kill you, Nigger, like tone. That hate-filled ignorance will try to discredit or take away your total existence.

☙☙☙

Jude called me the third level Nigger.

My next thought is three White men have me in a secluded area. I know Valentina has gone out of the tunnel. She is safe, but can I count on what I think are open-minded MPs? They might feel pinched to follow the orders of this sadistic prejudiced ass, and if not, they could face a court-martial if they don't follow orders.

Time to tuck in some pride.

"Master Sergeant Jude, it is late or early depending on how you look at it. I'm tired and so are you...right? I need to finish this rifle for one of the MPs. What do you want? Why are you here?"

"Another dead woman – they found her in the next town. The captain wants you in his tent at first bugle." His tone's temperature boiled high enough for his brain matter to bubble over his hair follicles. Jude fought with the canvas as he stormed out. One of the MPs nodded to me, and shrugged his shoulders as he left. The other MP chuckled.

I checked to make sure Valentina made it out. She can't be discovered. I knew if caught, they would never accept her word as truth. They would say I inappropriately took sexual advantage of her in the worse ways, or maybe the Army would imprison her in some hellhole as an accused spy of some kind. I'd never see her again. At the worst fate, I'd be court-martialed and led to an open area with a blindfold over my eyes, and I'd wait for a bullet to end my life. They might make me do hard labor for life. Shame, in the form of a government letter to my folks, would wound them with an American pride seal ripping their hearts apart until their deaths. The message would say, your son spied for the enemy. No equivalence of truth would rise, but sometimes examples made out of men kept order in Uncle Sam's Army.

I can't avoid knee-deep muddied perceptual thoughts as my boots slush in the mud. My blurry contemplations matched my eyes' sad sight of tents sagging from the deluge in the middle of the night. Rain here is no different than the Seattle sleet. It's cold, and wet, and near to the bone.

In the field, a cow is tied to a stake as it awaits slaughter. The men pooled their money to purchase the cow for a feast. Thinning bodies and taste buds have worn down with a lack of daily canned rations we used to receive. Early on, what seemed like unlimited rations of high protein canned goods such as canned salmon, stewed meats, and peanut butter with plenty of boxes of powered eggs, kept the weight on. Those foods put a lot of lead in a man's pencil – meaning large portions of protein keep you wanting to have sex even more than a young man already wanted and needed. As of late, we have seen less of those rations as they moved them along to the frontline soldiers. I do have my supply, and I treat the soldiers close to me. We need good ole' red meat done up for steaks and barbeque. Several of the men have butchering skills and plan on feasting next week. On my way to meet with Captain Castellani, I see Valentina across the field with her signal – one of her colored scarfs. With a green scarf, she is telling me she is okay. A black scarf means she needs or wants to see me. Red means something is in the air, be careful.

She is wearing green and black.

Episode 15

"Master Sergeant Preer, the brass – the men with more stars and stripes above me – have said a stop must come. They want names of who is responsible for the deaths. You and I know the meanings of such news. Your men, in some way, will be in the sights first as scapegoats, and I will not have any control. Men with bigger balls than mine will cut mine off.

"You and I can't waste time on whether it's right or wrong. Your endeavors, and frankly the freedoms you and I have, it is the least of my worries. I'm grateful for what you have done, saving my son-in-law, but I know you understand my position. The commanders will do all they can to protect their investments. The whores and the men's pay, it greases wheels to keep things turning.

"Your men will be sent to the deserts of North Africa to fight and most likely catch bullets from behind them. You understand so-called *friendly fire*, but you know it's not. It's us shooting at our own to get rid of the Negro soldier in front of them."

As I heard the captain, I also heard soldiers outside marching, talking, and laughing.

The captain's gray eyes were darker than usual when he kept talking. "If this war ended today, what goes on here now will stay in place for as long as we rebuild this country. No one will speak ill will of our wrongdoing because of the good we do. However, murdered women in or around the brothels in these countryside towns, you and I know, it is a problem."

"Captain Castellani, I'm going to be frank with you, sir."

"We need to be open here."

"Then, sir, please stop filling my boots full of cow shit."

His eyes didn't open wide or show shock. He did take a deep breath and looked away from me.

"I know you have someone else looking into our problem. Whoever they are, they can, with the simplest of false evidence pin me as the person who is killing these women. But you understand if I'm sent off with my Colored men, you won't be far behind, or you will be somewhere you don't want to be also.

"I can do a lot better if I know I'm not setting myself up. Meaning, who else is on this case? I assume if they can't find the killer or killers, they will want to look good by any means possible. I'm snooping and asking questions of people who don't want to be in the middle of this."

Captain Castellani avoided eye contact to the point he has turned away from me. "It's Master Sergeant Jude."

"Captain, in the Bible, Judas Iscariot sold Jesus for thirty pieces of silver. Thirty pieces of silver, which an insulting price to pay for a slave who is killed by my ox, and you compensated the owner with only thirty pieces of silver, as in, "Oh well, sorry...here is your reimbursement for your dead slave."

I stared at the back of the captain's head as he faced away from me. Without me asking, I knew Jude swindled his way into being the other man on the case. I just needed the captain to confirm. It got back to me that Jude probed and questioned people who hate him. The White boys who did speak to me, they talked freely of their dislike of his ass because of his arrogance and under his boot disrespect.

The captain turned, and a zip-out window allowed light and views of what is going on outside the tent. The dim light casts a silhouette of a troubled man speaking with some anxiety.

"The higher-ups threw Jude in my direction to rid themselves of that pain in the ass. He is a thorn in my side as his nose pushes up the food chain of asses to kiss. I assume there were reports on me, behind my back, and the orders came down to put him on the case. He doesn't understand I have friends too. I have you and some above me who don't like his brown-nosing," the captain spoke toward the kerosene heater instead of me.

"Can I assume this Judas...he doesn't know I'm working the back channels?"

"No! Certainly not, if he did, we both would find ourselves tied to an underbelly of jackasses. He only thinks you are asking questions of your men."

"Okay, captain...from here on out, stop giving me half information. I know why you have been doing so, but it must be different now. If I find out who and why these killings are going on, you can't let it be known how and who found out the information with me being a Negro soldier. Captain, you want to walk away from this war in one piece, and so do I. I don't need anything more other than what I requested of you after I saved your son-in-law's life.

"I need to know what you know. Do I have the correct number of women murdered? Did some commit suicide? How many soldiers have been in the other towns and why? I need the correct and full information. You can't give me partial intel, hoping for me to figure it out, and then drop it in Jude's lap. Please don't..."

He turned and faced me in the green drabness of his tent. Our eyes met.

"Captain, we both have each other's bone collection to hide. I know where yours is, and you know I have bones I want to protect."

"I'll tell you what I know, and I'll send you more info over by my special man. He will approach you in a way – maybe... he's not so nice to protect you and him."

I know he's only thinking of saving his ass. There is nothing wrong with self–preservation. But then again, I have hearts and homes to protect in my world. I have a mother and a father. I don't want their hearts broken by the ugliness of this war in any form whatsoever. I have a son, and I pray I can be in his life again one day. I have the respect of the men I'm in charge of here on this muddy French soil. I want them to go home to their relations. As I look past the captain, I visualize Valentina. She...we depend on each other, and we love each other. I must leave her better off than when we came into each other's world. The captain watches my body stir from me chuckling slightly aloud while wondering, *how do I do all of this?*

Thinking of Valentina, maybe I can delay a bit returning to the States somehow, and after some time, I can have her come to America. I don't know how any of this works or how to ask. Nevertheless, no matter what, I need to go back to my family when this war is over...alive. I can't stay here when the ships or planes leave from here.

Episode 16

I walked toward my side of the camp and with weighted information. The captain said more info is on its way. Some of the girl's throats were slashed with a wicked type blade in the brothels, and some appeared strangled. On my list of soldiers who traveled to those towns with orders, only a few of my men worked nearby details, and no single person was consistently in the areas of these murders. The best thing out of a bad situation, all the Colored soldiers are accounted for at nighttime. The White soldiers had more opportunities, but nobody had a reason or made a way to be near when a young woman met her demise. The killer is ghostly-mystic like in their movements, and managed to make it seem as if the women themselves slashed their throats or strangled themselves. It's all so bizarre.

The best I can do is drink coffee and think it out in possible visions in my mind. The smell of coffee in the early morning hours on these shores will be a distant memory one day. My motorcycle recovery operation has led to over 300 cycles already back in the States, so I will have a business to start when I return home. It made me think of the future, although right now it's cloudy with turmoil.

A strange sky cleared with no clouds over the Colored side of the camp. Quickly, the attitude of my men also became lively. There were shadow clouds on the other side of the base. Still cold, the burn barrel smoked, and laughter and conversations rose with the smolder.

The conversation of the GI experts around the burn barrel...as usual, the talk of sex dominated. The debate today: the ins and outs of oral sex. Most men would never admit to putting their mouth on a woman's sex. From what I heard from most men, they were not trying to satisfy a woman, although they thought they were. The repeated theme, "Once I give a woman this hard meat, she won't want anything else." A skewered mindset dribbled out of men who I would think couldn't get a woman to like them, and much less keep a woman.

I'm not so sure women felt empowered or felt stifled to tell men what they wanted and needed, or how they felt. I don't know if men heard women wanted more in the bed. I asked women what they wanted, and most felt shy in telling me what they wanted. A few women who did tell me, they said men would act intimidated and upset if they brought up what they wanted to be pleased. Some weak men exhibit a wariness of a woman's needs by sometimes accusing their woman of wanting an old lover or wanting a new lover instead of them. It could turn out to be an adverse outcome for a woman to feel pushed into isolation or even having to live with violence. Me, I always wanted to feel I pleased a woman, and I did as many things as I passionately thought possible.

Since being with Valentina, I would heat a washbasin of water, and I would sponge her body like using a polishing cloth to put a shine on the expensive crystal on a glass shelf. I washed between her toes and between her thighs from anterior to posterior. I let the rinse water run down and ski jump off her firm, miniature cherry nipples. I'd shampooed her hair with lavender oil I found in a cottage. I'd dry her body, and then let my tongue roam her sensual figure as I knew where to go to please her.

My uncle shared with me, "A woman wants our hands, lips, and tongue all over her body, besides a hard pounding," and for sure, Valentina wanted my tongue caressing her womanhood. It turned me on even more hearing and seeing her reactions. I treated Valentina to all I knew. She told me, she knew nothing about making love before me. She never felt desired and pleasured until making love with me. I wanted her to see I'm not a simple man. I wanted her to feel exceptional as a woman, despite all the past pain absorbed in her in life. I wanted her to know the desires of my heart and my physical love.

My uncle also told me, "Men and women have to lift each other no matter what. Males become men for the glory they are allowed to see in a woman's deeds. Females become women when they support the actions of a man who is trying to be worthy of the love of a woman. All others stay alone, being less than when they choose to keep their eyes closed, ears covered, and their minds asleep while letting love pass them by."

The dark clouds made their way over to my area, and rain is dropping. The burn barrel pops and sizzles almost like it's telling the liars to stop. I'm listening to men brag and lie. My mind is somewhere else. As of late, I avoided the conversations about women knowing Valentina and me one day would be over. She and I both understood.

Do I genuinely love her? Yes! *Am I like a creep of a man who touches a woman's heart and then he disappears?* I don't want to be a heartbreaker. I know what it feels like to have my heart ripped out. *Then, what am I doing?* I'm in a war zone and treating our flaming hot love as if it's a home, when time is running out on us, and our house burns down. Time is the big bad wolf, and it will blow our world apart when I leave. Sometimes when I observe her crossing a field, she's dressed as if she's Little Red Riding Hood. She'll have on a long, tattered, brown dress, a black shawl over her shoulders, and a red scarf tied around her hair with her streak of White hair flowing over her face.

What do I do, or don't do, with Valentina's heart? If I break it off now, and I'm here for another six months, how can we avoid each other? If one day, I'm up and gone, will it kill her soul?

Walking on a muddy path, with confusion stalking me on the insides, I headed to the mechanic's tent, and I walk into a White soldier with my head down.

"Hey, Jig–a–boo...watch where you're going."

I walked into hate. We are both standing in four inches of mud, almost a foot apart from each other. I look around at my surroundings, as he is on the wrong side of the camp. The sky is dropping a steady flow of rain, and the trees are swaying from wind sweeping hard from east to west. As far as I can see, there is no one near us, but I look back, and I can see my men at the burn barrel a hundred yards away. I can see them all looking my way.

In my men's eyes, only one thing could be happening – a form of disrespect being thrown in my face, and I know my men want to know how I am handling it. My existence is theirs in many ways.

"Hey, Jig–a–boo, watch where you're going. You hear me speaking to you, or do you speak jungle–jig?"

Another 200 feet away is the mechanic's tent and repair area for trucks and jeeps. My area. I have several guys working who should be on duty by now. *Where has he been?* I'm wondering, but I think I know why he is here.

"I'm Master Sergeant Preer. You're in my area."

He casts an eye over me as if he thinks I'm not telling him the truth. He spat on the ground. It landed next to my boots. I'm sure his spittle hit my boots as the rain dropped on them.

"So, you're the head Negro in charge?"

"What are you doing in this area, and who are you?"

"The info is in my front pocket," he said.

I lowered my voice, although no one could hear. "I'm going to poke you in your chest a few times and take what is in your pocket."

He lowered his head, and I poked him hard with stiff fingers, and it moved him back each time. I slipped the note out of his pocket and then one last poke. I made it count. He fell backward. I walked over him and never looked back.

Captain Castellani said he'd send a man I could trust with some more information. It did feel good, and know my men were watching. Leadership sometimes is taking a risk and acting a badass. Most soldiers, and much of the associated personnel, have a role to play in the theater of war. Acting can be tool of survival.

Outside my detail area...the main mechanic tent, truck, and jeep hoods were up, and my crew worked. I keep the tools in smaller tents, and I allow the men to go in and retrieve what they need for them to do a job. I checked the duty list I made the day before, and the men of both crews – morning and afternoon – checked off what they needed to accomplish, and finished their details. I did not want the guys to spend all day working in one area, and it allowed me to keep more men busy.

The White soldiers around us maintained lazy bones as a way of life of being no-account when outside the combat zone. Not funny. Colored soldiers are labeled lazy and no-account when we have the dirtiest and nastiest details and still manage to do them. My uncle said Colored folk were labeled lazy the day slavery ended. It's the privilege of America who stole men and women from Africa to do the work that they did not want to do, but they have the nerve to call *us* lazy.

A college professor said one day to me, "The Colored man will raise up and march, and boycott, and protest, and will gain the right to vote all through the South. The White man will fight before they give up controlling power, but the Negro will make strides and do what is right by God's will. One day, segregation will be a thing of the past."

Well, it's the mid-1940s, and I walked by a White soldier, and he whispered loud enough, "Hey go back to Africa, Nigger." All the Negro soldiers have heard the same thing while we were in basic training, as if feeble brains could only conjure up simple slurs. Those White boys rarely took on a Negro by themselves – they usually came with a gang of cowards. So, I can never see it happening to where America will ever see me as an equal and treat me fair. If change comes, Redneck-Whites will attempt to seize control back. Power is worth dying for, worth stealing for, and worth killing any amount of people to have it. You can kill people physically. You can kill the spirit of any human by them by putting them in prisons or withholding or taking money, property. One can hurt a group or in a singular situation with forcing one to work for dirt poor wages. You can hurt people for generations to come by blocking or limiting travel housing and education. It is an awful history for Negroes in America, by enforced immoral laws.

I'm sending the morning crew away for the rest of the day, and the afternoon crew will come a few hours later. I needed a nap, and I want to go to my private hideaway area. My dog keeps any potential intrusion from bothering me in the tent with a growl or bark if need be.

I've given it some thought...*could there be a way for me to have my dog, Jerri, come all the way home with me to Seattle, and be my son's companion pet if I'm ever near my son again.* Jerri never barked when Valentina came, even though she approached from concealed entrances, but she knew the dog before me. Jerri will let me know Valentina is nearby making a short low–volume, high–pitch yelp. When my dog wags her tail and makes her little yelp, I can go back into my hidden sleeping area, and Valentina will be sitting on my bed.

Back in my hidden tent, I read the note of information, and now I'm going to take a nap. In my sleep, I often solve my problems or wake with new things to ponder.

Episode 17

BOOM − BOOM − BOOM − BOOM − BOOM!

My body feels itself falling out of a dream. I'm lying prone, and it feels like I'm helplessly going one way and my mind is going the other. I feel like a ragdoll in my dream. What the hell is going on?

BOOM − BOOM − BOOM − BOOM − BOOM!

I'm awake. Violence is near me. The ground trembled. What the hell...? Bombs dropping from the sky, and there should be no bombing anywhere near here. A siren pierced the air from the other side of the camp. The last time we experienced a deafening sound like this, it had been many months ago, and even then, our immediate area went untouched. In the region where bombs did land, alarms alerted us to German fighter planes with 20 mm machine guns which are huge bullets tearing human legs off or any body part clean off. We destroyed those fighter planes and the last of them, as we found the airfield they were hiding some 100 miles away hidden in a forest of tall trees. What I hear and feel this time − bombs dropping from a plane flying slowly and high in the sky.

The ground quaking is shaking me off my cot. Startled, I jump up out of my bed and bump my head on a low hanging mental pipe holding tent material which helped hide my hidden sleeping space. *Shit.* I'm bleeding above my eye.

BOOOOM, the loudest of the explosions came from a distance. I heard an echo as the ground shook. Slipping out of my hiding area, I quickly pour water from the freshwater supply I keep hidden for myself, and clean the wound above my eye. The siren kept blaring.

Jerri cowered under the truck, but she barked like crazy. I heard yelling approaching.

"Sir–Sir."

Hearing my nickname called, I make it out of the mechanic tent as some of my soldiers from the afternoon crew approach me on the road.

"Master Sergeant Preer, a Nazi bomber looks to have crashed upon the mountainside. A huge fireball seems to have set the mountain on fire." Lanky Slim's down-from-the-deepest-part-of-the-Bayou Cajun accent squeezed his throat with fear, and his Negroid nose flared to inhale much-needed air from being out of breath from the long run. His light brown boyish hair stood as if electricity charged up from the ground.

"Master Sergeant Preer, as soon as you can, can you check?"

He stopped himself, realizing another soldier stood next to him. I knew what he wanted. He needed to know about his male lover over on the White side of the camp. His emotions seeped with fear.

"Where did the bombs come down?" I tried to sound calm as my chest pounded as if the mythical legend, John Henry, were nailing spikes in the ground with his hammer. My fears, on a scale compared to his, might be the same.

The men pointed to the other side of the camp. As the siren kept blaring, no emergency alert rang out from the Colored encampment. My men have often wondered…if, by chance, if all of us Colored boys died in one blast or battle, who would bury us? Who would send our dog tags to our families?

"Sergeant…the far end," Lanky Slim said again as he kept pointing to where black smoke lifted to the dark sky. "How did a bomber get this close to us here in southern France, and yet no one shot it down before coming this far?"

"Good question." I patted him on the shoulder in an attempt to calm him and his fears, knowing he hoped his lover had escaped harm. I looked up at the skies and realized the peace in this area played a tricked on all of us making us think we were safe.

A jeep sped in our direction cutting across the cow field. The soft ground out there – it invited the jeep to sink into the mud, but the jeep slipped and slushed its way through. It stopped next to us with two MPs inside – the friendly ones. They jumped out, came in my direction, and stood at attention before speaking.

"Master Sergeant Preer, a Nazi plane dropped bombs near the washing station area and has trapped a bunch of men. Some are dead, and a few bombs did not go off. You are the only one who can disarm bombs. The captain requested you to come now."

I stared for a long minute, thinking. How is it, they – many of the White soldiers demeaned me when given a chance? It seems they can't, or won't, show respect unless they need me to save their asses. *If it wasn't for the God in me!*

I know the captain sent an order for me to come, as he should. I held a finger up, wanting them to wait. "At ease, soldiers," I said, allowing them to relax a bit if they could, because it's not their fault, they are merely delivering the message in the middle of a bombing.

I trotted to the tent, and the followed in the jeep. Maybe in a bit of defiance of what could happen from trying to disarm bombs – the fear in me made me move slowly. I grabbed tools and tossed them in a bag, and then I pushed my soul to jump in the back of the jeep.

"Take the road, don't go across the muddy field, my extra weight will sink us in the soft ground."

We sped along the longer distance to the undetonated bomb. Deactivating bombs is not something I love to do, or think I'm special because I can do it, but I'm good at it...I'm living proof, right? My parents paid for my mechanical engineering degree to build, restore, save, and survive, but I don't think disarming bombs was in their plan.

The far end of the camp is where the mess hall is. It is a series of circus-like tents and cooking stations. The White side of the camp holds over 1,500 soldiers. The Colored side, we have nearly 200 soldiers, and 100 assigned to outposts. I have corporals who report to me who oversee those Negro soldiers in the outpost bases. In the mess hall, we Colored soldiers have a separate eating time in the tents.

The jeep hit potholes and jarring bumps in the road as my unstable stomach tumbled into vomit levels, but I maintained.

The washing stations look blown apart. Now, Captain America soldiers who clean up in barrels of gas before they trek into the whore houses for a minute of pleasure, they have nothing at the moment. We Colored men have to walk out of our way in order not to visually see the devil's works, although we built the area and fixed up the brothels. Like anything in life, one minute you could be a joyful person about to receive a treat, and in the next moment, you are suffering. Men, who were clad only in towels, now lay naked with broken and mangled body parts. Purple gas is running along the ground as well as standing still in puddles. The aftermath of the undetonated bombs that landed near barrels of gas, caused those barrels to fall over, but there are no flames...yet. It's just a matter of time if I don't defuse these bombs. The town and brothel houses were almost a quarter of a mile away, and that's not far enough away. Valentina could be house cleaning.

Nearby, more structures are in shambles from other bombs, and I'm sure men are under piles of rubble. Death lay on the ground along with other injured soldiers carted off to the MASH unit.

Strange maybe, but I'm the Head Negro in Charge. The rednecks who call me a Nigger before, all did what I told them to do now. I need it still around here. No movements. No one walks. I don't want to hear talking or yelling!

I stared at undetonated bombs, knowing sometimes they implant deep into the ground and can go off much like a land mine if stepped on. The men who were hurt and needed assistance would have to stay right where they were for now, or they would be taking their last few breaths. I gave orders, and everyone listened and heeded.

The bombs were small in composition, and were meant to spread shrapnel like shards of glass piercing the flesh with dirty metals spreading infections quickly. If detonated, these bombs will kill life nearby including me. Each of the unexploded bombs, if shifted the wrong way, would make a hell right here. I approached a bomb, and I felt panic inside my head and stomach, and my walk felt weak. Never much of a drinker, I wished I could toss a double shot of bourbon back, and for a minute, feel the warmth to slow my heart. I walked toward the bomb with my tool bag.

Sweat on a cold day, and the smell of a mixture of amatol and TNT, and aluminum powder, naphthalene, and ammonium nitrate, is in the air from exploded bombs. They were pressure contact bombs meant to go off on contact. There were several bombs lodged in the ground, and those were either duds or were on timers.

Right now, I want to live to see another day, and live to see my son, my mother, my father, and...Valentina. I want to see my home.

The bombs are my height, and as wide as my body. My sweat dripped on the metal portion of the bomb, and I kneeled over a timed killer. I exhaled a sigh of relief. I felt fortunate the access plate faced me on the top of the bomb, and not underneath it. This would allow me to gain operating space to do the mechanical operation.

I removed the hatch and saw wires and connections. The Germans set many of their bombs on timers – they did so to ensure a variance of explosions. I recognized the wires allowing me to live or die. I prepared to cut green, red, and White and black heaven or hell connections. The sequence of the disconnect procedure, and the life of those already hurt and hanging onto life, had my nervous hands sweating. I kept drying them. God or the devil wanted me to deal with the blame of whatever happened, no matter the ending.

I heard men moaning, and death rattles. As much as I knew they were in pain, I needed them to shut the hell up. In the balance of all, empathy ran low with me at the moment as I needed to focus.

My undergarment felt soaking wet from swimming in sweat, or I have peed on myself with each wire I cut. One kind of electric time–delay fuse could be set for any time between two and seventy-two hours after dropping, and another type could be set to detonate within minutes. To prevent the bomb from being defused, I first swabbed thick axle grease to any metal near the wires as a barrier to keep any contact of a hot wire, or to enact a ground wire from finding grounding. A mechanical anti–withdrawal fuse is fitted with a simple spring-loaded detonator to prevent the removal of the fuse---------- ----- yet it's still possible to do by a few who are skilled, such as I am. I had been successful up until now.

I learned bomb diffusion from a dud bomb from previous bombings. The ins and outs of how bomb triggering mechanisms work is a sequence pattern. Dud is the byproduct of the Germans trying to make as many bombs as possible, and I'm sure quality controls were lax. There is no way to know if the bomb in front of me will go off, so here I am, and one wrong move can cause an instantaneous explosion if the detonator moves more than 5/8's of an inch.

5/8th of an inch is slightly wider than my forefinger. I lifted the internal device to what I felt like 3/8th of an inch would be. I slid a stiff wire through a long narrow hole. I pushed a spring-loaded pad down to keep in place as I lifted the detonator. With the electrical wires I cut, I would hear a *click* letting me know I have ten seconds to run in a safe direction if lifted too high, or missed the spring-loaded pad with the stiff wire. Ten seconds might save me, but could still tear me a new one. I and all those near who couldn't run for life, the journey to the hereafter would commence.

I went from bomb to bomb and defused them – the last two, and just to the left of me, a man lay on the ground laboring to breathe. Without medical attention, death poured out of him. I tried to focus on the bomb. He distracted me with his wheezing lungs omitting guttural distress. I shredded apart from insides listening to him and seeing his left arm mangled, but waving at me. Under the bomb, I see his right hand pinned. The bomb lodged two feet into the ground, leaving his arm contorted with an ugly compound break. The bone breached through the skin. His facial expression – a sinister, almost defiant glare tried to hide indescribable pain exposing itself through his stressed pulsating veins.

I stared at him instead of the life and death task in front of me. Something caught my eye of his torn, almost gone, sleeve of his arm. Strange markings. I stopped working on the bomb. His markings took my total focus. From his upper forearm up to an enormous bicep, it showed tattooed non–English words with a woven crown or circle emblem. The circle seemed to have a dark skin man woven in a circle, with words intertwined all through.

A GI? I froze. I paused to reason. The letter of info Captain Castellani sent by way of his carrier highlighted information that one of the girls survived an attack. Whoever mutilated her caused her to nearly bleed to death, but the woman survived. Under some trance or drug, she did not remember much about her attacker, but thought he might be a soldier because of a tattoo or strange marking. I'm supposed to interview the woman held in a secret place. Only Captain Castellani, and supposedly no one else, knew she lived through the experience, except a madam at a brothel. Now I see this wounded GI with non–English tattooed words with a crown-like a circle insignia.

I walked over to him. His eyes are defiant. But the pain he's experiencing – it must feel like lightning strikes with each heartbeat.

I turned from him and slowly walked away from the gravely injured man. I'm walking toward the MPs who were stationed somewhat safely in the distance. I know they are waiting for me to say it is safe. I'm still a ways away from that, and they are gesturing for me to signal. I give no signal as I keep walking their way. I look up to the sky and clouds parted slightly, letting the sun is peaking in and out. I look north, and there is the sun. I look south, and rain clouds are gathering. I'm not sure who will win the battle. The smell in the air is of fire, destruction, and fuel-ready to explode. My eyes water, and my nose and throat feel dry. As I step lightly over splitter smoldering wood and mangled metal, I spit, as I'm trying to clear a nasty taste from my mouth.

The two MPs, both west coast boys who I trust for the most part – with one eye open, they met me at the perimeter.

"I will need one man removed! I will not save the others until we remove him. I have to save him first as a bomb pins him. If I can release him, I will need you to retrieve him, and then I will save the others."

They looked at me and then at each other.

"What are you saying, Master Sergeant Preer?" the blonde one from southern California asked, his face twisted in confusion.

"There is a man...I feel he is not one of us, or if he is, well...I feel he can help us with a problem we have here. It is sensitive, and I'm sure Captain Castellani will respect you two to the utmost by doing what I ask of you."

"Is it safe for us to come?" the Seattle born soldier queried with his head cocked as he closed his eyes. Maybe he's visualizing what could happen.

"I will disarm the bomb he's pinned under, but the moment I do, I need you two to come before anyone else does and recover the man I speak of and take him to a place away from all the others. Maybe one of you can go to the captain now and let him know what's going on, and then return here, as it will take two men to remove him. He is hurt badly, but I don't think he's going to lose his life. Death for him right now is still up to him."

The Seattle soldier nodded and looked to his friend, and they both nodded. Then he moved away quickly. He yelled back over his shoulder as he ran on his way to the captain.

"Wait," I called out, and he stopped and trotted back. "Where is Master Sergeant Jude?" I asked. I know the tone in my voice sounded guttural. "I don't need for him to know anything."

"He is out with a small band of men."

"He doesn't need to know anything. He doesn't need to know, guys, I hope you understand,"

"We do, and he is no friend of ours. He's a prick. I think he went out to locate the bomber plane, which we think went down over the mountain."

"And he won't know a damn thing, sir," Southern California responded.

"Give me your note pad," I requested.

Southern California nodded and handed over his note pad.

I wrote a quick note and folded the paper. "Give this to the captain. Hey guys, if we make it back to the States, I'll assemble any motorcycle of your choice, and they will be faster and handle better than all the rest."

I shook hands with both of them, and then I made my way back to the man pinned under a bomb. I assumed both he and I wanted to live.

❈❈❈

I disarmed the bomb I first started on before I notice the man and his arm. The man stared at me the whole time I defused the bomb. It unnerved me a bit, and it sliced into my focus at a time when I needed all concentrate instilled in me. Now, this man under the bomb spoke.

"Please, God, don't let this last bomb take my life."

Sweat ran down my back, and my whole body might have sent out an unpleasant musk.

I stared him down and spoke loudly. "I have to move the bomb. By chance, it might free your hand, and it might twist it some more. You have to try to stay still until I tell you to move. If your hand comes free, lean to the right, and fall away instead of trying to pull your arm out. You have to do as I say, or we both die." I said sternly and gave him the cruelest face I could hurl into his eyes. He kept disdain in his eyes like a welder torch trying to burn his way out of a 10–inch thick metal box. His discomfort right now is not my concern. I knew nothing of him, but by his tattoo markings, I have to believe he is trouble.

The rain started to pound on my helmet, drowning out my thoughts of him. It helped to center my focus on diffusing the bomb. I handled the bomb gently. I tried to roll the bomb with baby care over on its side. I struggled with an 80–pound, deadly baby lodged two feet in the ground. The bomb would not budge. I felt fear run through my chest and move into my testicles as if waiting for the firing squad to fire the deadly bullet.

The man, suddenly despite his pain, reached over his body with his less–injured arm to assist me with just enough help as the bomb turned into position.

Twice wires touched. I should have been dead, but God made other plans for me. I disarmed the bomb and gave the signal for help for the two MPs who knew what I needed. They removed the man. The pain he felt from the dragging away sent a scream up to the sky, and I will never disremember the scream piercing of my eardrums.

As I watched the MPs remove the man, all I could think of from being near what felt like evil is, I wanted a hot bath. I wanted a hot drink. I want warmth. My mind traveled from disarmed death, and I sought comfort. I felt a jolt in my soul—Valentina. Where might she be during all this? We concealed our life away from others, but there's no telling if we've been found out. A killer hides amongst us. The man dragged away...*could he be an angel of death?* I felt fear.

With my need to know Valentina's well-being, it hazed my vision, and I walked blindly. I headed in what seemed to be ten different directions with much on my mind. The downpour turned to mist as the MPs walked me into a tent with a bunker going deep into the ground. Captain Castellani opened a door at the end of a tunnel. He waved me in. I read between the lines of what the captain hinted of in past conversations as there's a place only a few knew of, and this is it. I stand in a damp, dark dungeon-like dwelling.

The man in question sat in a chair naked with a medical sling wrap to support his arm. In the presence of the man stood the request I sent in the note to the captain. Tiny Taps, the New York–Puerto Rican boxing champ stood positioned behind the naked man. I went over to Tiny, and I whispered the story of why I needed him here. He nodded. Tiny Taps exhibited a look on his face signifying he wanted to hurt the man on my orders with pleasure with all five feet of his powerful body.

The captain and I moved to a corner. "Master Sergeant Preer, you're right. There is something different, and the difference is, he is not one of us, he is not an American soldier. As far as I can tell, he is German, or I don't know, but he has enough knowledge of being and acting as though he is one of us."

We are two men standing in uniforms serving the same country, but yet I'm wet to the core and cold, hungry, mad, and scared for what has been, and what needs to happen. He used the term, *one of us*, as he held no power over me right now. He needed me. Without me, the unidentified man might harm all of us.

Most Colored men, our lives were hard one way or another under the thumb of being ruled in America unfairly. I doubt nothing will ever change, but right now, I seized total control. Negroes, we wear our beast of burden – as Africans were shipped into slavery – and never wanted for much else. We Negroes live in a country that despises our race for surviving, and yet we wear the weight like a badge of honor because we do survive. My people have lived on – one way or another – while being against a barrel of a gun and Jim Crow laws of hanging at the end of a rope. We made it in the dark when many times we thought there to be no light at the end.

I believe the man is German. We have evil tied to a chair. *Just how evil?* A foreigner passing as a White America soldier – he can salivate on wickedness he can create. I'm where I am, along with thousands of men of several different races, because of Hitler. Many White men don't understand Hitler doesn't want them in his fold. He wants an exact type of White man. If the American White man can put aside his hate for me, he would see Hitler is just a pure killer of anyone who doesn't have his idea of purity, and think like him.

The word is...there is a special kind of bomb in the making, and it might be able to damn near destroy whole cities and regions with a firebomb effect. I wonder will they use it on White men, or non-White men, as an experiment in terror.

I spoke in a whisper. "Captain, I need you to leave. I don't want this man to think he has a choice. I need to do whatever it takes to gather information from him, so turn and leave like you don't give a damn."

"Sergeant, I do believe in the Geneva Convention. We both know the Germans are evil killers of the Jews, and have been awful to captured American soldiers. We are here to put a stop to evil."

I gritted my teeth and kept my voice low, laced with aggression. "Someone strangling, and knifing the life out of women and our soldiers are over here damn near raping for a fee! We put evil between these women's legs, in their mouths, and then a man is squeezing their throats down to string or slitting their throat. You have a choice, but not really."

I shifted my weight to show my contempt for the do-gooder bullshit.

He moved from my face and yelled in the direction of the tied naked man. "Do whatever you want...we need information!"

The captain turned and left the room as if he didn't give a damn as I needed it to appear. I wanted the captured man to sense his life garnered no importance. I nodded to Tiny Taps. Then, as if a baseball bat held by the greatest home run hitter of all time, the great Josh Gipson swung at a watermelon...Tiny Taps fist exploded off the side of the man's head. I knew the damaged sent a message, as we were not going to torture him for long.

War is ugly, unfair, unjust, and inhuman when it comes down to victors and losers.

I walked around the man and saw blood slowly drip from his ear. I knew the pain prodded his thoughts on what to say to save himself. From early on, with his arm lying twisted under the bomb, he played tough, or a superman to pain. No one could play that tough, and he did scream when they drug him in here, so he knows pain.

Down the pipeline of truth, rumors, myths, or lies, I heard the Germans developed a "courage drug" called Pervitin, and sometimes they called it D–1X. The drug it is a methamphetamine-based experimental performance enhancer tablet made with equal parts of cocaine and painkiller. It's the Nazi's dream of creating super soldiers. Funny, all the Colored men, whenever we encountered a Nazi soldier in hand–to–hand combat of fist and feet, we beat the shit out of them. Jesse Owens wasn't our fastest Negro, and he ran circles around the Germans in the Olympics. So much for taking a drug to boost fighting ability, but if this man is on any drug to have increased pain tolerance, it just meant a terrible beating is coming his way.

I needed to decipher the tattoo on the man. However, the anger directed toward me is not the usual hate Whites have for a Colored man. This man hated me even before having his brain bounced around inside his skull from Tiny Taps' fist. I knew if Tiny Taps hit him on the other side of the head, he would be without any hearing. I put up two fingers. Tiny broke a few ribs and then broke the man's nose by driving a sledgehammer punch up into the man's brain cavity.

Now the sound of the pain lifted to the bunker ceiling. He roared with intense pain. I felt my ears melt earwax from the fire of his roar. Tiny Taps' face sequenced several facial expressions, it was from the discomfort of the volume from the howling the man released inside the contained small space.

I waited for the man to catch his breath the best he could through his mouth and broken ribs. I know each breath is painful. If he is drugged to withstand pain, his drug finally lost its battle and the war to Tiny Taps' Thor–like fists. I place my lips close to the damaged ear.

"Who are you?"

"Kaspar Österreicher." His voice was less defiant, but it still held on to some antagonism, considering his thrashed condition.

"Okay Kasper Österreicher, it's rather apparent you are German."

"Austrian."

"Yeah...same shit – no matter how close you are to Hitler and his birth country. What are you doing here? And you speak with such good English, so let it out quickly."

"Darky, they call you darkies – jigs in your USA. I go to your schools in your USA and I come back to find truth in neither your country nor a madman as Hitler."

"You call me names, when I own your nuts at the moment, and maybe not even a minute away from a beating," I smirked and made sure he saw my face.

He smirked with blood dripping from an ugly face, and spat on the ground. "You are not a darky like you might think, as I have said. You, and most of your people, are living in the dark. I have no love or hate for your kind, and your race or color. For you are a shit pile for America, as you and the Indian and the Asian immigrants –if you became as one people, you would be the power over the gun and whip, and the colonizing of the world," he laughed through shortness of breath. "You second class fools."

I ignored his insults. His people never felt the end of a whip. Ignorance of a man to think just 100 years ago, the enslaved African Negro and the American Indian, and others spoke the same language, or were entrenched in the same battles to fight. He learned his offenses and views in the country that often insults me.

"What are you doing? You spying? You killing? You have anything to do with the women murdered near here? Who are you working with? How did you move so easily amongst the White soldiers? Answer any of those questions."

"I don't have anything against you personally. But, you Americans...are you not killing the whores with diseases and unwanted American babies? Are you not paying a penny to whores and charging your GIs a lot of money? I believe in America they call it the procurement of sexual workers –pimping. Unmoral America, you steal the wares of a woman for profit."

"So, are you killing the women to stop what is wrong? By killing, you're supposed to make it better?"

I walked back to the wall and leaned against it. My back ached a bit from all the moving of the bombs, and being in extended awkward positions in doing the disarming. Tiny sat behind the man. I believed he hurt his hand, but he waved his other hand to let me know, if need be, he's ready to do more damage.

"I don't give a damn if you do or don't. Start answering my questions or Tiny is going to make you feel your end is near in the most painful way –long and slow, but dreadfully impactful as you take your last breaths."

"You are not my king! You're nothing like my king! And I will kill for him. I will die for his throne. He will lead me to what is right so that we will rule over all nations of race, color, or religion of man," the captured man spit and displayed strength through his voice in his defiance.

"So, Hitler is your king who you will die for if you don't answer my questions."

"Hitler is a fool. I live for my king."

The man lifted to a standing position with the chair attached to his tied legs. He hopped to the wall and thrust forward, then banged his head against the wall with such force it made a sound of two boulders colliding from up high. He fell backward and landed on the back of his head. Blood pooled. Before Tiny Taps or I could react, the man summoned enough courage and overcame his pain. He killed himself most horrifically. Blood ran from his mouth and eyes like a well pump pumping.

"What fool cracks his skull wide open like a tomato can in order to prevent from telling us what we want to know?" Tiny Tap spoke to the dead man as we stood over his bleeding corpse.

We stared at the ghastly death as we both sat down and viewed the dead man.

❈ ❈ ❈

I wanted to sleep, as I felt pain in my body from lifting and digging bombs. I needed this to be over, and my ass to be back in the States. War is death, but seeing a head split open in a self-inflicted murder is not what my soul needed to see. My soul hurt.

And then, what the man expressed about some weird, "King." What the hell? If it wasn't Hitler, then who? Maybe he tried to throw my scent off from understanding he has to be a Hitler lap dog.

I needed sleep to think.

Episode 18

Hours into the night, Valentina's warm soul and soft touch put me to sleep. We might be safer together than any place on the war-torn land, and at the same time, we were a danger to each other. It doesn't mean anything to those White soldiers if her skin is less White – she wasn't Mulatto-brown, but Mulatto-White in the eyes of jealous White men. They would see her as something they don't have, and a Negro shouldn't have. Even here on foreign soil in France, there is no woman a Negro soldier has the right to be alone with or near.

Then there is the killer – the one who is strangling and slashing, I cringe with fear if he finds my secret lover. I need her near me as much as possible. Her way of being safe when we are apart is to stay close to other women during the day and evening times. Then when the night comes, I'm anxious as I wait for her to appear in my hidden lover's den.

She massaged my physical pain slowly with hot olive oil. She started at my cold feet and worked on each inch of my skin. She worked her soft hand into the stress of my face. In my hideaway, the oil lamp cast shadows on us. Valentina's hot hands touched deep into pain and eroded my tension. Her accent, laced with her sensual fire, whispered mental cooling in my ears to make each breath I took one step closer to an intoxicating sleeping potion.

"Valentina, my love, bring your ear near my lips so I can whisper how I feel."

She moved her ear to the point of touching my lips. I lightly kissed her, and I whispered,

"My love, your voice is light rain on a summer night.

Your words, they embraced me

My heart is a warm salve in the snow when you are near

You erase muddy footprints from a world that walks over my daily rising

Like pure cream, only you are whole in my drifts

My blood is a river of spills of past deceptions

You captured and held my soul when the world seemed to fall apart

Feel my love flood your soul

I want my soul to drain into a new ocean

Only you and I sail to a world we create and live on, and nary a storm shall part our love."

"Sirletto, you are the only soul inside other than mine, no matter where you lay your head. I feel your love as the only love I can have. I can never love another love, as you have sealed me so no other can touch my being, and your love will hold me into another life as the love instilled in me from you will hold my soul."

I tried to speak not knowing what I what to say, but Valentina placed her parted lips over mine and closed my lips tight. She pulled back just far enough to let her lips kiss my eyelids. I'm drifting away, but I believe I hear her talking to me.

"I have heard the gypsy women say, *men say too much when there is nothing to say.* I know you are going away one day, but I have told you...I love you until there is not another breath to keep me alive, and even then, I will still love you."

❊ ❊ ❊

My dog nudged my arm to wake me. I knew Valentina left before daylight. I made it to the burn barrel with much on my mind about all I needed to do. The men were laughing it up with coffee and French toast in hand. I procured eggs from a farmhouse a mile outside our camp. The Germans forced the farmer to supply food or die. I came to help the farmer and repaired a broken well pump with parts I made. He gave us many eggs often. Nutmeg and cinnamon came from Valentina in her travels near and around the countryside. Tanks have cast iron plates, and I removed an iron plate from a bombed-out German tank. Now it's used as a griddle sitting on top of the burn barrel. I made a deal with a baker, I repaired a generator for his bakery, and he supplied me with pure syrup from the forest. He gave us bread just short of molding, and as we did all our lives, we cut out any mold. Bread dipped in an egg batter with seasoning...it's the best we have tasted since we landed on the French shores.

There is no sweetness or satisfaction in what Tiny Taps and I did last night. We made a dead man disappear. We missed the mark on burying him six feet down to cover his busted head and limp body, but we still dug down far enough to make sure he's closer to hell.

Tiny taught me how to bury a body through tales of hard knocks of living in New York. He told me stories as we dug. Something I already understood, but I learned more about, is that many of our people, through time, did not have the pleasure of being sent to an undertaker and having a ceremonial funeral. Tiny Taps came from an island of barely getting by and burying his kinfolk in the ways of the land.

Muscled Tiny Taps stood by the fire looking okay. I'm sure his hand landing like a hammer against a hard head, and then helping drag a man and dig a grave, he must be exhausted and feeling some discomfort. I wanted to let him know he's a good man. He looked up at me, and we nodded as we scarfed down some sweet bread and coffee.

A jeep with two MPs and the captain drove into our part of the camp and kept on heading toward the mechanic repair area. I knew to follow and meet up with him. Strangely, the weather broke from the rain and dark gray clouds of the last few days and weeks. It's bright winter – almost like a spring day, but cold.

I wanted to stay by the fire and isolate myself from the outside world and let my mind think of all the things Valentina whispered to me. She knows one day I'm going home. My mind is somewhere else, but duty calls.

"Sergeant, what do we know? Tell me we know more."

"The man – the now dead man – he and at least one more person and maybe others, are bringing death to the women. He took his own life before we could extract more info. He received his schooling in America. He spoke good English, but came from Austria, and claimed no allegiance to Hitler. But I think he used that German pain killer drug, but it made him extremely neurotic."

"Did he work with the Germans?"

"Captain, I'm betting no, but he worked with someone or someone's."

"We have no leads to his alignment?"

"A king."

"A king?"

"Yes, sir, some weird belief I cannot make heads or tails of."

"So, we are nowhere?"

"Captain, I have a plan to attempt to draw out the killer or killers."

"I'm listening, but you do know we are under a microscope and clock. It is a matter of time before the Germans surrender. Hitler has taken his own life, they say. Some think he staged his death and has left the country and headed to South America to hide out."

"Either way, he's a coward, sir. I need some coffee, and you may want some more yourself with all I have to tell you."

"Right, come to my tent and tell me what this plan is."

He turned and walked away to his jeep. I watched them leave as my head spun with insanity. I turned to the open field and shielded my eyes from the bright sun. I'm blinded in many ways as the killers of these women have me in a bind and steering blindly to stop the madness. I'm trying to disconnect from all the madness, and it is trying. I can't see how one day soon, I will be on a ship headed back to the so-called land of the free, but leaving a significant part of my soul chained to a woman who loves me.

❀ ❀ ❀ ❀

"Captain, my plan will take a lot of moving pieces."

I sat in a chair in Captain Castellani's tent. A long table held maps, toy soldiers, and tanks, and airplanes were stationed over the diagram to show mountains, rivers, and forestlands, which were divided by lines of what country had control of what area. There were American and England flags over toppled German flags. Outside of the tent, sounds of troop movements and machines escalated in the distance, causing the ground to have slight tremors I could feel coming through my worn boots. The bombing from yesterday put a sense of war back into the actions of the camp to do something, even when not knowing what to do.

Repairs are in the works, and some of the minor wounded walked seemly aimlessly. Sadly, there were a few deaths. I sent a small band of my Colored men out to do some searching nearby for possible Germans. It could have been possible the bombing is a last-ditch attempt to serve as a decoy for left behind Germans in the area, in hopes of those soldiers could return to Germany to help defend the approaching Americans. But it doesn't make sense. The German leadership proved to be less than smart enough to have a plan to work. The dumb ass Germans tried to overtake Russia in the middle of the winter, and their asses got handed to them, all the while trying to take on the U.S. and England. Now Hitler turned coward and has run or ate a self−inflicted death as his main course.

I laid out a general plan to the captain, but I spoke as if I had a master plan and made up a lot of what was said. I made it up as I spoke and while he asked questions. My dad made it clear, *if you don't know what you are doing, act like you are in total control, and do it with conviction, and that is your plan.*

An hour later, and with the captain's coffee, he poured a bit of whiskey in my cup. "Master Sergeant, we have to find the killer or killers. As this war ends, more brass will come here to rest and restore before they return to where they have beaten down the Germans, and have to go back to help rebuild. Troops will come through here. Your band of brothers will be moved along to other places or sent home."

I guess he shared a drink with me to ease the discomfort of telling me the services of Colored men would not be welcome with an increase of White soldiers coming through this camp. The trouble for him to control rednecks would be a job he feared. Then, to have murder going on in the brothels with Colored men nearby would be an instant, *let's lynch us some niggers.*

Nothing is for free with angles and actions forthcoming as time is moving fast. "Captain, with time moving us all along, would you please use your men to go around the countryside gathering up the left behind motorcycles, and have them dropped off near my mechanical area. I need wood for crates, and then we need to step up the shipping of my crates headed back to the states."

Many crates have already made it back to the states, and my uncle received them and then relabeled the containers for a fake contractor moving parts to the Seattle Washington area. My uncle dealt with an Italian politician named Rossellini in Washington State, and my containers are freighted to the Northwest and stored. Once I return home, I'll have a motorcycle restore and repair company, and will be a legit business. As they say, it will be the American way to pull yourself up by the bootstraps. The part they leave out is, most pull themselves up by using other people's lost or used soles or souls.

"Sergeant Preer, your plan...this trap is going to take a lot of men. Who do we trust? Then your other request...we must control our favorite asshole—Jude, and keep him at a distance. He can dismantle all we do."

"Well, I'm glad we, I mean, you have moved on from thinking he needs to know who, what, and where, as to when I find the killer or killers, so he swims in the applause as someone else may drown in the blame. I have a plan for him. You're going to have to be okay with I might have to hurt him, but he won't die. War is a dangerous thing, captain. Hey, we might even make him a war hero, but a hero on his way back to the States."

The captain smiled and stared at the toy soldiers on the table. I'm sure deep thought-controlled him about all of what could go wrong.

Timing. Master Sergeant Jude called loudly from outside the tent and asked permission to enter. I interrupted the silence from the captain. I told him quickly what I need from him in order to control Jude.

The captain walked out of his tent with me behind him. I know I wore a slight smirk on my face. Jude squeezed in a tight scowl, trying to slice me in half with his hate. If he could whip me like a slave, he would, and then he'd throw salt in my broken skin.

The captain is right – the Colored soldiers will have to leave from here before the thongs of White soldiers make their way to this camp near the war's end. The White soldiers, here in this camp, have fought alongside us, and most don't care for us but have accepted us as fighters to save their asses. New White soldiers coming into this camp to stay, and wanting or needing to have fun using our Colored asses as a game, is not in our plan for any part of a Colored soldier's life and or possible death.

"Master Sergeant Jude...what is it, soldier?" the captain's voice waivered. I'm sure he understood he signed a man up for hurt, again. This time it's an American. The dead man from last night, his body is almost six-feet down in the ground, and now this asshole – soon...I'm not going to kill him, but his life is in his own hands.

"Sir..." he spoke to the captain, but his eyes were on me. "...out on patrol, we found three of our men dead, and one man is unaccounted for from last night. Their throats were all cut. They were naked with only mangled dog tags. We were still able to make out the names."

Hearing this made me cock my head to the side in wonderment. It did not sound right.

"Missing or found dead? The captain asked with puzzlement in his voice.

"Sir, three are dead, and one is missing. I have searched for the missing man and other men."

"The names of these soldiers? Did you leave them out there?"

"Yes sir, we left them in shallow graves." Jude pulled out paper and read the names. "The three dead: Dean Marron, Carl Sanre, and Reed Cuchillo, and the missing man – Kasper Österreicher. I should have sent Reed Cuchillo to the Colored side of the camp, sir, as he appeared to be a Mulatto or a Brownie or a wetback parading to be a White man, I felt. His skin tan and his broad nose resembled a Negro."

As the hate-filled fool told of his doing and unmasked thoughts, he became brave in his delivery, maybe thinking he pleased the captain. I knew better. The captain moved into Jude's face. Being so close, I knew they could smell the other's breath. I stood leaning to the side and to the right of the captain. I saw a vein in his neck pulsate as if it pumped blood outside of his body to fill a bucket fast. With Captain Castellani being of Italian descent, his people have felt insults thrown like bricks into their world, and if not him, his elders felt the ugly side of America. Then again, when his people became White Americans, they joined in on stepping on the Colored man's neck. He has been as fair as he could to my men and me, and accepted us on our merits while seeing the redneck of Jude and knowing his character.

I looked down at my boots with smeared dried mud and what looked like specs of blood. I started to crack a smile at Jude's ignorance, but then saw the uncovered tracks of my deeds. My paranoia created a slight fear inside me. The blood on my boot could have come from anywhere.

"We have over 1,500 to 2,000 men in the camp and between the outposts. I'm far from knowing all the men under my command, but the last name is different."

The captain acted as though he never heard that name before, of so-called Mr. Kasper Österreicher.

"Captain, we took in a band of four American soldiers lost behind enemy lines, but who escaped some four months ago, sir. Those men, strangely they are dead, well, three are dead and one is missing."

"Who took them in, who made a report, who assigned them, and who else knew of these men? Master Sergeant Jude, give me some fucking answers now!"

Hearing a usually low–key Captain Castellani speak with ass-kicking anger made me feel a twinge of how it felt when my grandmamma told me to pull a switch off a tree. She was going to whoop my ass for throwing feed at chickens instead of throwing feed on the ground for them to eat. She didn't whoop me, but she just wanted me to know the difference between right and wrong by scaring me with a threat of pain.

"Ah, ah...sir, I did the intake paperwork to save you the trouble, sir. It was when your... When he got badly hurt, and I knew your main concerns were with him. I inspected all their identification and I assigned them to the north-central outpost. I saw the four of them earlier in the day before the bombing. They came to our camp from their base to pick up supplies. Then the bombing. I've accounted for all the men – the dead here on base, and injured here, but those three were found dead. I found the three by where the plane went down in the forest, and one is missing."

"The four missing, for which you are responsible for them being on this post, and you never followed protocol. All records of transfers, deaths, and captures, is to come to my attention, anything less than is a violation. Something is not right, sergeant. I want all their paperwork and have it in my hand in twenty minutes. Then, when you return, you will be under Master Sergeant Preer's command. He's the new First Sergeant, and you're losing one of your stripes! I am busting you down right now to a Staff Sergeant."

Jude's face went from red to ghostly flush.

"Yes, you are hearing me right. You are now under the command of First Sergeant Preer, and if you don't follow his orders, I will put you up on charges of subordination. He is now over you, and you are going out on patrol with the Negro soldiers to the foothills. You show First Sergeant Preer those shallow graves."

"But, sir..."

The stern anger from the captain's face stopped Jude from saying another word. He tried to look in my direction, but surrendered.

After fifty feet of distance away from Jude, the captain turned to me. "If you can fix this, you do it by any means you think are necessary. You do understand, we may have, or there were spies, or killers infiltrated into our camp, and who knows who these men are, or if they have tricked Jude into thinking they were American soldiers."

"Captain, how did they get paperwork? Or maybe Jude is just a fool, or in cahoots with them. Those men were all together before the bombs dropped and they survived, but they were then killed out in the foothills? Bullet holes, or stabbed dead, or were their throats slit? They were left buck naked? But one man, Kasper Österreicher, he managed to beat the point of the bomb drops? I must see for myself what the hell Jude had cooked-up. Things aren't what they seem to be, captain."

Episode 19

Hours into the foothills while looking out for Nazis, or any enemy, we arrived at where Jude buried the bodies of the three men. I brought with me a fighting crew. Clement trekked along for his muscle, but not his brain or honesty, but he will kill the enemy with his bare hands if need be. Also, with me as part of the crew was my sharpshooter, N−Booty, with his beanpole body, and the opposite stature − Little Roy, who, despite his size, was a hell of a soldier, and he could move quickly and has staying power. If they ever let Colored men play professional football, Little Roy will be one of the best. Lanky Slim, he's a medic when we needed him to be, and he a fighter. He loved a man, but he is the best damn soldier to have by your side. I guarded his secret because he'd be there for me no matter what. Also, with me was a true warrior, Tiny Taps − a one-person wrecking crew.

As we came upon the shallow graves, we all took a break after we uncovered the bodies. One of the dead men, his light tan skin, he could have passed for several different races.

Their throats were all cut, and they were hogtied with their wrists and ankles tied with twine. They looked ghastly. It evoked a visual of the women in the brothels who seem to have wounded and killed themselves. I stared at Jude and then back at the dead men, and played chess in my mind of trying to see the moves all made before this all happen. I saw the board now, and visualized everything, comparing it with all I knew.

I pulled Jude aside. Looking out of place with a sulking attitude, Jude came across as an unwanted hobo. I didn't disrespect him as he would have done to me. I stepped away from the other men and spoke to him.

"So, tell me how you came upon these bodies?"

He scanned my face in defiance. When he did, it reminded me of a recently seen face of resistance. Now, I'm asking questions from a position of power he could not fathom. However, I possessed the control over his ass, and his ass told lies. I connected those lies to find the truth he must have known I knew.

I outwaited his stalling with mine until he spoke. "We came out of these woods and saw them by the stream over there."

"We? How many other soldiers saw them dead?"

"I came upon them. My men didn't. As I went to take a number two at the edge of the wooded area over there...fifty yards into the wooded area, hoping maybe to spot and catch enemy or plane survivors. We never spotted any from the plane crash. The plane burned completely, and no one could have survived."

"None of your men saw them prior to that? None of your men were down by the stream?"

I found my head leaning to the side, and I caught myself. I tended to do that when I spoke to Jude as my defiance. I looked past Jude to the stream running fast, and from where he said he took a dump. *He said he came down here to take a dump?* We are trained to all go in the same area for several reasons, and we watch the time each one is gone unless ordered. Most of all, we did this not to let the enemy capture all of us with our pants down.

He's lying. He found three men dead with their necks cut open...NO! Two of the women who died in the brothels had their throats sliced open, and so, did another woman who escaped. I finally talked with her before heading out to find the other bodies. It took her a long time to remember at first, she did not remember much as she had told the captain. By the time I spoke to her and I asked several questions, she could recall more, and she described a White man and light-skinned Negro who attacked her as she traveled from one brothel to another brothel. In the middle of the attack, she felt herself cutting her own throat, and she could not stop. A jeep with some MPs came down a road and stopped because of shadows they saw off the roadside, and the two men ran off. She lived, but is severely damaged for the rest of her life. She could write as her only way to communicate, as her throat vocal cords were destroyed beyond her ever being able to talk again.

Jude did not know I knew this. The captain kept that information away from him, per my request. I did not think it possible for Jude to be one of the assailants, but as he continued to lie since the conversation with the captain, I knew he had something to do with the death of these women. There is no covering his ass, as he kept spewing his ignorance as he talked.

"I let the guys know I needed to take a dump, I felt the runs coming on, so I took a dump. As I headed back to the guys, I saw something strange down by the stream. I went down to the stream and saw what I saw. I blew my whistle, and then my men came."

Jude – maybe unknowingly – he sounded silly and unconvincing, but it did not matter.

I asked, "Their throats cut, huh?"

"Yeah, their throats were."

I walked back over by the dead bodies, and he followed. I looked at their throats. The cut looked similar to the same curve of cut and depth as on the woman's throat who survived the attack, and the same trajectory of wound described on the other whores. My guys all stood around the corpses. I whispered to Tiny Taps and Lanky Slim about what we already knew, and they told the other two who then slowly moved to another position behind Jude.

"Jude, I want to cut the ropes off of them. Do you have a knife?"

"Ah, no, I don't."

"You are a high-ranking sergeant, you carry a knife."

I faced him and let him feel my breath. A cold breeze blew from the direction of the rambling stream, making a loud rushing sound.

"I'm not that high ranking anymore," he laughed, but his laugh sounded sad and deflated as his life has turned to bogus existence.

My men, except Jude, pulled out a knife, as no man in this war went without a blade. Jude arched his back and groaned. He felt a bayonet poking into his back. Enough so, I'm sure warm blood ran into his underwear. Lanky Slim, the Cajun raged with enough hate for Jude to slice him for gator bait. Lanky Slim's lover–Francis W. Cutter and Jude...they hated each other, and Francis had the duty thrown at him to dig the shallow graves, and he reported this to me.

Unknown to Jude who was now stripped down from his previous rank, Francis watched Jude's every move. Jude thought he pulled a slick move by telling his men to go in another direction than him, but Francis followed and thought he saw a meeting between Jude and another man, but he couldn't be definitive on what he saw as he spied from the distance to maintain his safety, but it all added up.

So much for the claim of Jude having the runs. He is about to get the shit beat out of him. I froze my eye movement on Jude's face. I knew he could tell I recognized the lies he told as his body language signaled, *I'm caught.*

"No, these three men...you did not see them anytime soon, as you said. They were not on the base. They made it to a German airfield. They must have secured a German plane with a crew, and made them fly over and bomb us. Then, what happened is, you came out here away from your men and met up with these three men who were waiting for you. Maybe they signaled you, and you made your way to them. Perhaps they were on the plane, and they parachuted before the crash. They must have forced a crew of Germans to fly. The flight could never take off near here and not be spotted. From whatever airstrip it took off from, they must have run out of fuel.

"Yeah, Jude...you know these men must have parachuted before the plane crashed. Afterward, they waited for you to contact them. Maybe they trailed your unit, waiting for you to separate from your men, but you met up with them, and now there are three dead men. Somehow, you made two of them end up on their knees, and the other one tied them up, and then you made the last one drop down on his knees, and you slit his throat. Then you cut the throats of the other two who were tied up. From there, you hogtied them all. Then you blew a whistle for the men to come down and find them dead, and you acted as if you just found them that way."

Jude did not respond. Clement and Little Roy positioned themselves in front of him with just enough room for me to see his face between them. I pulled out my gun and put the barrel tip on a grotesque looking pimple on his forehead. My men moved a bit. Lanky Slim removed his rifle bayonet from Jude's back and came around behind me.

"Search him."

Clement ripped Jude's coat off and then the shirt, then Clement took his knife and cut through the leather belt and pants Jude wore. Inside Jude's jacket, Clement found a strange blade which was curved and thinner than a combat knife. Clement touch the forearm of Jude with the knife, and with the slightest touch, blood came forth. Jude's pants slipped down to below his knees. Pee ran down his leg. One could hear him peeing.

Clement, handed me Jude's knife. I put the knife a half-inch away from Jude's throat and pressed the gun barrel hard against his forehead.

The tables of racial fate were flipped. A group of Colored men controlled the life of a White boy in the woods, and it would be rare if the other way around. So many Negros understood beatings, torture, rape, and then being killed by a group of rednecks for mere sport.

My dad made it clear to me as the elders preached to him as a young man to do my best to avoid being cornered by a group of White men – especially in the woods. He said when we were slaves; the rape of male slaves was a way to control large groups of slaves with fear. Then later, when there were no real laws to protect Colored people, we faced the same awful treatment by sexual predators attacking and torturing both males and females, young and old.

We were not going to rape this fool, but he will feel an insertion of pain to get what I need. My mind tried to piece this strange puzzle of deaths in how all these different people ended up dead. It is clear; Jude is a crucial connection to these three dead men, the dead women, and the man who used his head like a brick against a wall.

When we stripped Jude naked, I saw the markings of a small tattoo under his armpit. It resembled the same one on the captured man who now had a self−inflicted head crushed to mush.

"Tell me, Jude, tell me all you know." I pushed the knife into the razor rash on his throat, and blood ran down his chest. "Jude, you better start talking or you will die right here naked like the men you killed." His face showed defiance. "Oh, please don't try to play fearless when fear is making you piss down your leg, and it is going to turn cold like your blood, so start talking!" I yelled, and spittle flew from my mouth and landed on his nose.

Words rushed out of his mouth with pain. A bayonet pricked his butthole. Blood ran down Jude's leg, and Clement smiled.

"Those three were to die along with the other one who I can't find. He sent a signal up to the bomber flying above by flashing a mirror. The bombs landed where we wanted them, so he must have done his job. I think he died in the bombing, or you already know where he is. If you have him, he will take his own life before he lets you take his life. They were all supposed to die for our king. They were to die in the crash, but somehow, they defied our king. We were to kill as many whores as we could from the bombs dropping. These three stole a bomber. The Nazis have no reason to fly back this far − they are losing their whole country."

With a bayonet pricking his asshole and the pain of the knife at his throat, Jude still resisted telling me all that I needed to know. Maybe he's on the same drug as the other one, or he can take the pain.

"So, is this some secret society?" I asked.

"We are here to take the world away from you Americans, Germans, Russians, English, French, Italians, and whoever believes in colonialism. We are here to take the ugly life you surround the world with, such as using whores, and telling who can rule over a country, and starve who you think should be starved and make rich."

I chuckled, "And you serve a king, huh?"

My men laughed, knowing kings started this shit of killing to steal land and enslaving people.

"So, Jude, what is your connection to all of this? Your ass is a hate-filled American cracker even though you have all the advantages of skin color."

"I know that's right," Clement honed in.

"I think he also hates his White brethren," Lanky Slim's Cajun drawl sliced though with a mad tone. Jude had mistreated Lanky Slim's lover a few times.

"You are right, you perverted half–White dog," Jude retaliated with hate-spewing in Lanky Slim's direction.

I pushed the barrel of my gun like a hammer hitting a nail into a wall against his pimple and made it pop. I needed to silence Jude's mouth. I did not want to take a chance he might know of Lanky Slim and his lover. Worry went up in red flares inside me out of fear of exposing such knowledge to the other men. It would be hard for most men to understand the association of a fellow soldier and that the fact that soldier loved a man. The way Jude said what he said, I believed he knew the connection between Lanky Slim and his White lover Francis.

I side-eyed viewed the men around. I hoped they were none the wiser of what Jude might have meant. I could handle the chronicles of Lanky Slim's personal life, as I didn't care what another man did for the sake of love.

The men focused on the ass whooping they hoped to hand out. Beating a White man to death and realizing there is not the threat of being lynched, it could make some Negros salivate. If only the white man understood we didn't want to beat them, we only wanted fair and equal and respect.

The thought ran across my mind, Did Jude know of my lover – Valentina?

I had to focus, and I quizzed Jude about his knowledge of it all. "I need to know your part in this...talk!"

"My king...I met him in the forest when we arrived, and when he talks to you, you will then become alive and follow. These were my comrades in horning our king, but they did not complete the mission. They failed our king. I did nothing to them. The king entered their mind, and they knew to cut their own throats."

"What are you saying? That shit makes no sense. Where is, and who is, this king...and are there others like you?"

"I say no more."

"You will take a beating, or you will talk. Is this some mind-altering drug that is making people cut their throats? Tell me where this king is so we can rid him of this drug."

Listening to Jude...it came to mind and I thought about the man who bashed his head into a wall. I suspected he might be on drugs.

"Talk Jude, tell me more," I jabbed him with the gun.

"Let me beat on this cracker!" Little Roy, he wanted to lay down some violence on Jude. Sir–Sir, this motherfucker, he pulled me aside a few times and said he wanted me to meet someone. I knew this cracker ain't shit-talking all nice to me when he treats Niggers like dirt."

I cut my eyes at Little Roy, "Don't call yourself or any of us a Nigger in front of this Klansman who would lynch any one of us and celebrate our death by toasting to a Nigger."

"Your right, Sir-Sir. I am not beneath this piece of shit. But I know now, he tried to see if he could trick me and involve me with these dead dudes. He's the one who told me of the dead girl over by the shit houses. He said to meet him over there, and then he told me to tell you the MPs gave me the information. I didn't want to say anything to you. You know this dude could have made life hell for me. Let me beat him to death now!

I held my hand up telling him to hold still and wait.

Clement spat in the ear of Jude and yelled in his ear. "This peckerwood talked to me the same way, and he wanted me to meet a man in the woods. I just thought this asshole wanted to have his boys beat me down. I thought I was keeping my ass safe by always talking overly nice to him and down at his boots in hopes he would leave me alone."

"You darkies think I hate you. A nigger can be a White man, a Jew, or you. When I came over here, I acted as I was supposed to act toward *you people*. I hate anyone who is not with the king, and I will die for the king."

Jude lunged forward with his full body weight onto the knife I held at his throat. In doing so, he sliced his own throat wide open. I jump out of the way of blood shooting. *Fuck*, now twice this has happened—a man took his own life for this king. This king must be giving them a super strong drug with a kind of power that twists the minds of these idiots. I have seen heroin addicts, but they only fight and steal for more of that high, but not to take their lives in this fashion.

Jude's body stood slumped a bit to the side while blood spurted, and then he fell hard to the ground.

Looking down on the death of four men and seeing the one of a darker hue with the broader nose, I began to think maybe Jude, or this king, planned on putting that man in the middle of my men. It seems they tried to recruit Little Roy and Clement, but those two were too headstrong in their personalities to follow. And, those two were amongst my strongest meanest fighters, so I can see the draw of wanting those two. He may have put all of us in the face of a hangman.

We burned the bodies. The gore of doing so with us Colored men had long passed. It's a job they gave us often to burn the piles of the dead. Before we headed back, I explained most of the doings, including about the man who killed himself. I kept my personal life out of it and a few other details.

"Hey guys, no matter what, with the murders of these women, it's a danger to our Colored asses. It doesn't matter if it is some cult-like drug controlling these fools. Understand...no one will believe us Colored men. I...we must put a stop to this, and I may need you at a moment's notice. What you now know, stays in your head and never comes out of your mouths...forever! If this is some cult-like crazies, we don't want to be a part of the story, and they –the Army – wouldn't mind coming back to send us to prison to keep it all hush-hush, and blame us as the only killers. What you know, you can't tell any man or woman – no matter how good the lovin' a woman gives you."

They chuckled, but they understood what an Army prison meant for us Negros. It's a place of hard labor, and a place to die.

Episode 20

We made it back to camp just as it turned dark. We were all worn out, hungry, and on edge from the whole experience. On our legs since daybreak, and now it was dark, cold, and we were in need of sleep, but I asked them all to meet me between the mechanic tent and the burn barrel. I poured each man a couple of glasses full of apple wine from several bottles I found in a farmhouse. We toasted to living.

On the trek back from death and truth in the forest, Clement approached me. "Hey, Sir–Sir."

He never called me by my nickname, and he always said "Preer" with some tone of contempt. Other soldiers called me Master Sergeant Preer, but those closest to me called me Sir–Sir unless addressing me for official reasons, then they would address me as Master Sergeant Preer. Sometimes the men slipped and out of habit they called me Sir–Sir at the wrong time. We Negros learn at an early age: manners, protocols, and respect in how we address others. Oftentimes, having and using manners and etiquettes, it is a matter of survival in being a Negro. Down South, a Negro knows to cross the street when a White woman is coming his way, and never to stare into her eyes to avoid being jailed, hurt, or lynched. When we Negro show respect toward each other, it is a way of showing love for each other for surviving in a world with no desire for us.

This time, Clement did not have his usual disdain for me when he spoke. "Man, you took me out here to see the truth. You didn't have to, so thank you. I do have your back, although I know you think otherwise, I do have your back. I have no hard feelings toward you. I never did, but I felt you were the one person who might think so little of me with all your college ed-a-ma-kation'. It made me feel and act strangely toward you. I know it's my problem I pushed onto you. And shit, man, back home in Hobbs, New Mexico, we all carry a gun, but ever since I joined the Army, most White men have a pistol and a rifle, and all we have is rifles. So sometimes, I have kissed their ass hoping to stay on their good side as a Negro."

"Clement, if we're shot dead right now, who would remember now, or in the future? If you still have folks back in the States who love you, you must live the best moral life you can for them. I'm like you in many ways, as I want to return home to see my momma and eat her good cooking and sleep in a warm bed. I have a son who means the world to me. I want to be a man to help raise him into being a man to survive this ugly world. He already has an uphill battle being Negro in America. I need to be with him. I pray I make it back to him. I may need you, and you may need me, to help our friends and family. So, let's make sure we have each other's back, period. All my education can't stop a bullet, and neither can all your strengths and courage. If you and I use all we have, we can be a force of might to return us home to our people, right?"

"Yeah, you're right."

"Clement...you and I have problems with each other without knowing why. It all goes back to when one plantation owner bet on his tough young Mandingo slave to fight another young slave from a plantation from another county. They thought of us as pets and livestock as two slaves fought to a bare-knuckle deathmatch, for no reason other than those slaveowners' enjoyment. They called us Niggers, and said to us, 'Niggers, fight to the death.' Then, no matter who would lose, if you weren't dead, you might lose your life or at least take a beating and or be tortured, and death might have been a better option. However, if we understand our greatness, no matter what they think of us, we are more than warriors for their pleasure. Mandingos are people from West Africa, and the language they speak is Mandingo and is what the Spanish and English called the Mandinka people of Sierra Leon. They came to Africa in droves of ships, and they stole our people who created much of their wealth in this world.

"We were used for entertainment in a gruesome fight between two men who did not have a reason to hate each other. Both slave boys came from a Negro slave mama who wants to know her child is alive and well, but what happens to her soul when they sale her baby? But here, you and I, we can act like slaves trying to outdo the other, or we can take the freedom we have and live the best we can and help each other survive. I may have the tools you need, and you may have the skills I need, and with both, we can live a better life if we share brains, brawns, and experience. I hope I've made sense."

"Sir—Sir, it makes sense. I want out of this war to see us both live to go home. And when we do get home, I want to buy you a drink and a pretty woman to enjoy."

"I'll let you buy me a drink, but...nah to buying me a woman. We use women way too much. Both you and I understand what happens to women, and we have to stop turning a blind eye. A mindset we take all too often, is one of we don't treat our women as if they are worthy of good love. They birth us and love us. And then think of the daughters we could have one day – we need to care how a man treats them. Do me a favor, and it will be a favor to yourself...find you one good woman by being a good man. She may not look like a New York Satin Doll, but settle down and have a family and help deliver some children into this world. You and a good woman will make a better world for them when they see you loving one woman. Make those children go to school and learn, and make them feel needed by loving them and protecting their lives. You having one good woman will make you a better man in this world as she will know how you feel, and she will help make the world around you a better place.

"My daddy has done a lot of hustles, and many could have gotten him killed, but he made sure I completed my education. He wanted better for me as a man should want for his children. He loves my mom in a way – I know he never does her wrong. The world wants to believe men don't love and love right, and the negative talk...we can't be a part of making it true. He always told me his wife is to live for, and he puts no others before her. I know my daddy's dirt, and so I know he has never stepped out on her. And when my mom asks for something, he made a way. Find yourself one of those lives."

❦ ❦ ❦

Reflecting on my conversation with Clement, who seems to take in all I have said, my heart hurt thinking of having to eventual leave Valentina. In the town, an old church bell rang at six in the morning, noon, and six in the evening. At midnight, that is the last time, it rang each night. She came an hour later than midnight to be with me.

"Valentina, I saw some crazy unexplainable experiences. I don't understand any of this. Someone, or some people, have a mind possessing cult-like control over these men who kill women. The best I can tell, it has to be a powerful drug given by a group or what they call a king. These women strangled themselves or cut themselves, so I guess they are controlled by maybe a drug also. I plan to trap whoever it is and end this craziness."

"Sirletto, you must be careful. I need you to live."

She went silent. Maybe I scared her. I waited for her to say more, but maybe her mind traveled to somewhere in the future, with the thought of me leaving, it must be looming. Perhaps the weight of the future is crushing us both.

Selfishly, I wanted to have sex. The tension of all I had seen and done had me wound up and I needed to release the pressure, but we held each other until the morning came. I disliked that Valentina creeped out of the short tunnel to crawl through the tall grass to make sure she made it back to town.

∗∗∗

We moved into the time of years where we have four different weather seasons in one day. It is either fog or rain in the morning, or breaking clouds or sunshine throughout the day, and wind, and then cold at night. I'm sitting in the dark and cold.

I set my plan in action by the light of the full moon. The captain is twisting in the wind with my plan. Why, because I'm using my trusted men. I chose to set the trap in one of the nearby towns and set up highly-visible regular security MPs at the brothels, except where we set the trap. I wanted to funnel the killer or killers to where we could take them down. The little town where I sat the trap did not let soldiers come in after dark to partake in the use of the prostitutes. This brothel lived more of a normal life of cooking, cleaning, and relaxing after nightfall.

My men…we talked and planned, and did dry runs. There could be no room for the unexpected. In all my planning, I stayed troubled as I could not wrap my head around what has gone on. The men who took their lives gave me some information, but at the same time, they gave off an extreme defiant attitude. Something, or someone, controlled them, and they were willing to die. It made me wonder if anyone among us might have slipped into the cult-like mode. I looked for triggers and signs of insubordination and arrogance. For that one reason, I took Clement along on the trek with Jude. I needed to know about him, and we found peace between him and me. Our heart–to–heart talk allowed us to realize we misunderstood each other's intentions, and it caused fears, leading to mistrust and dislike for each other. From our conversation, I gained an empathetic sentiment to grow and teach in situations when it derives from another Colored man who comes from a different background. It is upon me to do so to give more to my people. A White man put me in charge of these Colored men, but it's up to me to lead.

✼ ✼ ✼

Here I am a week later and as if nothing had happened, soldiers repaired the damage to the brothels and were open for business for soldiers coming in for sex. Our base personnel is growing with men who were now not needed in the field.

Episode 21

With my men stationed in numerous cloaked positions, they viewed the brothel from different angles and passageways. We all came early each night before the last of daylight. A few of the men dug shallow foxholes and covered them with brush. They peered through the cover with the best binoculars we could obtain from the command post, and the moonlight allowed them to see quite well. The other men hid in trees, and two men were under the house crawlspace. Under the house could be a place a killer might come to hide, so we made it only possible to come in one way and leave one way. The men under the house hid behind a fake wall allowing them to see if anyone tried to hide under the house.

I spent days, and put many hours, into planning the setup, attempting to trap the killer or killers, and maybe lead us to catching this king, and whoever they were. All the other locations - the regular White soldiers overlooked the more popular and usually busy brothels with a highly-visible presence. I hoped to make this brothel appear comfortable to attack without resembling a trap. With all the connected death, I hungered to stop more destruction from happening, including life for my men and me.

❈ ❈ ❈

This Sunday morning, we gathered around the burn barrel as usual for a kind of a church like service where I would sing or lead some gospel hymns, but this morning, I had a lot on my mind. I may have caught a little Holy Ghost, and I talked to the men, and few men said I preached a bit before singing.

"My brothers – and I would say my brothers and sisters if we were back home – we have gathered here at a time that is so important. This time right now, it is necessary for us to give praise and worship, and to give God the glory who has given us more than we can and do imagine. We are alive and breathing, walking and talking, and the food is food, and we have survived the worst situations. Can we say Amen?"

I heard deep and high voices shout *Amen* in unison like a choir. It inspired me more.

"Although there are those of us who have not gone the whole journey, we pray and ask God to cover their souls as we keep asking Him to give us another opportunity to live to stop evil to save our souls. We ask the Lord to cover our mothers and fathers, and or children, and ask that we return to be better sons and fathers. Many of us are going to go home to become fathers. Let us be men and take care of what we help to bring into this world. We pray God helps us understand that woman is here on this Earth to be by our sides, and we must protect them from harm as we have fought for this county for that right. It has not been a place we want to be for sure, but for many reasons we know, and some we may never know, we are fighting more than one enemy. We know love can conquer hate as we have God above to lead us to endure, and with that, I want to play a song for you."

I heard another chorus of *Amen*. While I preached, I kept my head bowed, and when I looked up, I saw behind the Colored men, there were more than a few White soldiers. They usually made it over to our side of the camp for our

Sunday service. It would be a reasonable thought some had taken to a fondness for Negro gospel music depending on where they lived. Some might come over, because they don't consume the same hate in their souls some of the rednecks harbored. I saw the two MPs working with me as a part of my team to capture a killer. Also, in the back, stood Lanky Slim's White lover - Francis.

I held my guitar, played, and sang.

I don't know about yesterday, Lord

I don't know if I could have used me,

I don't know, but I'm here for you

Oh Lord, I don't know if I was the right man to be a wise man, yeah – yeah, to give gifts to a newborn who came to save the world

I don't know about yesterday, Lord

I don't know if I could have used me,

I don't know, but I'm here for you

Oh Lord I don't know if you could have used me to part the Red Sea

I don't know about yesterday, Lord

I don't know if I could have used me,

I don't know, but I'm here for you

Lord, I don't know the many things you could have used me for

I don't know about yesterday, Lord

I don't know if I could have used me,

I don't know, but I'm here for you

But if you need to save one or many

Lord if you let me see another day, please use me

Use me, Lord, please use me

Lord if you let me see another day, please use me

Use me, Lord, please use me

Lord if you let me see another day, please use me

Use me, Lord, please use me

Can we catch the killer or killers? I'm positioned in the attic crawlspace so I can easily maneuver from one room to another room. If the need arises, I can come down and into a closet in each bedroom. There is also a small room I observed with enough room in it for me to move around comfortably. It's like a little small walk-in closet where the women store a small wardrobe and a pullout washbasin to clean themselves up after doing their business with men. I procured flashlights for all the men, but they are for limited use, and batteries were few. I have two flashlights on me. The moonlight and stars helped the guys outside, but I'm mostly in the dark.

Carl, the MP from Seattle who looks like Cary Grant, he devised another way for us to communicate with each other. His father taught him how to make bird callers out of thin reed slices from small tree branches. He made the bird callers in his spare time all the while on the base, as other soldiers laughed them off as a toy. They sounded real, and the sound traveled. We all rehearsed how to use the bird callers by going out in the foothills and mocking the birds we heard. The season of late winter started kissing early spring, and the birds were coming alive–chirping and calling out to other birds. For practice, we positioned ourselves around the base and communicated with each other, and no one caught on to what we were doing.

It's the fifth night, and we were losing the moon's best light as it's down to almost less than half a moon. I've been up since sundown in the crawl space each night.

I wished for some hot coffee, but I sipped on cold tea instead. I'm trying to be as cautious as possible, so I'm keeping as still as possible. I rolled onto my back, I'm staring up at the wood, wishing for a lush life, so I daydreamed of a dancing Valentina.

All the women in the house gathered in the living room. If one woman moved to any room in the house, they all went at the same time to be nearby, and no one is allowed upstairs. They read or listened to the radio in the parlor. They stayed there all night, and this is the fifth night in a row. I have N–booty in the parlor hall closet with a curtain hiding him. His marksmanship skills were ready to shoot to kill if the killer came into the room near the ladies.

Through the air vent, I heard a bird call. I held still. I waited. I listened to the birdcall again, and I heard it clearly. My men made bird calls all night to sound natural, but we had different calls, and this call gave the warning of someone approaching. I peered out the air vent to see outside. I saw a figure walking. Whoever's out there, they stopped between the three outhouses the johns used. Once the figure cleared the location of the outhouses, they moved toward the back of the brothel. I made my way down into one of the closets.

I staged one of the prostitutes in a room alone. I have no intent to sacrifice her. She is aware there is danger in her helping us. I told her we were trying to catch a robber. Her look said she knew the truth. Word of a killer on the hunt for the working women could be no secret by now.

Her name is Ms. Porlena, and she sat in the corner of the room. There were no other women in the adjoining bedrooms near hers. I hid in the walk-in closet behind a curtain, as I waited and hoped with a twinge of fear. I heard doorknobs turning. Part of the setup, I wanted to make sure I directed an entrance to lead through the kitchen, and on up to the upstairs portion of the brothel. Whoever is checking inside the bedrooms, they entered through the back doorway as we wanted them to come. Now they have made their way up the back stairs, and doorknobs to empty bedrooms turned. Each room, we made them look as if a woman might be coming back soon. Oil lamps burned bright, and the beds were unmade. The doorknob to the room I'm in turned, and slowly footsteps entered. I stay stooped low in the closet behind the curtain.

Ms. Porlena yelped, and said, "Who are you?" She spoke French and gave me a signal to let me know whoever was in the room was someone she did not recognize.

It is a man who is speaking in Spanish and then French, and now in English. "You are the kind of woman who makes men pay for what God gave free. You are the kind of woman who gives the money you earn on your back or knees to a master. You are a slave of your own making. You must die. Rise. You must die like the others. I said, rise!"

If she felt in danger, Ms. Porlena was to say *leave* as the code word. She said nothing, but I heard her lift from the chair. I placed the bed and dresser between her and where someone would face obstacles. I staged it all in hopes of helping me capture whoever this killer is.

I burst through the curtain, pointing my Walter PPK revolver, and with my Bowie knife on my side. What my gun is aiming at is a man whose skin tone is much lighter than mine. He has dark hues under his eyes, and his hair is like mine. His nose is like mine. Thick eyeglasses magnify the darkness under his eyes, and his loose clothes did not hide a body sliding into chubby. He is not a military man.

We are staring at each other.

Ms. Porlena said in English, "Sir, please don't hurt me." She stood stiffly. I did not know she could speak English. When explaining to her what we were trying to do, an interpreter translated the plan to her.

The stranger held a knife with a curved, jagged edge. It looked to be right for the damage done in the brothel killings of women. It resembled the same type of knife I took away from Jude. He might be from an African country, but he's not an American Negro. I assumed.

He grinned. I see evil. He pressed his lips tight, and they spread wide. He placed the ancient-looking knife in front of him as if he is worshipping or praying.

"Put the gun on the bed," he said to me.

I kept my eyes on his eyes, and I chuckled, although nothing is funny. I feel myself placing the gun on the bed. *What the hell?*

"She is mine," He tells me.

"You don't own anyone human," I'm trying to sound defiant.

"I control you, and you will never control me," he spoke with a sneer and snicker. "You just put the gun down as I said, and your knife. You stand in place under my command. I will bleed your life away, but first, I will make you slit this whore's throat. I am more powerful than your mind. I reach into your soul, and you do what I say to do. I am the king, I rule over all."

I feel like a puppet, controlled like a rag doll, as if someone is moving my arms and legs by strings.

"Come to me," he said.

My feet placed one step in front of the other beyond my control. I fought, but my body felt like hot metal, and a magnet is pulling me. I'm losing the struggle of my mind to say no, but my body is under the control of his command.

Oddly, I'm reaching out for the knife in his hands. I'm able to resist some, but my hands inch forward with each breath. I can hold in place, but then I reach forward more. A tug of war raged.

I thought of my grandfather's backwoods country tale of never making love to a flaming redheaded Negro woman from the Bayou. He said I would be under her control if I strayed from her. He said, "A flaming redheaded Negro woman from the Bayous can make a man take the life of the woman he cheated with, and the reason some Negro men are on chain gangs down South is because of a Black Magic Mojo."

What the hell is this? This is not an old wives' tale or fable. I'm way more physically fit than the man who is ripping away the domination of my motions. I can tolerate a decent amount of pain, but my head feels a pounding and heat. I exerted all my effort to stifle a scream.

The knife handle is fingertips away, from me – his body jerked hard and stiffened. His eyes divert upward. I feel some relief of his control, but I'm still in the grips. I'm able to lower my hands and take steps back, but I can't pick up my gun.

Oh damn! Valentina is standing behind the man. She has a bayonet – her two hands hold it horizontally against of his neck, I can see she has cut him. Blood is oozing onto his collar.

"Let go of him," she said to the man who holds mental control of my actions. Valentina is wearing Army combat fatigues, and under an Army helmet, her silver mane of hair peeks. She is more than the average beauty, which is a power to have, but right now, she is the most powerful woman in the world, as she is controlling a madman who is controlling me with his mind.

"I am the king! I rule him, and any man or woman I choose. Oh, but wait, ah yes ...I know your voice. I know who you are. You are my sister, Valentina. Oh, my dear sister –a daughter of a whore, it has been some years since I last saw you. Now you hold a blade to my head."

He said, "Sister." He knows her name. She is behind him, but yet he knows who she is.

"You are no king! You are a tyrant living with the blood of the soul of evil. You are your father's child with even more evil pouring from a wicked soul."

"Ahhhh, my sister, you are the reason my father is dead. You killed him."

"You bastard! Your father raped me, your sister, and he killed my mother. He did this while you sat in the other room, barely being able to feed yourself at ten years of age. You played a childish game in wanting to be served as if you were a prince, when you were nothing more than a lazy boy."

I'm still frozen in place listening to them, unable to move, and so is Ms. Porlena – the woman in the corner of the room. All I can do is try to decipher what is going on. Somehow Valentina slipped past all of our security and might save my life...again. First on the mountaintop, and now in this room, my lover is more capable than any human I have met. I'm trying to remember all Valentina shared with me of her early life with her brother, and now the brother who is opposing her – they share the same mother's blood.

Valentina reached around her evil brother and removed the ancient knife from his hands. She moved in front of him with the ancient knife across his throat. At the same time, she pointed the bayonet to his heart. His throat trickled blood from the front and back of his neck. His shirt started to sop with redness. The bayonet, the one from under my pillow, I'm so glad I did get rid of the tool of an ugly history. The bayonet, the one that Nazi left me a scare for life, and later I learned, he damaged the body of the woman I love. He cut her from her breasts down to her womanhood, and left her unable to bear children. Valentina has the tip of that bayonet against her brother's heart.

He remained verbally defiant as he dripped blood. "You speak of our mother who sold her body for the game of man to put food in your belly. She was put here on this Earth to serve me as a young king, and to be subject to my demands in the same manner as my father. You speak like the same mother who hundreds of men did whatever they wanted to her, all so she could have money to feed her half-breed children. Yes, my sister, I speak ill of the same horrible mother – our mother, the whore who bore us both. Then you killed my father trying to protect a whore and your little girl virtues."

I wanted to reach for my gun and end his hurtful words. He threw spears of hurt to her soul, and twisted them deep inside the woman I loved, but I'm still frozen, unable to release myself from what...a spell or whatever controlled other men and women. He possessed the power over the man I captured, but that man took his life under his control by bashing his head against a wall. Jude killed for him, and he was a bigoted pig, but he died for a dark-skinned man. He used his power over the women who submitted to his control to execute themselves with their own hands without a scream.

I waited for my men to storm the house, but I needed to birdcall back for them to move in, but I am under the control of a madman.

Valentina's voice spat rage when she spoke to her brother. "Your father...in my sleep, I kill him again and again, a hundred more times. You are not worthy of life here on this Earth." Her head turned toward me, and she said, "Take your eyes off him." She told me firmly, "My dear love, try to take your eyes off him. Think of your son, or mother, or anyone you love, and you will break his control."

I've never felt this kind of fear as I'm trying to do what Valentina has implored me to do. As I try, my heart pounds at my temples. My head is going to explode, or bull's horns gore through my head through my ears. My heart pounds in my ears as I'm attempting to concentrate on breaking away from his control. With my eyes wide open, and as if I'm in a movie house, I'm watching my son playing in the park on the swings, then he is jumping into my arms. My son seems to respond to me as I'm saying to him, "I love you, son." I'm gaining strength to tear away from the man's exploitation of my internal controls. I'm able to look to the wall, and I see a framed painting. I picture my mother's smile, and she kisses me on my forehead. I shift my eyes upwards to the peeling ceiling paint, and a flickering movie plays of my father putting his arms around me. Now I can focus my eyes on Valentina standing in front of her evil brother with a knife to his bleeding neck, and one pointing at his heart. I picture her smile. I lock onto a daydream of us making love and melting into one another, with her beauty overwhelming me as she always does.

Her control overwhelms her brother's power, and I feel myself becoming me again.

Ms. Porlena, she still stood mummified. My eyes can slide vision back and forth between her and him now, and my feet moved a little. My hands are free.

"Free them, my brother. You are using the blood of good for evil. It is passed down through generations for good. You are using the Soul of Cayor, which came from our ancestors, and was never meant for evil."

"You, my sister, are the image of your whorish mother, and it appears you have fallen for a man who has a child by another woman. How fitting...you are just like your mother."

Valentina laughed and placed more pressure on the knives. "You are the image of your father, a madman. My brother, you are no more powerful than I am with the Soul of Cayor we share. You can't control me and this, you know that. I am here to stop you. I will use my powers to end your life."

Valentina quickly pushed the bayonet into her brother's chest entering into his heart. My hands have become free and so has my body. I picked up my gun. Stiffly, her brother stood as she kept driving the knife into his heart with ease of force and strength as she pushed the knife into her evil brother. I felt my body jerk as he did. The woman in the corner exhaled a loud sigh and fell to the floor. The man fell, and Valentina stepped on the handle of the knife. I knew the blade went through. I had sharpened the blade until it could cut and butcher a cow with no restriction for the men when they prepared a cow for our meals. Now the blade is stuck in the wooden floor through a dead body. His eyes dimmed, but he wore an obnoxious grin.

Blood covered Valentina's body from each spurt of evil dying. I'm calling her name, but she seems as if she's in a trance or something.

"Valentina," I say louder, and she turns in my direction and falls. I rush over and help her up.

"I'm alright, Sirletto. I'm okay." I held her tight as if she would fall again. She did not push or pull away, but eased out of my arms and turned to Ms. Porlena who is now free from whatever spell was on her. I'm listening to Valentina speak in French, and Ms. Porlena nodded her head.

"Sirletto, I told Ms. Porlena she is safe, and to never speak of this. She must safeguard all she seen and felt and never let another soul know.

From the look in her eyes, it is apparent Ms. Porlena's fear should push all of this deep down and away in her soul from wanting any part of this to rise. Valentina turned to me and explained, "If there were others under her brother's mind control, with his death, they are free from his power."

I helped Valentina climb up in the attic needing her to wait until I cleared the house. I blew the bird caller, and my men came. They saw what they saw – a dead man stabbed to death and they assumed a story that I must have killed the man, a so-called king who brought death and terror. I did my best to lead their thinking to follow their assumptions. I felt troubled not being more forthcoming when their lives were on the line, but I must protect Valentina.

I ushered Ms. Porlena downstairs to be with the other women, and assured them all they were now safe.

Episode 22

Days went by. My head and body all began to feel like one again. The captain and I are relieved the nightmare is over. He and I draw long breaths through cigars now that I have reported, *all is clear*. Before we set the trap, another team of soldiers brought back the bodies of Jude and the others, to help cover our tracks. We twisted a tale of Nazis fleeing from the area and killing them.

A few nights later, Valentina and I finally talked about all that happened with her taking her brother's life. There is no way of knowing where her heart and head might be, but she tries to tell me.

"The power, it is called the Soul of Cayor. It transcended down through generations from my great grandfather's tribe. The power is for good and not bad. There were a few times it fell to evil uses, and they had to die. As my half–brother went on an evil path as his father led him to evil ways, and my brother had to die. The power passes through the mother to a male, and it can pass through a mother to a daughter, but a daughter cannot hold onto the power. That daughter can only pass it onto a male child. My power will go away when I use it to stop the more powerful male energy. I have some concern my brother may have a daughter out there, and one day she could have a son, but that son will not use his power the wrong way unless he is taught evil ways."

"Valentina, have you used your power? I mean...you have been in some troubling matters with your brother's father, and then again with the German who hurt you inside, making it so you can't have a child."

Valentina fell silent, and her body felt stiff. I held her tighter, but wishing I had shut my mouth.

"I did use my power on my brother's father as I made him insert the knife into his own body and take his life. I did not know I processed the power, or I would not have let him do any harm to my mother or me in the first place. My power did come out until the height of my anger rose, and I could feel the power. With the German, he hit me from behind with so much force, I could not gather my senses to protect myself, and he did what he did."

"I'm sorry, so sorry."

"I'm not sorry, and you should not be sorry for me. I lie next to the man I love even though I never thought love would find someone like me. How could it be in this wrathful world? You know all that has happened to me, but you still love me."

"I have your love no matter how far away you are. I have a piece of your soul of the good man you."

We made love well into the morning with the power of love. We lay in silence until the morning birds were awakening. Sleeping in late with Valentina by my side is dangerous, but strangely we felt safer with each other. This morning, she held onto me tightly while kissing me all over. She gave me a thinking man look of love before she left this morning, and it was deep from within her eyes. He gaze made me breathing deep. I'm sure with the sadness of her brother's life gone, but knowing now at least that danger is over – it might have her feeling freedom to intensely love me.

❦ ❦ ❦

Later in town at the inn, there were fewer restrictions as a gift from the captain. Women from the brothels were allowed to party with my men. I put in some strict rules, though. I told the men, "No vaginal sex, and no oral sex." They could, however, enjoy the soft, warm hands of a hand job from the women, or they could have a woman put on a visual show for them to jack off if they wanted. I didn't want my men to go home to the U.S. infected with anything. I felt guilty of even letting the man have a little pleasure after Valentina's brother said, *we used women.*

I understood men women use women. I hadn't fully realized how true it is, though, that we use women as expendable tools without regard to the damage we can do to a woman's mental stability. *How do I, as one man, stop the oldest thing since the creation of time – sex and sex for sale?*

I made sure Little Roy made his choice of the woman he wanted to talk to, and I also made sure no one would make a move on her as she held his attention. I couldn't have him beating down another man over a woman and ending up court-martialed. In many ways, the men were respectful and just wanted to have conversations with a woman.

❦ ❦ ❦

I want her just as soon as I make sure all my men make it back to the base, and I'll be with her again. With the midnight bell in town striking midnight, I did a headcount, and all my men were in the tents, and many of them were drunk. Some hit the woods to go beat off the female stimulation built up inside of them. I head to the mechanic's tent –my sleeping quarters.

My dog...I could hear her whining a bit while sitting outside of the tent.

"What's wrong, girl? I fed you before I left – at least I think I did." I'm entering the tent, and the oil lamp I left burning had started to flicker out. "Come here, girl."

My dog sat near the truck where I go into my hidden sleeping area. She's sitting there and not coming to me and whining. I know Valentina is not inside my hidden bedroom. Her signal to me is the second oil lamp would be burning, and both would be refilled to burn bright. But wait, the lamp, it's flicking its last of flame, Valentina, she always refills the lamp.

I remove my sidearm from my holster. I'm now one of the Negro soldiers allowed to carry a sidearm, along with my crew of men who helped me take down a killer.

I'm lean down and rub Jerri's head to check to see if she is hurt. She appears to be okay. She stopped whining. I stood and eyed the room to see if I notice anything else out of place. At the same time, I tune my ears in for any abnormal sounds. I hear out on the road a jeep going by the Negro side of the camp, and it's just shifting into fourth gear and is picking up speed. It's heading to the White side of the camp. The night security team circles the base on time intervals, and they are switching crews.

I keep listening and not moving. I trained my eyes on each item and square foot visually dissecting the mechanic's tent. Each workstation looks normal. Nothing seems missing or out of place. Besides, Jerri would not have let anyone inside without tearing the flesh off the bone. I allow no one to pet or play with her. The only person who can touch her is Valentina.

Valentina. Valentina.

I ease into my hidden area. A bee's wax candle is burning low on a scrap metal table I made. On the bed is a lock of hair tied to a silver ring. Paper with frayed edges, but not wrinkled, is in between the pages of a book. The hair is from Valentina's silver Mallen streak. The ring is the one she always wears on her left index toe. The paper is in Valentina's handwriting, but written in Spanish. A book is on the bed – the book I purchased from the town bookstore. Once a week, if any Colored soldier wanted to go to town to shop, we were allowed to do so, and often, I frequented the bookstore. The book is an English-Spanish translation book. I also own a French-English translation book.

Both books captured my attention enough to attain them. I wanted to be able to say more than a few words to Valentina in different languages. I bartered with the Frenchman who owns the store for the books. He needed a thermos to preserve his cream fresh. I procured the thermos from the captain. The French bookstore owner and I love to chat with one another over French coffee with fresh cream. He's an interesting fellow. When the Germans controlled the area, he pulled all his floorboards up and stored all his books when the area was taken over by the Germans. He plays chess in his store with other town folks, and with several chessboards setup in the store, others often come in and play. He and I played to standoffs as neither of us can claim victory. Sometimes though, I believe he held back in beating me just so he could make sure I would keep coming back.

Valentina often read the books for translations. Her English is good, but sometimes she used the wrong words in sentences. My Spanish is littered with the wrong word choices too, so I used the books as well. When Valentina left me love notes, she wrote them in Spanish, and the letter in my hidden area is written in Spanish.

I pulled off my clothes, and I slipped under the covers. The things on my bed, I knew why they were there. Well...I believed they meant Valentina is gone. She isn't coming back. Valentina must have held my dog before leaving, and my dog is hurting read each word she penned.

She wrote a poem no different than when she spoke in one-line meanings.

The one thing you need to know

Now, my memory of you is, for the first time, a memory

I'll away be with you, as your love is from a place inside you helping me

understand love

I knew nothing of love and passion before you

I knew nothing of a man wanting to know how I feel inside my soul

I knew nothing of a man who could remove my hurt

I always thought I was a vessel for a man to do his pleasure

You kissed my mind

You kissed my ways

You kissed the things I love

You fed me

You clothed me in pretty colors

You sang to me

You held my hand

You stroked my hair

You bathed my feet

You loved me in the best ways in the middle of guns and bombs and death nearby

You introduced to me images of dating if I was in America

You would take me to fine dining and walks around lakes and riding a

bicycle for two

And you would take me to hear music, and it would make our feet move and slow

dance to violins

You told me of family dinners

You talk to me of the love of giving honor to God

You gave me a treat meeting me on the mountain and facing the sunset and being
held in your arm – you did this for me

You gave me a piece of home when meeting me in the cabin and having a candlelight
dinner – you did this for me

I pray my imprint is left upon you too in my essence of how I loved you

I would have never gone from you

If I knew how I could change the world to be with my love

I would do this for us, my love

The world is what it wakes up to be and goes to sleep as

Maybe I would have never been with you

Perhaps

But you came to my life, and I take the chance to love you

I will keep our love with me

But you must go

I must go away so you can go

Our pain is shared until we breathe no more

In your heart I hope, I pray, I stay, and always you see me when you close your eyes
I will be every kiss no matter whose lips you touch
If they feel one cup of the love I have felt from you, they will be happy
I have been born into love from your hands and soul
You need to know, and I will forever make love to you after 30 ticks of the
clock after midnight and after 30 ticks of the clock in the afternoon
I'll make love to your soul every day

As I walk in the sun, I will have dreams of your love
As I stroll along streams, I will dream of adventure with you
When I come through doors and no matter the world cannot hold me away
from thoughts of us as the moon and sun
My memory will be us as stars circling the Earth
Our love may be a past life someday
I have a part of you
I will hold onto, and no space or time will remove your love
You have a world I cannot see me
You have a life
I have your love for me to love forever
I pray I am more than a memory
For me to live in the world as you know it to be, I would have to come to your
world, and we know that cannot be
Emptiness I will feel as depraved times of no love, but you have taught me,

your love is all I need, and it can never become less over time

You and I have known this time will come

We arrived in each other's hearts

Our presence in each other's world cannot be

You must leave

I must go

The stairs we climb will be the dance of your life, and I embrace your flight home

I know your heart is with me

Two things you need to know,

I can't believe you went from sea to sea to love me

I'll miss holding you in your sleep

Three things you need to know,

Your kiss

Your embrace

Your whispers made me submit to you forever

Four things you need you to know,

I adore you

I'll take care of your memory

You are beautiful

You made me feel beautiful

Five things you need to know

Under many moons, I wait

I will take care of what you placed above me and in me, and love the life you gave to me

I believe you are the only man who could grow love in me

You are indeed the only one for me

I know you must go

So, I leave no fresh oil in the lamps

I leave you my hair you stroked as I fell asleep next to you

I leave my toe ring, and you first bathed my feet you made me feel like a woman

You loved me from my head to my toes, and captured my soul to be forever yours

I love Sirletto

From me Valentina

Be well my love

Episode 23

I felt myself breaking. Tears stormed. I fell into a state of crying uncontrollably. My dog started whining again. What have I done, and how could I not...war kills in so many ways. It rips apart souls. After the French rebuilds, is there a place for her? She has no family, but I'm going back to a family. After America returns to normal, as in keeping Negros and Whites segregated, and all the other ugly things have been pushed aside to fight a war, will I be whole...ever?

I pulled on my clothes and went outside. I paced, while my mind raced to where I might find my love. I traveled from and through the foothills, open fields, ponds, and rivers. I knew not where to start to find my love. But what then if I did locate her? My stomach released my hurt, and I hurled all my inside contents until the dry heaves broke me down to my knees.

I walked to the ever-constant fire in the burn barrel. I stood and paced around the flames all night. I wished I could burn my pain. I'm sure, at some point, every soldier here lived a moment of sadness and upset while standing at the barrel. The barrel became a cross for transference to give my soul hope of redemption.

Episode 24

Twenty–five months later, I'm back from the war. Initially, I still had time to serve in the Army once I touched down on American shore. I used leave time to visit home, and then I spent the rest of my enlisted time on different bases around the States. But now I've been discharged back into civilian life. I have only been home for a few months. I didn't come back with Valentina, and even if I had found her before I left, there would have been a slim...no, I mean...no chance they would have allowed her to come back to the States with me.

I did have all those motorcycle parts waiting for me, and I also have my dog, Jerri. The commander, upon my request, made it happen. He got it approved through upper brass by saying I retrained the dog after the Germans used her. He stretched the truth, stating Jerri saved some of our soldiers when we were bombed, by finding wounded men. Strange irony of it all – if I wanted Valentina to come back she would be on a lower status or nor status at all. Well, life is bizarre. The affirmation of the dog's hero status secured Jerri a new life away from the war zone. Now she is my watchdog at the motorcycle garage, and she spends time at home with my parents. My mom is a walker, and she and Jerri are like best friends.

I'm sitting at the dinner table with my mom, my dad, my uncle Sonny, and his girlfriend. Since I opened my motorcycle shop, things have been going very well. I'm selling cycles as fast as I build them. I have a large inventory of parts. The men who helped me, I kept my word to them. I built and shipped cycles to Clement, Little Roy, Tiny Taps, N–booty, Lanky Slim, and his White male lover–Francis W. Cutter, and the two MPs. The one MP from Seattle is now a good friend, and we often go motorcycle riding in the countryside of the Pacific Northwest. It always helps to have someone who looks like the locals when riding into small towns. Although the Northwest is not like being down South, being alone as a Negro…it is as in anyplace – a Negro needs to be careful of the redneck citizens, or racist police.

I'm thankful I'm able to see my mother and father again. I'm grateful to sit at this dinner table, although leaving the love of my life in France. Before I left France, I searched behind each door and inside buildings. I scoured the forest, the mountains ranges, foothills, farmhouses, and fields. She didn't want to be found. *Did she watch me while I searched for her?* I doubt so, because I had Jerri, my dog with me, and the dog never detected her. She loves me, I believe, and I love her and miss her.

Each night I spent alone from Valentina while still in France, I dreamed of her, and I would sulk when I awoke. She knew and understood passion in the middle of a war, and she made all my senses come alive. Some nights we talked until daylight, and some nights she would meet me wearing sheer silk or thinly woven crepes. Once in an abandoned farmhouse, Valentina met me there for one night, and in a sense, we played house as if we were married. She made dinner for me, and then we made love by the fireplace.

While my dog, Jerri, guarded outside the house, Valentina danced to no music, but I hummed and sang to her. I would take her in my arms, and we would slow dance to the wind blowing. I miss her lips, which were always so warm, ever so sweet. At times, her passionate kisses made beads of sweat run down my back. Then still, sometime during our lovemaking, she would kiss the salt of my sweat from between my shoulder blades. When she lowered her ample hips over mine, her hands would brace on my chest. The warmth and softness of her spread fingers – they felt as if she reached inside my body and controlled my heartbeat and my breathing. When I woke in the early morning, to have her eyes open slowly and meet mine, we reached inside each other in love before we made love again.

Our hours of talking and laughing and holding each other, I missed what another woman may never fulfill, but I have to move past what I can't have. The war on another shore dictated our fate. Fate allowed me to fall in love. Another love will come one day, and the love of Valentina taught me lessons of love, and all of this whole experience would make me a better man. It has too. This must make me go on to do great things for others as a payment for the love she gave me when I needed love. Valentina killed her brother to save my life. My grandfather told me there is always a love we can't have, but we live on to honor that love by how we give love in the future. We can dream of love gone away and hear love lessons guide us to be great at giving love.

I have not shared much of the joy and pain I experienced in France. I wouldn't know where to start and how to tell the end. I have spoken of some of the battles, but I have only shared wartime stories, and none of the background of my personal life.

As we are sitting at the dinner table, there is an awkward quietness. I look around, and I can tell a conversation, or conversations, have taken place, and I am the subject.

"Son, it would be impossible for me to be your mother and not say something sooner or later. I have waited for you to find your way, but something in me tells me a part of you is lost. I know it has been hard on you, but we have found your son, and you are traveling to get him. It will be a joy for all of us when he comes back. I know you are dreaming of him daily. But Sirletto, it may seem you have other dreams inside of you. You seem restless, and I find you pacing at times. You have buried yourself into your motorcycle business, but is there something going on with you? You never go out. I look over at you while at church service, and you appear to be traveling while looking out of a train window instead of worshiping. I keep seeing one of the prettiest girls at our church trying to grab your attention. I see her making her way over to you as soon as church lets out, and her smiling in your face. You know I'm not a busy body, but yes...I talked to her mother, hoping you two might hit it off. She told me, her daughter, Marjorie, mentioned to you the sax man Louis Jordan is coming to the Civic Auditorium, and she would love to go, yet you have not responded.

Then, another pretty woman, the one who teaches Sunday school to the teenagers – Ms. Isabella, you know the one all the men can't take their eyes off of her hourglass figure...well, some may feel she is a bit too old for you, but I don't. She rid herself of a no–account husband back in her early twenties, so she has been divorced for ten years. *Them* old dirty-minded deacons whose wives have passed away, they are trying to grab her up for themselves to come and be their new young wife and take care of their old behinds. But she needs a good young man like you. Although she is thirty-seven, she is only five years your senior. Now, she is a nice woman, and she has no children but loves children. She came to me and asked if it would be to forward for her to ask you out, to see the person everyone is talking about the blind piano player. I think his name is Ray Charles, who opened for T–Bone Walker at the Black and Tan Supper Club. I told her she should ask you. Then, when I ran into her at the supermarket, she said, you said, you were busy. Baby boy, you only go riding on your motorcycles. What is going on with you? What did the war do to you, son?"

My mother is a rich chocolate brown-skinned woman with a cheekbone smile even when she sleeps. My mom, she is straight-forward honesty. I never want to aid in anything which makes her sad, by not responding to her with the truth.

My mother touches my face and lowers herself to eye level with me. "Sirletto, it has been on my mind to ask you questions, but I have waited. I can no longer let another day go by, not knowing what is on your mind, and what is going on in your heart. Did something happen in the war – is it troubling you?"

My family is staring at me. It's almost like they know my story, but are waiting for me to tell it all. How do I say that I fell in love with a woman during the war, even though, so few women were near?

My father stands and leans down on the table to look into my eyes. "I'm so glad you're back, and you are healthy. I'm happy to see you have your business going, but it saddens me when I can sense something is going on inside you, and you haven't, or can't, disclose what it is with us. If you can, please tell us. What's going on in your life, son? I'm sure the war left horrible memories, so maybe you should let us help. I have heard some men came back from this war and things are not well for them. They have repulsive dreams and have become angry. Some drink way too much, and some have...taken their lives. So, I say to you, I want to help my son in any way I can. Let us all help."

My father stands up straight and looks over to my uncle, who is staring at me. My uncle's girlfriend holds his hand on the table, but her head turns toward my mother. The room feels as if it is shrinking, and the wood floors, with the paisley printed wallpapered walls, and wood archways all seem so close. My mom has tears in her eyes. I knew the time had come to tell them about my life in the war.

I shared my story of how I met Valentina, how I felt when I was with her, and how empty I feel now. I told them of the murders, and how she helped me solve them. I left out the parts with anything to do with all the mystic type Louisiana voodoo.

"Valentina saved my life twice. Meaning, including the fact she killed someone—a blood relative to save my life, but they were evil. Her name, Valentina, it means strong.

Then one day, she went away, but she left me a letter, a lock of her silver hair, and a ring." I pulled the ring out of my wallet. "This is all I have of her. She has all my soul, and I miss her. Am I to live like this all my life? I thought, after some time, I could move on. I have thought of going out with the two women you speak of, mom...but if I start something with either of them, I feel I won't be able to finish what I start."

I'm talking to my mother and all those in the room, and I realize I'm sobbing. My father comes up. He stands behind me with his hands on my shoulders, reaches around, and hugs my head.

"So, you are the kind of man me and your mother would hope you would be. Even after all these years, your mother makes me feel the same way you feel when I hear you speak of this woman you miss – there's nothing in this world I wouldn't do to be with your mother. Maybe you know, or you don't, but I put you in your mom's belly before we married. Not only was it the right thing to marry her, but God blessed me, and allowed me to be her husband when you entered this world. Go find your woman is what I say to you."

My mother lifts out of her chair, rubs my father's back, kisses his cheek, then she kisses my forehead. My father's voice is rich and thick, like the low note of a cello. "Son, you have to go find her, you're going to have to go back.

You cannot let this situation burn a hole in your soul. Maybe, as you said, she doesn't want to be found. Possibly...maybe she felt you needed to focus on coming back and finding your son. However, many of the White men are bringing war brides home from Germany and England. Why shouldn't you have the woman you love? It will be an undertaking. It will take time and resources, but son, what have we not done in this family if we wanted to?"

"One thing at a time though, let's return your son back home. Please bring my grandson home, now that we have an idea of where he is. Afterward, will we all help you make plans to find the love of your life."

My mom's words soothed some of my sadness.

Episode 25

I'm in California. We have located my son, Baritone. I'm riding one of the motorcycles I assembled to deliver to the MP who helped me in France. I'm now entering the Los Angeles area. I'm grateful to have the skill to be able to build two-wheel dreams as I promised, and I finished the other bike for my soldier friends and shipped them.

My uncle found valuable information. My ex-girlfriend, the mother of my son, is in Southern California. Some time ago, before I returned from the war, Kathy called my mother once to tell her that she and my son Baritone were okay, and they were living in Los Angeles. Mom thought Kathy was reaching out for help, but lost her nerve. My uncle knew a guy in Los Angeles who located people. A war veteran like me, put himself to work by finding people for other people, or fixed things the police can't, couldn't, or wouldn't. We Negros police our own in many ways, as American justice often played games with Negros as a sport. This guy, Easy, he specialized in private investigations. My uncle Sonny wired the man a thousand dollars. It turned out to be money well spent, as the man delivered as promised. Easy sent a telegram two days later, stating he had located the mother of my child. My ex-girlfriend, Kathy, and my son live alone. She's not with the man she left Seattle with, and my son is stable and safe to a point, but not in an ideal situation.

I did not tell my mother, but I shared with my dad and uncle how I reacted when I killed the German in the forest. Right before the overkill, I got lost in a daydream – a nightmare of me dreaming the man Kathy was dating had her pinned on a bed and having sex, and then my son came in the room right in the middle of it. I reflected on the experience leading to me killing the German in the manner I did – who would have killed me if his rifle released a bullet as he hoped it would do, so that he could take my soul and send it in a direction. The outcome of it all, I killed a man with the rage of having to kill 100 Nazis because of the drama playing out in a nightmare I had.

Easy met with me, and he drove me around, giving us a chance to get to know each other. I thought he might be almost interviewing me to check my character. He and I swapped war stories while we headed to different destinations as he handled more than one case at a time.

Easy held a cigarette in the corner of his mouth when he spoke. "I killed a lot of men in the war, but when the Army reclaimed my rifle and sent me back to America soil, I found a Negro had so few choices of how to make money – although I fought for our right to have opportunities – so they say. Anyway, back in the States, when it came to making a living, I fell into what I'm doing – handling problems for people.

"Of course, money helps to drive me to where and how I make more money, and almost every time it involves the love of a man and woman, or lack thereof." He blew cigarette smoke out into the hot air of Los Angeles as he turned a corner and hit the gas to speed up.

"You know what...sometimes the pain of loving a woman, and receiving the love they give back, is a minefield of the heart stuck in dreamy romanticisms or defective emotions. Sirletto, I'm glad to be able to help you find your son. You know, the seriousness and calamity of love is a war all to itself. The battles over love have killed many good men and women. Why? The trying to be morally upright, they cross paths with the evil sides of life.

"The fire of love between two is beautiful until it crosses paths with other souls who are of crude oil, and then it can get too hot or dose the flame. Men and women die over what loves is, or what love is not, more than any other reason to die.

"You and I have fought in a war over in Europe, and possibly, if the right or wrong king or queen slept with the right or wrong person from another country, it could stop, or ended, or it started a World War. Think of the man who slept with Hitler's mama, or if another man had sexed her up, we might not have ever known of a Hitler, but maybe instead, a woman named Barbara would have been born in Hitler's place."

He laughed, and I contemplated.

We went to the flophouse where Kathy lives with my son. Easy has the respect or fear of folks as he entered other people's business. He mentioned he had a friend who killed or hurt first, then asked questions, it put fear even in bad people.

At the flophouse, I looked at what someone called *clothes*. My son's clothing is less than desirable. I left them right where I found them. While they served their purpose as adequately covering my son, a new life is coming for him. I will buy him new clothes before we return to Seattle.

We drove up to the school where my son attended. He had listened to what kind of man I am, and believed it was time to gain my son back into my life. Easy told me to go to the office, as he knew the school secretary, a Ms. Carla, and he said she would help me.

I walked into the school office and saw a strikingly beautiful woman. A breathtaking visual of Negro woman greeted me at the counter. She could pass – her fairest of skin tones, some folks among us Negros called it "passing" when you're a Colored person, but White folks think you're another White person. Oftentimes, a *passing* Negro will live a secret as a White person for the advantages that came with being integrated into privileged society, instead of being treated as less than because one is a Negro. Her skin tone reminded me of my Army friend Lanky Slim, the Cajun, but he refused to pass.

I explained my story to Ms. Carla. She knew some of my narratives as told to her by Easy. I stared at Ms. Carla kind of mesmerized by her beauty. She spoke of concerns about my son's life as she hoped it to be better than it is.

"Mr. Preer, your son is gifted in many areas of his education and music, and it drew attention, which brought care and protection from the staff." Ms. Carla has a sultry voice, but spoke with sadness in the tone of her voice when speaking of my son's well–being. "Mr. Preer, I believe your son is not happy…no he is not." She placed her hands on the bridge of her nose as if to pray or to help compose herself. Her head dropped a bit and went side to side, shaking her head no to a question.

Then her voice entered me and made me a bit weak. "We have kids at all schools that don't have, or receive, the care or love they should. Your son is not deprived of love, but care is lacking. However, your son exudes love." Her deep breaths made me feel a bit emotional inside with fear of what my son might have gone through. "I, and others at the school, made sure he ate good food, and I found clean clothes for him when I could. However, I did not give him clothes that were too nice as someone might want them more if you know what I mean.

"I do know his mother brought him to school by way of the city bus. One of us here at the school drove him to the flophouse he has been living in after school. Otherwise, he would have to walk too far."

She reached down into what might have been a purse. She lifted a handkerchief and wiped her forehead and patted her pretty face with her hands which were equally pretty. Valentina had caught my eye as a rare beauty, and when I came back to the States, I went to the movies that stared a stunning Dorothy Dandridge. All the men thought Dorothy was the finest-looking picturesque woman ever. I'm looking at Ms. Carla, and I made love to Valentina. I think I know what beauty is, and there is no one single woman who can be called the prettiest, but some women's visual attractions can go to levels we men cannot handle or appreciate. Sadly, a woman's vivid wonder can distract weak-minded men from looking pass her intellect and soul.

Ms. Carla pulled paperwork from a filing cabinet, and made some changes to the information on it, then handed the paperwork to me. "You will need this paperwork to enroll him in school once you are back in Seattle. Let me walk with you to your son's class, if you don't mind, and I want to make sure the teacher will release him to you."

I could not help but engage envisaging eyes as she never took them off of me. I believed she wanted to say something to me, or wanted me to say more. She stopped along the way at a water fountain, and slowly placed her pretty hand in her hair to hold it from falling in her face as her lips pursed to kiss the water entering between her lips. After she finished drinking, she faced me with her wet lips, and she fastened her eyes on me.

"Mr. Preer, for a man to come this far to find his child, it speaks volumes of what kind of man you are. And, if you are a friend of Easy, and he has brought you here to pick up your son, I know you are a good man."

"Ma'am, I'd like to think I'm a good man – for sure, I try."

"Please don't call me 'ma'am.' Umm, I'm pretty sure we are near the same age." She smiled, and it almost intimidated me. "Are you going to be in town long? I mean...no forwardness or incivility, but I'd love to at least have a chance to prepare a home-cooked meal for you while you are here in Los Angeles. I mean, if you are traveling back with your son, you and he should have a good meal before you leave, and I do love cooking for a man."

Her smile, and then a light bite down on her bottom lip, made me smile. I might be blushing, and she did affect me.

"Ms. Carla, you are really nice, but you don't have to do anything for us. I think we will be fine."

"Mr. Preer, I'd like to make sure you and your son have all the right things going for you, and so maybe I can pack some food for you and him so you don't have to stop to eat at places along the way where you may not be sure of the food's preparation, or service."

Her face wore an expression, and it made me wonder...*am I missing out on something?* She is sweet and caring, and I like her assertiveness without being too fast. She's wearing those stockings with the line up the back, and her heels let one red toenail peek through an opening. She's not passing for White. She intently wants me to look at her Negro-ness.

Her fingers touched the back of my hand and trailed down to my fingertips. I didn't jump or move my hand away. I longed for a soft touch.

"Mr. Preer..."

"Call me, Sirletto."

"Sirletto, I love your name, but...ah...if I ever come to Seattle...you know, like catch the Greyhound, would you show me around? I'll be no bother. I'll find a rooming house to stay at, and you can come by and pick me up whenever. Maybe I'll be able to see if I could find a decent paying job while I'm there. Just maybe...I can make a life there. Maybe I'll find myself a good 'husband,'" her voiced toyed with the word. I felt her words.

Her smile is perfect with a gleaming shine, and her lips were a parting of sensual allure. Her hazel eyes held me in yielding containment. It felt good to have a woman flirt with me. Valentina made it clear…I should move forward in life, and our love will never change or diminish, but an empty feeling overcame me, knowing I might not be ready for another woman.

It is best I do not confuse or hurt someone, especially since I did not know what might happen when I go back to France.

"Ms. Carla, the war was long and left me feeling many things I don't understand about myself as of yet. I don't know what is in store for me right now. I know I need to spend a lot of time with my son. I hear your compassion. I look at you, and I know I'd love to know you much better, but give me some time to sort out my life. If too much time passes, and you don't hear from me, I'm sure a good man will give you a good life. Besides, I'm sure if you ask Easy to look out for you, he will make sure a man treats you right, I do believe."

"Fair enough. Maybe, just maybe, I might be someone who can help you figure out what is for you, but I should not say more along that line. I am a lady, and you are the man. I must let you take the lead."

"I hear you, and I understand. I do not take your kindness and passions for what could be a blessing to the both of us as to, you are not too forward. I'm intrigued by you. Please, have no misgivings. I can sense your intelligence to bring about great conversations, and you are…hmmm, beautiful."

"Thank you, Sirletto. I will say though, no matter what, I thought I read you right, Mr. Preer, I mean…Sirletto. You are a good man to be upfront as you are. I haven't been so lucky meeting a good man while living in LA. I'm from Louisiana, and I came out here to go to school at UCLA for Journalism, but all I can find is secretarial work."

"You went to the same school as Jackie Robinson, the first Colored man in the major leagues."

"He was a classmate of mine and dated one of my dormmates. I'm a good woman down here in LA, Sirletto, and if you ever want to take time to know me, I'll be here...you have the number to the school. I can come to you, or you can come to me. Inconvenience, it never has to be a barrier. Also, Easy...he is my cousin, so you can always contact me through him."

I took her hand and held it for a long moment. "Thank you, Carla. Thank you for making me feel special. Thank you for looking out for my son. What you have given me at this moment, I did need."

She held my hand as we walked until we were right outside of my son's class.

When I walked into Baritone's classroom, I saw my son at the blackboard writing a math problem. I watched with pride as he explained the method to figure out the math problem to his classmates. He put the chalk down and turned to go to his seat. He saw me, and he ran and jumped in my arms in front of all his classmates. It startled the teacher. It's a good thing Ms. Carla escorted me to his class to explain.

Outside, Easy gave me some time to walk and talk to my son on the school playground. A rebirth happened. We held on to each other as if our lives depended on each other, and to some extent, it did. I made it back from the war, and now I'm here with my son.

We drove to where Kathy worked. Earlier, before we picked up my son, Easy told me that my son's mother fell into drugs, but she has since cleaned up. She, and the man who is no longer in her life, owed a couple of people money. Easy and his friend who corrupt people feared, they made those accounts go away. Kathy did some hard living by doing things her man made her do, of which, I didn't want to know the details. I understood what he meant.

"Preer, all you need to be clear about is she is clean from drugs now. She is working an honest job as a waitress working for tips in LA, which means she is barely making ends meet, but she is trying to provide the best for your son by working for tips."

We pulled up to a diner. People with less than they needed—the have-nots, they were up and down the streets standing near cheap hotels and older cars, and wearing worn clothes. More frowns than smiles on faces told stories in how they struggled. My mind painted pictures and created tales of better times, or never any good times.

For a long minute, I stared into the window before I exited the car to tell my son's mother I am taking him home with me.

Easy pointed me toward the door of the diner. "Leave the young man with me and go handle your business with care."

Easy and I exited the car. He leaned on the hood of his car and puffed on a cigarette and looked me in the eyes. "She has been through a lot just as you have. She has fought battles to survive, whether she put herself into a war or not. Don't start another war." Easy poked his head in the car window, and then he looked back my way. "Go ahead and go inside. Your son is sleeping from all the excitement of seeing his father alive and well." With an unlit cigarette hanging from the corner of his lips, he stared back at me when he spoke. "Offer her a feeling of peace to continue as a woman with a child in this world."

Easy...he made a point of who I want to be. To go inside and treat Kathy with hostility, I would be wrong. I felt my heart weighting heavy with regret.

I did not need to start another war. I walked into the café and saw Kathy turned away from me. Instinctively, the crisp ringing of the door chime made her turn her head to acknowledge a new customer walking through the door, but she did not make eye contact or give a personal look at who might have come through the door.

"Have a seat. I'll be right with you." Her songbird voice caressed my recollections of better times.

A flash of heat went over me. The woman I once loved looked thinner than I remembered, but her curves were still in place. Her skin is darker, maybe from the Southern California sun. Her hair is much shorter, but it's feminine. Kathy is still soft and seductive in appearance, and her walk always made me freeze in place with her sway. Reflections of the past kept me still to simply observe a love gone away, but why? There is a place in my heart for her, but not as being my woman. It seemed as though I'd known her forever, from back to a time when my mom used to teach her music.

But things happened. Mainly, the woman did not want me, and then she took my son away from my family. She broke hearts. My pride wrote angry thoughts inside the walls of my soul with my sense of right and wrong. I wanted to be angry about my son's living conditions, and clearly, he is not happy. I wanted her to feel my anger, but whatever we shared at one time in our lives made me grab my tongue by pressing my lips tight, and I quickly reminded myself of words told to me, "She has fought battles to survive, whether she put herself into a war or not. Don't start another war."

Maybe I'm wrong, but I needed to move on, and she must also move in another direction. Back then, possibly, it was lust with Kathy more so than love. Maybe it was merely young love, but now, as grown-ups, we should know better.

"Kathy, it's me, Sirletto."

She looked up and dropped the empty coffee pot she held. The few people inside the café went silent for two seconds. Then folks went back to talking as if the shattering of a coffee pot was normal as they turned the pages of a newspaper. The jukebox is playing the blues of Elmore James. He shouted that the sky is crying, but here I am in the sweltering summer heat of Los Angles in a diner with hot grease permeating the air. Kathy asked the cook to cover for her, and we walked to the back of the café and sat down at a table.

The hot-cracked vinyl poked me in the butt, and I wasted no time in telling her a change was coming. "Kathy, I've come to take my son back to Seattle. He is going back with me, and he will have a life with his grandparents and me. If you want to come back to Seattle, I will make it happen for you. I will help you find your way back to your feet, and you can see our son as much as you like, but he is going back to Seattle to be with me."

"Sirletto, maybe we can...ah...maybe we can begin again? I mean...you made it back from the war, and..."

"No!" I caught my voice slicing through with some agitation, and took a deep breath to reel myself in. "Kathy, that boat has sailed on. But we can be friends. You are my son's mother, and I am going to respect you, and I will not be at war with you over our son. His best interest is why I am here. I'm going to respect my son's life more than anything, so he's coming with me, and you are welcome to come back with him."

She placed her hand on top of mine. It's the second time in an hour a woman touched my hand, but this time, I pulled it away.

Episode 26

Easy drove us to a friend who sold cars. We traveled to the far outskirts of town in the desert, and I bought an excellent running car and headed back to Washington with my son. Kathy decided to come back to Seattle with our son and me after a long conversation. I believe we had a clear understanding of the boundaries of our relationship. I told her I loved someone else. I saw the anguish in her eyes, but she let me know she understood how life changes, and if we both could turn back the hands of time, we both might see things differently.

❧ ❧ ❧

Once we arrived in Seattle, my mother set Kathy up in a furnished apartment. My mother made sure Kathy felt welcomed to be back at home with all her family who missed her. My mother is not one to hold a grudge. On the way back from taking Kathy to her apartment, mom talked with me.

"Sirletto, sometimes a woman feels as if she has no choice in making certain decisions in life for herself, and once she has children, her life changes and keeps changing. Sure, she ran away with your child, and I know it hurts, but you two were having problems long before you left for the war. When women have children, it puts us in a circle of joy and anguish of choosing what is right for us and our child. Despite what a man feels is right, and what he wants, men demand things to be their way or no way, for the simple point of having control. A woman has to look out for what seems and feels like number one. Oftentimes, the choice between her and a child, and what the future for both will be, is murky waters to tread. Maybe Kathy felt short-changed for not living long enough before having a child. She saw your dreams, but maybe she didn't see her own. Sometimes it's hard to see dreams when you don't know what to dream for."

My mom's word put a knowing in me that I helped create a part of her choices. It helped me to start to look at Kathy's circumstances differently. I understood a woman, or man, could make decisions which resulted in no one being truly happy. Kathy is gifted with musical talent as she can sing, and before I went to war, she earned her college degree, but having a child with me may have stolen moments of joy from her. One day, she will have a life with someone else, and I should expect and be okay with her choices in life. I need to be happy for her. We both accepted we needed to be friends for the sake of our son's future. She and I, we have to prepare him for a world that ships young men over to a foreign land to fight wars for older men.

Weeks later, I saw my son shine with the joy of love all around him. Baritone is blessed with different talents when he sang and played a musical instrument. He has traits of my mom and dad, and his mom in him. I noticed he could take something apart and then reassembled much as I did as a child. He loved being in the shop with me, and I am amazed at how quickly he learns. I made it clear to him if he couldn't afford to buy something, the mind within him can create what he desired.

With Baritone back in school in Seattle, I to his school daily to meet him after school was out. I want him to know I will always be there for him, but I also needed him to understand I needed to go back to France and know the main reason why.

I decided to talk to him about it all as we were walking home from church. We strolled through the park, and I asked him to sit with me on a bench. We started eating some fried chicken wrapped in wax paper, prepared by the church mothers who handed it out in brown paper bags for all to enjoy. I laughed as I knew the church mothers cooked as an incentive for people to come back for the afternoon second Sunday service without the thought of them having to cook or go out to eat.

"Son, there is nothing in the world I can run from, and you are one of the most important people in my world. I made it back from this war because of you. What got me through each day – I needed to live on so I could be your father. I have a tough question for you. I want to know if it will be okay with you if I go back to France for a little while to find someone. I will not be gone long. There is a woman over there that saved your father's life – not once, but two times. She loves me, and I know I love her.

"I'm not going over there to fight a war, but to be at peace. I'd like to have a chance to have a good woman in my life – one whom I believe I can love for the rest of my life. If I don't find her, I'll learn to live without her, but I'd rather have her here with you and me, and I have to at least try. She will love you if she has a chance to meet you. I know the fantastic young man you are, and I want her to know you as well."

"Dad, but my mom...you said you love her too."

"Baritone, it was wonderful to hear your mother sing solo at church today, and her voice is of an angel. Your mother took a huge step in joining the church, and she is trying to be a better mom than before. However, no matter what, I do love your mom for bringing you into the world, and now she is changing her life to make herself be the best she can be. Your mom and I are friends, and we will always try to be friends for you. Your mom and I don't have to be a couple to love you."

It's a cold day with a light mist falling around us. I buttoned my son's coat up and made sure his scarf covered his throat.

"How long will you be gone?"

"I don't know, son. I don't know where she is. I have to find her, and a lot of things must happen for her to come back with me. Who knows, maybe you and I might move to France. Maybe I should take you to the library and check out some French books for you to start learning how to speak French."

"Dad, you mean we could go over the ocean and live? I don't think I want to unless granddaddy and Big Mama come too."

"Baritone, we are a long way from anything happening as of now. I was speaking in jest when I said we could move to France."

"What is jest?"

"It means kind of mocking or teasing with the thought of a possibility, as life has strange twists and turns on how things can happen. I have to go over there, and for sure I'm coming back, and then we will talk about all our futures. Okay?"

"Okay, dad, but let's hurry now so we can go see the man who plays the sax remarkably well."

We started walking toward 12th and Jackson to go to a place called the Black & Tan Club. It's a place where live jazz played nightly. On Sundays, they hosted music for the general public so that young people could hear the jazz greats. While I was stationed by the little French town and in the bookstore where I played chess, the bookstore owner tuned his radio in to pick up jazz from time to time, and I heard a sax player who people called Yardbird, but his name is Charlie Parker. The night before, with my mom and dad sitting front and center, we enjoyed hearing him play. I wanted to share the experience with my son. Yardbird is phenomenal, and I wanted my son to hear how good he is for himself. Charlie Parker has changed my love for music forever – it feels like an addiction to me needing to hear more of his music. My son plays the sax and piano very well for his age, and maybe meeting Mr. Parker can be arranged.

Episode 27

I flew to New York. It is the second time I'd flown in my life. Before, I traveled by bus, train, or ship. The first time I was on an airplane was thanks to Captain Castellani when I flew back from France after my tour of duty. I have stayed in contact with him, and we have become good friends on equal footing. He is back in France and helping the country find its foundation of recovery. We are assisting the French Army to reorganize so they can protect themselves. We are also protecting American interests – such as the construction companies who are most likely fleecing the French government.

I wrote Captain Castellani and finally told him of my relationship with Valentina, and that I wanted to come back to France to look for her. He agreed to help me. He has a cozy command post, and let me know I would have a place to stay for as long as I needed. He moved his wife, daughter, and the man I saved—his slightly crippled son-in-law there, along with his grandchild. All of them are in France with Captain Castellani, who is now Major Castellani.

Before I catch a flight to France as a guest of the U.S. Army and by way of the Airforce, I'm spending the weekend with my Army buddies. We all gathered to support Tiny Taps and to celebrate on each other. Tony believes he still has a chance as a fighter. He has won six fights in a row, and five of those wins were by way of knockout. The main guys from my troop have come to

New York to watch Tiny Taps in his seventh fight, and then we all hope to go out on the town and celebrate.

Clement from Hobbs, New Mexico, Little Roy from Chi-town, N-Booty from South Carolina, and Lanky Slim the Cajun...he's from near Baton Rouge, Louisiana. We are at the 3 Deuces Jazz Club located on the south side of 52nd Street between 5th and 6th Avenue. We survived an ugly war, so we are celebrating living through a tough time. We are having a great time throwing back drinks and beers while reminiscing and making fun of the times we shared while in France. Clement confessed it is his first time in the Big Apple, and he lied before about his New York experiences when we were all around the burn barrel back in France. Of course, I knew he bragged untruthfully back then, but it takes a maturing man to admit his past mistakes. It is a growth we love to share more than the lies we once told.

Clement is amazed by all the gorgeous Colored Satin Doll waitresses. They are working him out of some sizable tips with their coy smiles. He invested his VA money in buying a ranch. Although, he was forced to hire a White lawyer, in order to fight for his money and he received his American promised piece of freedom and liberty. It's not an uncommon theme for Negros to enlist White people to front for our rights. The lawyer fought the local authorities for Clement's rights for a Negro to own land.

"Damn, I can go kill a Nazi for Uncle Sam, but he didn't want to give me my money, and then didn't want to let me spend it on what I wanted."

We agreed with Clement and raised our drinks and crashed them together, and didn't care if they broke in a toast.

"Hey guys, I married a church girl, and she is six months' pregnant," Clement says during the toast.

For the next half hour, we treat Clement as if we are giving him a bachelor party. I'm proud that Clement took my words to heart from the conversation we had in the forest.

Little Roy is a bit of a different story. He came to New York to join us, but he had made a move to Detroit after he ran out of Chicago to avoid a gang of police beating him down and then doing jail time. A White policeman had insulted Little Roy in front of his woman, and he retaliated in his usual way. Little Roy recalled the situation for us.

"Man, me and my woman, we were enjoying ourselves at The Gatewood Blues Club and Muddy Waters made the women sway as if they were drunk on a fifth of bourbon. The club dripped sweat from the ceiling and down the walls, so me and my lady, we went outside to cool down. This cracker policeman comes up to me, and he tells me I can't stand on the corner. He told me to move along. He said my baboon-looking ass would scare people, but my woman could stand on the corner and maybe make some money. Now you know me. Before I could think, I grabbed him by the throat and lifted his cracker ass off the ground. That peckerwood squirmed as he held onto his last breath. He started to reach for his revolver, but he passed out before he could, and I dropped his ass on the ground. He laid limp and looking dumb for fucking with me, and I took his gun. Then I unzipped his pants and pulled his drawers down. I cocked the weapon and then slowly let the hammer close around the skin of his little pecker. If he moved the wrong way, he might have shot his thing off. The squeeze of the gun hammer had his balls turning blue, I'm sure.

"Well, I know they didn't have my name or anything to tie me to what happened, but I figured I should make a move out of Chicago before anything caught up with me. My lady and I have relocated to Detroit, and I got one of them car–manufacturing jobs at a General Motors plant, so it looks like I'll be okay. But that's some bullshit – we fight for these motherfucking States of America, and a damn flag dem motherfuckers once hung over us as slaves, but now, we don't deserve a decent amount of respect? These peckerwoods can kiss my big black Pontiac making ass."

We all toasted to Little Roy living through the experience, and to all of us surviving the America way.

Lanky Slim, the Cajun, has become a gym teacher teaching in the Colored Catholic schools in Baton Rouge, Louisiana. He took his VA money and finished his college education. Then he bought an old abandoned plantation property and has made a vacation spot for the Colored folks to come and not be bothered by Jim Crow.

"Sir-Sir, come on down and rest, and fish on the river and the lake on my property. Bring your son and bring your whole family if you like. It is safe. The redneck police leave me alone. My granddaddy and daddy are White, and they want me to conceal the fact we are blood. The town folk, they don't know I'm the Colored son, and if there are some who do know, they also know to keep it to themselves. My White half-brothers and sisters also keep it quiet, although we all played together as children. They allowed me to go to the White school with my skin tone being light and bright, and no one questioned my daddy when he enrolled me. Daddy and granddaddy own and run all the good and bad near and far.

"My mother is the prettiest dark-skinned Colored woman in the area, and she owns a fine house on the edge of town. Not one White person is offensive in any way toward my mother. My mama knows all the town dirt, so they leave her alone. My daddy, the White sheriff, he slept with my mama, a Colored mistress. He'd get drunk and tell all the town secrets with liquored-up loose lips."

Lanky Slim shared with me, away from the other fellows, about his White male lover – Francis W. Cutter, who helped us gain intel while we were in France. Francis lives on the property with Lanky Slim. He is the face of ownership over the property to help repress trouble. So Lanky Slim is living well and living as he wants. Lanky Slim also said Francis was troubled from the war as sleep did not come stress-free because of nightmares due to the war. Francis struggles with drinking too much, but drinking helps give some relief from the horror he saw when he transferred to Poland for a short while. He saw what the Germans did in the concentration camps to the Jews. So, Lanky Slim and Francis, they help each other in many ways.

Neflow Bonds, our Colored Clarke Gable who was known to all us soldiers as N–Booty from South Carolina...he is a train porter now, and takes assignments all around America. I noticed most of the women in the club gave N–Booty second and third looks. He is no longer so thin, and is handsome in his own right. He has developed a bright shining confidence making him smooth in how he moved and talked to women. At 6'3" and maybe 140 pounds while we were in France, he is now muscled and chiseled.

As he always did before, N–Booty smiles when he talks. "While in France, my nerves burned any food off as fast as I could eat. Coming out of high school as an exceptional athlete, all the Colored colleges wanted to enroll me at their school to play sports. I chose the Army. But once in basic training, I stopped putting on weight when my body was in the middle of a growth spurt upward and working so hard. So, I became a bean pole."

We shared good laughs at the bar while having a few drinks, but we all noticed our friend N–Booty, he's a sharpshooter with the ladies. He laughed and said, "I get around, but my daddy, he's still a rolling stone, and he made babies wherever he slept, so I wear rubbers religiously."

It made me reflect on what my mother said concerning a woman having tough decisions when she has a child, and the possibility of her not seeing her dreams as clearly as if she did not have the responsibility of a child. It gave me a profound respect for my friend who helped kill the German on the mountain with his sharpshooting skills. He is taking the past lifestyle of his father, and aiming his life in the direction of respecting his future until he is ready to settle down and not be a part of physically taking away a woman's dreams.

We left from the 3 Deuces Jazz Club and headed to Madison Square Garden to watch our friend Tiny Taps box. Ironically, Tiny is fighting the same guy he once threw a fight to due to being double-crossed. The guy is now the number five welterweight in the world, but he has been on the decline. Tiny Taps has been waiting to beat him down with revenge in his heart.

The fight world is enormous in New York Madison Square Garden. We caught the subway train to Penn Station, and there is a buzz on the street. Another highlight of the boxing night, we are going to see the great Sugar Ray Robinson fight. Our guy, Tiny Taps, is on the main fight undercard. We heard the excitement listening to people talk of wanting to see the fights and fighters, including fight fans wanting to see Tiny Taps. It's electrifying for us as we entered the Madison Square Garden. Tiny Taps made sure we are near the ring with great seats. When Tiny Taps came into the ring, he gave us a military salute, and we stood and returned the salute with pride. Then, one round later, it was over. Tiny Taps hit his opponent in a manner reminiscent of the time we watched him knocked out a German soldier. Then we watched the great Sugar Ray Robinson fight. He knocked out his guy in the eighth round. Sadly, they were forced to carry the guy out the ring, and it did not look good for him. It appeared as if life and death were in the balance for the guy.

We met with Tiny Taps later for a steak dinner. He told us, "One last fight in, guys, then that's it for me. The powers-to-be are offering me a title shot. Whether I win or lose, I'm hanging up my gloves."

He, too, saw the guy Sugar Ray knocked out, and watched him be wheeled away in an ambulance. The severely injured fighter planned on making his fight with Sugar Ray his last fight. We all agreed we'd be there to support Tiny Taps for the fight for his title shot.

I told the guys my story of Valentina. The fellas mocked me, and all wanted to punch me out. They joked about how I was getting some while over in France when their only options were a passed around dirty magazine to relieve sexual tension. They are supportive of my journey back to France, and the next day I'm on my way.

Episode 28

When I left the war in France, it was raining. It is downpouring as I land in Paris, two years after the war. Paris is clean and vibrant again. I guess one of the first things they felt they needed to do is to make it so visitors will come and generate money for their economy. It reminded me of how quickly the bombed-out area of our camp was repaired to accommodate soldiers to pay for a piece of ass.

I rode a military convey out to Captain Castellani's military base. It's good to see him, and to meet his wife, Kaitlyn. She embraced me with tears streaming down her face like I was her long-lost child. Then she spoke.

"Mr. Preer, I have to be honest, and maybe I may sound foolish, so please forgive me in advance in disclosing my ignorance. Before my husband's command, I never knew the presence of a Negro with a subjective view of your people as my life was in isolation when it came to skin color. Growing up near Quaker–like upbringings, there is no connection to your people for me to like or dislike. However, my Quaker–like beliefs taught me to try to see all God's creations as though they are my neighbor

"When my husband told me of the bravery, morals, and spiritual strength of your people, and how the world played gravely in your people's treatment, I did not know what to do. Then you saved my son-in-law, the father of my grandson, and your men courageously put a stop to some awful men who could have harmed my husband's career. You are an American hero, sir, and we are blessed by who you are. I can't say thank you enough."

I walked through the doors of the house where maids worked, and cooks were preparing meals. The grounds around the house with postcard-like flower gardens and walkways of a privileged lifestyle, I realized after listening to her, I am an object viewed for her praise. The house is cared for and kept up by lower-income French people. Class and race often escape the reality of do-gooders when they are acknowledging your gifts to them.

"Ma'am, I'll tell you something my grandfather shared with me. Some of us feel we have a measure of comfortability in our lives, and do not realize it could be that we are not a safe place. Misfortune can creep up to anyone's front or back porch. Some of us, we know we are not in a comfortable position in life, and we are safer as we see the reality of what is going on around us. Good fortune or bad luck can touch us all no matter where we build our castles, the sand underneath can wash away. Wind, rain, and high tides will come sooner or later for all of us.

"So, if allowed, seek knowledge and understanding, it is upon us to do so. Someone thought the world was flat at one time because they found it easier to not think of other possibilities. Others believed it couldn't be flat by how the sun came up over the horizon, and how the sunsets, they set out on a mission to find out the truth.

"Sadly, once many found out the truth, their next venture took advantage of what they learned at the expense of others. For my people, the American Negro, we became a scheme to take advantage of race and class for others to have control over our lives with slavery and now segregation, and Jim Crow laws." I made it obvious with my facial expression for her to see, I'm looking around. She's living an advantaged lifestyle at the expense of the class of people who worked for her.

"Mr. Preer, all you have said was not taught in my world. There is no doubt you are a new world to me, and I feel safer knowing you are in my world."

I don't think she understood me, but maybe I planted a seed. I wasn't there for race relations, or teaching, or hearing, or helping anyone gain a perspective. Perhaps at another time, or during different circumstances, I would...but I'm on an undertaking to find the love of my life, and I did not want my mind and heart diluted from my mission.

Captain Castellani's wife showed me around and escorted me to my room so I could take a short nap before dinner. Dinner was warm and welcoming, but I kept my conversation short.

After dinner, the captain, his son–in–law, and I drank Bastille 1789 Single Malt Whisky over ice. For saving his life, the son–in–law insisted that I take his Purple Heart and his Medal of Bravery. I knew I would hide them if I had them. Another man's medals were for him and his family.

After the war, people were moving around in groups trying to find housing and safe food, which became a big problem after the war. The Major made some inquiries before I arrived for insight with travel charts of those groups. He and I thought Valentina might move around with one or several groups. I knew it would be unusual for her to travel alone. She believed in safety in numbers, and although she could handle herself, I assumed Valentina would stay with a group, wanting to be one of the people to protect them. Then again, she could be a one band going it alone, knowing she could take care of herself.

Believing she probably moved around, we looked at maps of known towns in and around Southern France with populations of traveling people. My first stop...I will start where it all started. She might have come out of hiding when I went back to the States.

Provided with motorcycles, two guys will escort me to the outpost near the old base where my lover used to be. The next morning, we took off. The cycles helped us move quicker than being in a jeep, and as long as we made it from one military outpost base to another, we had enough gas.

❀❀❀

Rolling near the old base and the little town of demise, love, hope and loss...I took deep breaths trying to make it feel as good as possible. The two soldiers who escorted me, they rode on toward the outpost base. The base that once was, is now gone, but old markings and roads told me where I used to be. I stopped and gathered my thoughts of times gone by at the mechanic's tent and work area. I rode to where men once slept on the ground, and saw where the burn barrel once blazed. There's less vegetation in the area where the fire rose to the sky and men stomped in the mud.

The thought of the things shared of pain and sometimes joy of Colored men at war will be embedded in those grounds forever. It made me give thanks to God for surviving, and offered a prayer for covering the souls of those who were injured, or for those who never made it back to American soil.

Standing and looking in past directions, I reconstructed life as it was on those cold grounds. I viewed the foothills of the mountains to where Valentina shot a man to help me live to see another day and save my dog. I saw in the mountain range, a woman who introduced me to love, and I'm back to claim her love as a love I don't want to live another day without.

I looked out to the fields in an area where I saw people walking. They were going from the farms and the river to deliver their wares to market. I thought maybe she might be one of the women – she could be here. Valentina could be out of hiding since I left. I looked over to the brothels. I couldn't see them, but I knew they were there slightly past the outside of town. I would start my search at Frenchman's bookstore.

Riding past the now gone base, I relived what happened in the underground bunker of a crazed man who decided to bash his head in, taking his life. The captain told me they blew the bunker to pieces. I parked the motorcycle and smiled when I saw the town tavern opened for business. I entered the bookstore, and a full two-armed embrace welcomed me by the owner, Mr. Jole. When he pulled away, maybe we both held tears from falling. He put on some coffee, and let it slow simmer in a speckled blue kettle on the hearth of the fireplace. He emptied black coffee into two cups and poured from a glass jug of goat's milk.

We sat in front of the fire without a word. I'm sure we were thankful to be alive to share another moment. Mr. Jole survived through the hell of the Nazis and the Americans in his town.

A well-dressed middle age lady came into the bookstore. Her fashion sense looked to be of a high-priced New York shop. Mr. Jole stood and brought a chair over next to his. I stood in respect of a woman who entered the room. Although Mr. Jole only shared greetings of a silent celebration of each other's living, he finally spoke when introducing me to Mrs. Cinda Jole. I did not know thereof a Mrs. Jole.

Now with a lot of conversation going back and forth between the three of us, I learned Cinda spied for the French, retrieving information from the Germans. Born and raised in the French Alps on the border of Germany, she was assumed aligned to the German Nazi cause, but as a patriot, she bled the blue of the French flag. She came to Paris to model, and she acted in the theater, but when the war began, she used her circumstantial German background to infiltrate and spy for the Americans and English.

Mr. Jole had kept all knowledge of his wife to himself during the war. He worried about what could happen to her, of someone being captured and tortured into telling of her. Mr. Joel met Cinda while teaching literature in Paris, France, but this town will always be his hometown.

We were enjoying a fireside chat with a bit of French Cognac made in a town in France – the town of Cognac. I told Mr. and Mrs. Jole of my quest to find my lover. Mr. Jole erupted with a hardy laugh, knowing he knew Valentina dressed as an older Gypsy, but had to be a young woman. He downed his drink, and poured a couple of shots in now knowing I was her lover. Mrs. Jole, she insisted for me to come in the morning and pick her up on my motorcycle, she would help ask questions. Many folks in the little towns and countryside may not want to talk out of fear of an unknown stranger asking questions. The war has left scars, and for many, those rips of the soul may not go away for generations. Cinda spoke four different languages, and it would be a great help.

❊❊❊

I left early in the morning, after a good sleep on the base, with a feeling of no bombs or killers being present. I procured the use of a motorcycle with a sidecar to provide Cinda some comfort as she rode along on my quest.

When I drove the motorcycle with sidecar up to the bookstore, Cinda walked out, ready and dressed for the ride-along. She wore thick brown woolen and leather horse riding chaps with knee-high length boots. We rode to farms and cottages along the way to the town of the brothel of death for Valentina's brother.

No one claimed to know her or to have seen her. All the people we asked questions of were kindhearted. Most were happy to answer questions as they voiced the Negro soldiers were respectful and sympathetic to their countrymen, as opposed to some of the White soldiers who came in to take advantage of them and treat them as second-class citizens in their own country. I recalled a time when Little Roy laughed loud and hardy, thinking we Colored soldiers might have to stay in France when the war was all over, and we might feel more welcomed there, and our country—America might not let us come back.

I made one last stop – the brothel where Valentina killed her brother. I told Cinda the best version of what happened for her to understand. As we walked toward the house, our feet sunk in shallow mud, and my feet and knees felt a stiffening pain. Maybe too much riding on rough roads over the last couple of days has taken its toll on me. My stomach turned, upset. I felt pressure at my temples. I stopped walking and rubbed both sides of my head. Cinda placed the back of her hand on my forehead and gave me a worried look – she said I felt a slight bit feverish. I felt dizzy, and my stomach sent distressing feelings throughout my body. I re-experienced fear and the ugliness of a situation, knowing the woman I love killed her brother to save me and to save a lot of people.

We approached the door, not quite sure if it operated still as a brothel. But once invited in, I spoke with the same madam who ran the house back then, and she hugged me. I hope no one would get sick from whatever was going through me. I looked around and didn't recognize any of the other women, as my vision is a bit challenged. I asked for Ms. Porlena, the woman who helped me end the evilness as she sat in the room as bait. She still lived there in the house, and she came down the stairs when summoned. She looked at me and stared in my eyes for the longest time, and then she took my hand. I felt a little better as she led us to the kitchen.

We all sat down at the kitchen table, and although my Spanish and French were decent, I needed full understanding, and Cinda helped. I asked questions as I'm having trouble breathing. My focus is hindered by the tightness in my chest. Ms. Porlena reaches across the table, touches my hand, and I feel less ill. Every man feels a reprieve of life from the touch of a woman, from Eve to Mother Magdalene to the last woman on earth man always feel betters

"Yes, Mr. Preer, she came to check on me after the incident. She told me something to cherish."

Cinda kept translating for me. "Valentina told me, 'We have to protect life and live for life for all deserve life. Unless someone with life in their hands tries to take other lives away, we must do our best to provide a sanctuary for life.'

"I understand you may not know why she has chosen to do what she has wanted to do, but if you love her, then you must let her…"

I put my hand over Ms. Porlena's to stop her from saying what I did not want to hear, but what I felt she might say, and that is, I'd have to let Valentina go to be as she has chosen.

"Ms. Porlena, tell me what is going on with your life."

"I no longer trade my body, although I still lived in this house of sex for sale. The end of the war slowed the selling of a woman's body, but it did not put a stop to a woman's body being used for men's fun. The madam is my mother, and my mother went to the town folks and pled for them to let me – her daughter – teach in the local school again as I once did with love before the Germans invaded."

"Ms. Porlena, if by any chance you see Valentina, please let her know I love her. And please give her this." I pulled a letter from my coat pocket – a love letter poem I wrote while flying over the Atlantic Ocean to come to find Valentina.

WOULD YOU KNOW

If I thought about you 1001 time in the last 24 hours ... would you know?

If I kissed your lips in my daydreams 599 times ... would you know?

Would you know if I held you in prayer 24 times a day?

If I sang your praises to God twice an hour ... would you know?

Would you know if I gave thanks to God for just knowing you exist – morning, noon, and night?

If I thought about you 10,999 times in the last month, would you know?

No...no, you would not know...

But what those thoughts are and were, you have within your control

What you did,

What you said

How you said and did

Where you did

It all has to do with ... not how much ... I think of you,

Volume is nice,

But what is my last thought of you each time I have a dream of you?

If I should die in the next moment, would you know you were my last thought?

And what might have I been thinking ... that one...one...one ... time
Would you know?
I ask God to show me how to make sure you know my last thought will always be
I love you

I held Ms. Porlena's hand on the front porch as we were leaving, and then I closed my eyes and gave praise to God for saving her life. I felt better as I drove away on the motorcycle.

We rode back to the bookstore. Mr. Jole, his wife Cinda, and me...we all spoke of what to do next. Mr. Jole asked his wife to help me travel to the countryside heading south, and she did. It is now ten days later, and we have ridden to different places asking and not finding. Cinda and I even went across the border of France into Spain to a town called San Sebastián. Valentina told me she was born and raised there until her mother lost her life. She loved being there on the ocean, and she buried her mother out in deep water. Valentina told me she could look out over the sea and talk to her mother and feel her presence. We searched the town, asked the old-timers, and no one had seen or had knowledge of my lover. The town population presented a high number of African people who smiled when they saw me. I could tell they knew I'm an America Negro and not from any African country, as one young man told me so. The Africans we encountered spoke in Spanish and some English.

This town is a scenic place, and one day I want to come back and stay a while with the breeze of the ocean and the bluest warm skies. Cinda and I ate dinner in a seafood brasserie overlooking the sea. Our waiter, an African man, he treated us graciously and spoke good enough English, along with Spanish to talk to us. He wanted to know my story of an American Negro now in his town. We shared some good laughs and some wine, and then he directed us to a hostel for us for a good night's sleep before heading back to France.

I felt desperation. I missed my son, and I needed to keep my promise to him that I would try to be back in two weeks. Now my time is almost up with no results.

I thanked the Joel's as we shared a final dinner and night cap of brandy. I slept in their loft, it felt like family being there with them. It helped to calm my soul some, knowing I did not complete my mission to find my love. I invited the Joel's to the States to stay as long as they want to stay in Seattle with my family.

I rode onto the outpost base in the morning, and the two soldiers who rode with me to the outpost, they implored me to radio Major Castellani. Through a transmission line full of static, I heard, "Come back right now. I have a telegram of urgency from your family, and it has been waiting for you, but you were out of contact for ten days."

I asked him to read it to me.

"First Sergeant Preer, although you are no longer under my command, I order you to come back right now! Please...head back and read the telegram for yourself. Come now!"

Episode 29

Eight hours of hard riding on dirt, gravel, brick roads, and some paved roads, I made it back to the base. I almost dropped the motorcycle on its side, running toward the Major's house. He opened the door as I bounded up the stairs.

The telegram:

Come home, son, now, please. Baritone, your son, is gravely ill.

Love you, mom and dad.

Major Castellani thought it would be better for me to read the telegram myself, knowing the heartfelt strain it could cause when so far away in the countryside. A cargo plane was scheduled to leave in several hours and the major arranged for me to ride in the cargo bay on short notice.

The plane took off for England first and then flew to New York. Sixteen hours of flying, and then another flight to Seattle is scheduled for the next day on a commercial airline. Boarding a TWA that morning for a seven and a half-hour flight, it all seems like a month has passed since I read the telegram.

My dad and uncle met me at the gate, and off to the hospital we sped. My uncle drove as if no other cars were on the road. Dad explained in detail my son's condition, noting an infection in his brain. Baritone was playing one moment and become lethargic, and frequently became sleepy until he lapsed into a coma. In my life, it never occurred to me to talk back or raise my voice to either of my parents, but I wanted my dad to shut–up. I knew all he said I needed to hear, but I hated hearing my son's life hung in the balance while I went out on a failed journey.

I went off to fight a war, and I found love. I lost a chance at love, or it failed me, and if I lose my son, I would rather have a German landmine rip my body apart than to suffer defeat concerning my son and losing love.

For me, the birth of my son had brought life into a mad world of little love and so much hate for Colored people. It has meant I must do all I can do to help raise him. I must teach him who to give love as the answer to many of the problems he will encounter in life, even when love may not come back in an equal force. I traveled back to France – a place of war, and it could have taken me from him with one bullet, one bayonet, or one of many ways to die in battle – and all my son would have, are stories of his father as told by others. Tales of truth and lies often told and turned into a faultless fiction of a legacy of who and what his father was...*was*.

I don't want to be a story a great-grandson hears, and there is nothing but a name and picture of me as a young man in a uniform. The stories told might be of what I might have done or didn't do. I need my son alive to tell him myself of a truthful history, and most of all, I want to pass down a love for him to share for generations to come.

On the way to the hospital, dad told me that Baritone's room was on the tenth floor. I didn't even ask the room number, and as the car pulled up to the hospital and before the car stopped, I jumped out and ran inside, and headed for the stairwell – not wasting time waiting for the elevator. As I hurdled and bounded up the stairs, I passed a nurse coming down, and I knew I frighten her. She took on a flush-face look as she backed against the stairwell wall, as if, she were trying to push her body through it. I said, "Sorry ma'am, I'm in a hurry." How scary for a White woman to see a Negro alone in a stairwell, running. If down south, they would have the bloodhounds after me right now.

I made it to the tenth floor. I spotted my mother and Kathy. They both grabbed my arms, mom said, "Let's say a prayer, son, before you go in, and then we'll say another prayer with all of us in the room."

I pulled a bit from their arms. "What is the doctor saying?"

"Sirletto, let's say a prayer first!"

I yielded to prayer.

My mother prayed aloud. While praying, my dad and uncle joined our circle of prayer. My inner prayers were like the hour hand on a clock. I never ceased praying from the time I read the telegram in France.

"God, please forgive me for leaving my son. I was trying to find the woman I loved. But I guess we were only meant to be as we were during the war to help each other, and *You* know she helped me be alive. I ask of *You* – please heal my son. Please don't take him from me. I don't think my soul can take losing my baby boy. I may be asking more than I deserve, but dear God, please don't take my son away unless *You* have a better place for him. Please support the doctors to heal my son so his grandparents can leave this Earth one day knowing my son is in good hands, and he lives on with their love watching over him."

230

I held Kathy's hand in prayer. She knew of the reason why I went back to France. I knew it could not be comfortable for her as she still held out some hope for us.

❧ ❧ ❧

Seeing tubes in my son, and we all were forced to wear masks…it drove me mad, but ignorantly angry, though I knew it to be all the best for my son. Seeing the nurse wearing all White from head to shoes – the hat she wore with a red cross, and the nun adorned in all black with beads in her hand…I find it hard to take breaths. It's all nightmarish.

I wanted the room to change to a sandy beach with blues skies and the sound of waves washing ashore while the smell of fresh embraced my son and me walking, talking, and laughing. What I'm witnessing is the opposite. I hear, smell, and see my son lying helpless – defenseless to whatever he is experiencing. I sensed for my son what I felt when Valentina's brother controlled my body, and I was vulnerable to out of body control. I'm suffering as my mother wipes my tears, but she couldn't dry my face fast enough.

Episode 30

It is easy to observe and know we might be the few Negros in the hospital, but that is what is to be expected. But I step out into the hall, attempting to gather air. I noticed a Colored woman with pretty dark-brown skin, appearing to be early thirties. She is wheeling a food cart in my family's direction. She didn't have the Red Cross on her hat, but instead, she wore a hairnet crowning thick straight, black hair.

She came toward my son's room and took the time to pour my family some coffee and leave sandwiches for us while looking over her shoulder. Automatically, we shielded her, and acted accordingly to protect and to honor each of our struggles in a White--dominated world. For us Colored people, we have a sense of pride in each other when we break through and have a position anywhere in a White place of employment. For her too, she sees we were in a position of clout to be in a hospital where we are not normally seen.

We owned some influence due to damaging-influential information my uncle and father held over certain people's heads in city government, as well as they understood who to pay under the table. We were in the best hospital in the city because of a politician's wife, and her on-going affair with the hospitals head administrator, as my uncle Sonny had obtained some pictures of transgressing lovers.

The doctor came in. It gave me some comfort as he wore a Yakama on his head. From what we Negros experienced, Jewish doctors treated people who looked like us with no problem. Jewish people owned stores where many Colored people lived, and they spoke to us respectfully. There are some Jewish people who were known to sell us products, at higher prices, and the merchandise could be far from top of the line...but it's the few Jewish people who portrayed a clichéd way of life no more than any other people in America. The doctor's people suffered in the war, and for me, the Jewish soldiers were engaging and would share a drink whenever we encountered each other.

The doctor shook my hand, "I can tell, sir, you are the father, as you and your son are twins. I'm not going to paint this with veneer to make it look pretty. We are at a point where your son's condition is life and death, minute by minute, and day by day. We have pinned down that your son has an infection in his brain. It is causing a closing of some arteries which affect air to the brain. It is touch and go, sir. We are doing all we can to try to stop the infection from spreading, and so far, we have been able to do so. It's a good thing your mother and father brought your son in when they did."

"How did this happen?" I felt anger in my voice, although I'm not angry with anyone.

"We don't know – our medical knowledge is improving, but we have a long way to go. So, I know you are a praying people, so sustain your prayers – let them burn like a fire out of control, and I will keep conferring with others until we find a way to stop this infection, and bring your son back to a normal life."

I stared at the nauseating puke green walls, and the hospital smells seized control of my stomach. I went to the window and opened it a bit to take in some fresh air. After some more medical talk, the doctor left. Sitting in the room with my son, I reflected and started second-guessing ever leaving him and going back to France. My mom seems to read my mind and came over to me.

"Son, this has nothing to do with you being gone. This could have happened in the best or worse of times. This test is here for reasons you can't question. The focus needs to be on how you are going to handle this tribulation. All of us have to put this child's healing in God's hand."

I hugged my mom and decided to walk the halls to let my mind take in more than what I see in this room.

While trying not to worry myself to death on the flights back from France to be with my son, I dreamt of the woman – Ms. Carla, who I met at the school in Los Angeles. When I awoke, I felt a slight panic of what to do, if, by chance, I should contact her. Maybe not finding Valentina is giving me permission. I was incredibly attracted to Ms. Carla, and found her to be very nurturing, as it seemingly flowed inside and out of her. I have Ms. Carla's voice inside of my head. If I reach out to her...maybe she'll come be by my side while I'm going through what I'm going through. She cared for my son. But I couldn't involve someone in my situation and ask for comfort when she doesn't even know me.

Then my son's mother entered my vision, and I know my mom is holding her up. I know if let this situation bring Kathy and I too close, it could confuse our minds and our souls into crossing a line for all the wrong reasons.

Valentina...I wanted her still. But did I need her? Granddaddy would say a man and a woman should need each other to help with what the other one can't do – if not, their relationship is all about desires and wants. I believed that when I was next to Valentina, I needed her, and she needed me, but our life was enslaved in fighting obstacles. I think maybe me leaving was the very last hurdle I presented for her which she couldn't climb.

I'm standing in front of this payphone and I have Ms. Carla's number, but I'm returning to my son's room. I watch my son take deep agitated breaths, which is like my soul.

Episode 31

Day six, my son's condition hasn't altered, but he takes deep breaths, and the doctor told me it is a good sign his mind is prompting his body to do what it should do. He is fighting. I did go home to bathe and change clothes a few days ago, but mostly I have been sleeping in my son's hospital room in a chair. A few times, I crawled up next to him in the middle of the night. My body aches from not sleeping in a warm, soft bed. I need to stretch out.

The Colored woman who pushed the food cart to the patients' rooms woke me and said, "May I pray with you?"

"Yes, ma'am, please pray with me."

"No need to call me, ma'am' here – my name is IV. I'm from Albuquerque, and I come from praying people. I see you and your family in these people's hospital, and you are blessed to have, or to know the right folks. I see your boy here, and I want to pray for you, please. I have two little girls at home, and I know how hard this must be for you."

"You say your name is Ivory or IV?"

"It is IV."

Ms. IV took my hand from the other side of my son's bed, and she led me in prayer. She prayed in a way which took us both back to a time when our ancestors might have prayed while crossing an ocean as cargo with no understanding of where and why, but they needed and asked for guidance from the God they knew.

When Ms. IV leaves the room, the doctor comes in. He talks in a way I'm not sure I understand. My head is cloudy, and I'm not feeling well. I'm too tired to hear this right now. The doctor says he will come back tomorrow or the next day and talk to me about an experimental procedure. He is waiting for more information to be clear so we can decide our next course of medication or possible surgery. It could be a few more days, but a specialist from Germany – of all places in the world, I think – but a doctor with more specialization in cases like this is coming in, and my son's doctor says we should talk when he arrives.

I waited for my mother and father to come so I could go home and bathe and catch some sleep in a soft bed. I hadn't slept soundly since the night in the loft at the bookstore in France. The Atlantic flight was long, and I spent it in a cargo bay, sitting on the floor. It felt like riding in a jeep over 10,000 potholes within a mile. My body is sore and aching all over.

Mom and dad come into the room. I share with them that another doctor is coming in, but it will be a few days. Mom kisses my forehead, and my dad hugs me tightly.

Mom feels my hands and face. "Son, go home and get some rest, please."

They both plead for me to go home, knowing I needed some rest and a home-cooked meal, and maybe I'll have a more positive outlook. Mom left food on the stove for me. They both were right, I needed to get out of the confines of the hospital to attempt to sleep in a comfortable bed. Mom and dad rode in separate cars so I could take a vehicle home instead of a taxi, and I wanted to be isolated away from everyone for a while.

I'm feeling woozy. Damn, so much for getting home and have a drink that could only make it worse. *Oh my*, should I pull over. Mom said she left some food on the stove for me to eat, but I'm not sure I can eat. I feel a tension between my temples, and my stomach is rumbling. I have stressed myself out. Maybe I'm coming down with the flu, or I caught something while being at the hospital. Whatever it is, I hope I didn't give it to my son, he has enough problems.

Making my way up the stairs to the porch, and I feel like I'm going to heave. I know I've caught the flu now. I never did ask whether whatever my son is going through could affect me. I walk through the door and head straight to the kitchen. I wanted some Ginger Ale to calm my stomach. I enter the kitchen, and I slump against the doorway. Time froze. I feel like I am passing out...

I see illusions.

I'm back in my mechanic's tent in my lover's den. It's Valentina and me, and she is kissing me. She is telling me she loves me. Then we are back in the farmhouse – we are slow dancing. Then we are making love. Her lips are on my chest. Her hands play with my body. I lay her down on her stomach and enter into her warmness, we both groan. Then I awake.

She's gone.

I miss her.

Episode 32

I awaken, I think. Valentina is smiling at me. She is calling my name in a bit of panic. Her hair, with her White streak and her very light copper skin, stooped over me. I'm on the floor and she is touching my face with a damp towel. Valentina is here in the kitchen in my mama and daddy's house.

What is going on? Am I crazy in my head?

"I'm here. I'm here." I hear her say.

Valentina helps me stand, and then she wraps her arms around me. She is real. She is here. At the kitchen table, a child sat in a chair, speaking in Spanish and giggling. I put my arms around Valentina, and she moves me to walk over to the table. A child - a boy - sat with his legs dangling and moving back and forth. The child reached up and took my hand.

"He is your child. He is your son. He is here from the love you and I made."

My head jerked from her to him, and back to her. *Am I still passed out?* Then I let my eyes hone in on the young boy. The boy might be at least two years of age. I keep telling myself I might be dreaming. I needed to wake-up, but obviously, I hear Valentina's voice. I feel her hands on me and see her beauty. I stare at the child and he looks like his...brother.

"Yes, Sirletto, he is your child." Her head nodded.

"Valentina, I'm happy. I am immensely pleased you are right here in front of me, but what the hell is going? You have a lot of explaining to do."

Valentina helped me sit down. She reached down and picked up the toddler, and the boy reached out for me. I took the child in my arms. He has a thick head of brownish hair like his mother's hair color. I ran my fingers through his curly hair, and he placed his hand on top of mine and pressed my hand to his head firmly while giggling. His curly hair is like mine, like my father's, and my grandfather's hair. We have a loose curl in our hair – it has passed down to my son Baritone, who has the same loose curl, but black like the male family line.

We have a passed-down knowledge of our family line down to early slavery. Our name, "Preer" was once, "Pierre" a Greek-Frenchman – the slave-owner of my great grandfather. When great grandfather became a free man, he changed his last name to Preer. Master Pierre, the slave owner, my great-great-great-grandfather, impregnated my great-great-great-grandmother who was a slave. My great-great-grandfather killed his Greek-French, slave-owning father as a teenager when his father – Master Pierre made him fight another slave for sport. When my great-great-grandfather wouldn't kill the slave from another plantation so that the master could win money, the master set out to whip his flesh and blood. However, the tide turned amid a struggle over the whip, and the master lost his life. My great-great-grandfather ran-away with his mother, and they made it to safe living up North in Canada, but they thought he should modify his name from Pierre to Preer.

The child in my arms has the blood and the hair curl of a Greek-French, slave owner. The child in my arms has my mom's heart-shaped lips, much like my son and like mine. Girls teased me as a teen as my full lips look as if they were ready to kiss all the time. The child, his eyes were Valentina's eyes – or were they my eyes? She and I have almond-shaped eyes, and the young child who I know has to be my son, he has our eyes. As I pull my finger through his hair again, I see under the thick brown curls there is a White streak of hair just like Valentina's. I laugh. I'm joyful.

"Yes, he is your son."

"I don't know what to say."

"When I arrived and knocked on this door to this house, your mother answered the door. She is, as you told me, so very pretty, and you are the handsome look-alike of her. Right away, your mother called your father to the door, without asking a question of me. Your father said my name as if he knew me. Before I told either of them why I am here, they knew. Your commander's wife, when we fly to New York, she called them and let them know to expect me. Your mom said they wanted to keep it from you until they knew for sure...until finally, I made it here, and she said there is no doubt my son is your son."

Valentina sat down at the table across from me, while my child sat in my lap playing by touching my face.

"Padre. Daddy is Padre." Valentina pointed to me as she spoke to my son.

My son understands his mother's Spanish and English. The boy looked up in my face and touched and held my face with two hands. I didn't feel sick anymore.

"He is four months short of three years of age."

"I guess you were pregnant when I left because the timing would be right, and I can definitely see this is my child.

"I have missed Sirletto," I hear her say. I look at her and see I have missed her, but I knew I did.

"Valentina, so much is going on and so much has happened. I came looking for you, but I returned with urgency. I received news about my son – my son is ill. Now I'm holding a child of ours?"

She exhaled a long breath, maybe the air I her lungs traveled over with her from France.

"Yes, I know I'm delivering confusion."

We sat in silence while my son played with my face and then tried to scoot down out of my hold.

"You can put him down. He loves to walk and touch things."

I put my son down, he walked to his mother, and then he said something in Spanish.

He wants some water. I went to the refrigerator and poured some cold water from a pitcher. I handed the water to Valentina, and she nodded as he reached for the cup.

My son said to me, "Thank you" in English.

"He speaks mostly Spanish, but also some French and English."

I sat down at my mother's kitchen table, a place of many long family talks. Lessons were taught and learned at this table. Smiles and tears circled this table, and now I'm on a roller coaster of emotions and melting like the butter on the table, from high emotional heat. I'm melting inside from feeling sad that I was not there at the birth of my child, but joyful for his life, and Valentina is alive, and we are near each other when I thought I would never see her again.

"Sirletto, I tell you while we lay together, I could not have children because of what happened when that Nazi tortured me. After his attack, they told me my insides were spoiled to no use to be able to have a child. With the Germans around and no doctors near, the midwife cared for our medical needs. As a midwife to all of the women in the area, she looked inside me. She said I would never have a child. She determined I would be childless. The old lady helped so many women in the brothels damaged in awful indescribable ways, and she helped me with my condition as I did have infections and internal problems. We two – you and I – we made love some many times since the first time we made love. Then I felt something different inside me right before my brother...when...I felt something going on inside me when I thought I could not have a child."

She spoke of degrees of many actions and feelings and now outcomes while reliving the distress of taking her brother's life.

"We trusted the old lady's nursing knowledge, but she was wrong. With each time we made love, it could have been a time we created a child. Right before I ended my brother's life, I felt something different in me that I did not understand. I started to feel ill. It all became clear to me when my monthly didn't come. I knew your child was growing in me, and you were leaving soon.

I knew I must leave before you, and I left you a letter and my hair and the ring. I went back to my hometown in Spain to have my child."

"I traveled to your town on the ocean, and I searched for you there as well as many places."

"Sirletto, after the birth of our son, I ventured back and forth from my hometown and the brothel home of Ms. Porlena. I needed to go back there to face an ending and a beginning. Taking my brother's life – his death is his own disastrous doing, but I gave new birth – new blood that my brother and I shared. I birthed a new bloodline. Our son and I had to let him walk over old ruthless blood as it is in the ancient times of my ancestors. And, I was there when you came looking for me."

She reached into her breast area and placed on the table the letter with my poem. I do know you think of me because I think of you as many times."

"You what...? You were there?" I know my voice hit her like a hot raging wind. I watched her face seek calm as she closed her eyes and pressed her lips tight. My new son, his eyes became bright circles as he stared at me.

"Sirletto, yes, as you were there, my heart overfilled with scared and confused feelings of not knowing how you would feel. Our child grew inside me before you left the first time, and then when you came back looking for me...our son said, 'Padre' when you entered the house, and he said 'Padre' again when you left. I never taught him the word."

"Valentina, how could you let me be so close and not see you?"

"Our love was a secret, and we know the reasons why it had to be cloaked and veiled. I understand your sadness because of my choices. I have no cure for those feelings, other than to say I am sorry. What choices did we have? Sirletto, I'm here now."

"How are you here?"

Our son crawled out of his mother's arms and walked around the kitchen, pointing his little finger into the sun rays coming through the kitchen windows.

I stood and felt for my balance, and I felt fine. I picked up my son.

"What is your name?"

He looked toward his mother.

"She spoke to my son in Spanish in a motherly tone.

"Tenor," my son said in English.

I let out a breath, almost feeling out of breath. Squeezing Tenor, I held him as close as I could without discomforting him.

He hugged me, and he rubbed my face, and then he played with the tears on my face with his little finger tracing my tears.

"Valentina, when I arrived at the brothel looking for you, I felt ill. I felt the same nauseating feelings when coming through the door here. It's a strange sensation, it makes no sense, other than you were there then, and you're here now, and what does this all mean?"

"Sirletto, I know why, but I need to explain how I made my way here. I know you want to know how. We should talk about many things, and then...please take me to your sick son. Your mother, she says he is so ill."

"Okay, how did you find your way here?

"After you left the brothel, days later, I heard you were in my hometown on the ocean coast in Spain asking for me. I have a distant cousin there in town - we are close in friendship. He said you told him our story, but you did not know of our son. He served you dinner and helped you find a place to stay. He then asked a courier to deliver a letter informing me you were there. It bruises my soul, knowing you were searching all over for me while I withheld what is yours and mine to share.

"I began to recount the many times you spoke of your son, and you had to go home to find him, but you came back to look for me too – it let me know more than I already knew...you love me. I forced myself to believe you would go back to your home and forget me, but I learned your love crossed over an ocean when you came back looking for me.

"If you'll have me, I'm here. If not, I'll learn how to live here in your city, and we can share our son. I want to say much more, but I feel I'm not giving you enough after all that has happened, but I'm trying."

"Please keep talking, Valentina, I need to hear your voice."

"With your son saying the word 'Padre', which mean father in Spanish, and after the courier delivered the letter from my cousin in Spain, I went to the bookstore and met with Mrs. Joel and Mr. Joel. You told Ms. Porlena where you could be reached. Mr. Joel took me to the base outpost and spoke by radio to your old commander. The captain sent a jeep and brought Tenor and me on a long ride to his base. He arranged the paperwork, and his wife flew with me on several long plane flights. The planes made me so scared, but our son slept most of the time."

Tenor started moving fast around the kitchen, acting as if he were a plane. I reflected on knowing people took their time to get involved, and God guided them to help me. Major Castellani's wife, she assisted by traveling with Valentina and my son.

The Majors' wife, maybe her way of thanking me for what I did for her family in saving her son−in−law, she helped bring Valentina to the States. Maybe, I opened her eyes to what the world is like for those who are invisible to her. My ex- captain, now a Major, helped as we had helped each other through tough times. I admit, I'm gaining a new perspective on some White American people as it has not been good with the history I know.

I still have a fear, as of now, I have two young, Colored boys I am responsible for, and the world is only changing for the better in small corners. In those small corners, life may be better, but a broader view of my country dropped a bomb from hell on people who did look like them and destroyed an enemy with terror.

The British Imperialistic rule over India has been horrific troubles, and more are to come for sure in the future. There is news of a form of slavery taking place in South Africa from old European countries using colonization and the gun instead of whips and chains. There is the talk of sending soldiers to South Korea, and we don't know what can come about from that. We divided Germany in half, with America basically ruling one side, and the Russians ruling the other side. Then, for some strange reason, but maybe we will find out later, the world powers cut out a space in the Middle East and made it a Jewish state or country, but I understand they displaced the people who were there. That sounds like troubles in the future. All these unsettling world events, they have me worried for the future.

One would think after two World Wars, common sense would be the world's order. Nevertheless, now, I'm responsible for two Colored boys that someone one day might want them to go fight in another war. Then the war of segregation and Jim Crow is still a way of life all through America, and a burden on the Negro. I have much to worry about, including a son lying in a hospital bed, hanging on to life.

I'm standing by the kitchen window looking out to the sun with worries as Valentina came by my side. "I landed here in Seattle...or I should say, an Army base by a city I can't say the name well...ah, Ta–com–bah', and an Army car with a Negro soldier driving, he brought me here to your house.

"There are so many houses and so many roads. I think this is a nice place, but it is so much to take in. Your mother and father are such wonderful, loving people, and your uncle Sonny is a charming gentleman. Tenor really likes him. Your mother said this time is the best time, and right time, as you and your family needed some good news. Sirletto, I hope I am good news."

Episode 33

I'm overwhelmed and less unconfused, as the compiling of so much wore my already tired mind and body. I picked my son up, and Valentina wrapped her arms around us.

"Valentina, I'm more than happy to have you and Tenor here with me. My other son's health is hurting me, and I'm scared of what might happen to him."

We walked out of the kitchen and moved throughout the house.

"This is where I grew up as a teen, but I'm looking forward to having my own home, and I'm sure we can make a life as one."

"Sirletto, I'm here now, but I know nothing of how to make a life with a man. I will want to grow as a woman in ways I am uncertain of how to do. I will need you to guide me. I trust you will love me in ways I can grow as a woman, and help me feel I will be okay here in America."

I kissed her on the forehead, and Tenor copied me. It made me smile, but I'm tired, but I needed to understand this thing of why I felt ill. We are sitting in the living room, and my son is walking around touching objects. I'm sure he has not been near this kind of environment, and he should have curiosity. He and Baritone look so much alike and walk alike.

"Can you tell me why I feel like I have been feeling like cold or flu-like feelings when I'm near you...although, I did not know you were close to me where we had to be breathing the same air while in France at the brothel. And most of all, of today, I felt so uneasy, but I do feel better now. You said you could explain.

Valentina held my hand and looked me in my eye in a way – she made me focus on her lips as she talked.

"Our son, Tenor, has the same spiritual energy which my brother possessed, and all the menfolk people before. Soul of Cayor passes down through generations from my great grandfathers' tribe. It is passed down through the mother. I have the same energy, but it can only be for the woman to limit or counteract the evil use of an evildoer. As you witnessed, I stopped my brother.

"Our son has good in him and only knows what is right until if a man teaches him evil for gains of power against another. The same energy in our son can sense the soul of one of their blood who is in distress. When you came to the brothel, our son – who was in the house – without ever seeing you and knowing you, sensed your energy of suffering as being near his family. Much like catching a cold or any fever, the nature of your body wants you to rest. Our son, sensing you were in anguish over missing me, and maybe even now knowing how you are feeling stressed by the illness of his brother, he is sending you a message to rest your soul. Your son, Tenor, he wanted you to slow down. He may have sensed you needed to be home with your other son who is ill, before you even knew.

"As you were approaching home today, our son sensed his blood near him in distress. Tenor does not know this, but his Soul of Cayor was trying to warn you to slow down. There is a potent goodness to all of this, Sirletto. Your young son may be able to help heal your older son. With the energy inside Tenor, he might heal Baritone."

"My child...my son, he can heal?"

"There is healing inside your son. Yes, he might be able to heal your other son, but know this, he will lose his power. He can never use it for anything else ever again. If you remember, I thought I was losing my powers of the Soul of Cayor when I stopped a strong force in my brother, but the home of the power lived my heart, and it started moving into our child's growing heart to make a new home while he grew inside me. The power will not transfer to your older son because there is no male bloodline connected to my ancestors. But a healing can take place."

I contemplated all I heard. I'm God-fearing, and immediately, I am considering all of what I heard to be some kind of voodoo practice like healing. My son Baritone could die. I'm not sure I want him experimented on from a doctor from a country where they did horrible tests on humans and killed Jews. I can't help but chuckle in the middle of this critical time for my son when I think of what the awful man has done to people who some consider them less than human. My great-grandfathers were slaves. Then one of many atrocities of this country – some 16,000 Indians were made to march 1,200 miles on foot to move them away from White people. Four thousand men, women, and children died of disease and famine. I don't trust the government and their medical tests on Negros and people who are not desired. My history teacher told me that in time, we will learn of many times in which this country has done awful things to people.

So, voodoo from the Motherland for the good of man, and maybe God-sent healing through a child, might be the best.

On the wall in the living room hangs a picture of a Negro Christ sitting with little Negro children, and a picture of a Negro Christ with 12 Negro disciples for the Last Supper. My mother had them painted as she grew weary of seeing a European-looking Jesus from a land where people are of darker skin, but church fans and paintings showed a falsehood in many people's homes. My mother's painted version of Christ, if found in a Negro home down South, it might lead you to be left for a dead swing by a rope, or found dead in a shallow grave, and the least of possibilities is finding you have to run out of your home when it's being burnt down. *How Christ-like is that?* It's not by them southern crackers.

I believe God works in mysteries, and a man can never fathom how vast God's power is. I still needed to think it through. I didn't know if I should gather my mother and father and even confirm with Kathy – Baritone's mother, and tell them what is on the table. *How do I make it all make sense?*

"Valentina, I need to lie down. I need some rest. I need to think."

We went upstairs with Tenor, and the two of us sprawled out on my bed. Valentina went back downstairs, and a little while later, she brought some food up to me. I ate greens and chicken fried steak and then curled up with my son. Tenor crawled onto my chest, and Valentina curled up next to me.

I fell asleep. I must have slept hard, as the sun is coming through my bedroom window of a new day. Maybe twenty hours might have passed. My son, Tenor, is still sleeping lying next to me. I go down the stairs, and Valentina meets me in the hall leading to the kitchen. I can hear in the kitchen, my mom half-singing and loudly humming as she does and I knew the sound of my father turning and snapping the pages of the newspaper, and the sound of him putting down his coffee cup.

"You rested well thanks to your son. Tenor insisted as much through his soul."

"Valentina, let's go to the hospital."

She stared with what seems like a question-like expression, and if there was a question she is asking me, that is...*am I sure?* I woke up believing there is something in Tenor. I'm going to believe my son Tenor can heal his brother Baritone.

I kissed my mom and asked her if she wanted to go wake Tenor. My dad looked up over his newspaper and nodded my way. Valentina reached for my mom's hand, and they left the room. I poured coffee and went out to the backyard. I held the coffee cup with two hands and let the rich flavor be savored for a moment while taking in all the green and branches showing new buds of life. Spring is starting to bloom. I looked around and looked up to God.

"God, please tell me I'm doing the right thing."

At the same time, as I'm speaking to God, my son Tenor walks up to me and hugs my leg. I looked back up to God and gave thanks for the guidance.

I reflected on what Valentina told Ms. Porlena in France, and on what Ms. Porlena shared with me when I came looking for Valentina. "We have to protect life and live for life for all deserve life. Unless someone with life in their hands tries to take other lives away, we must do our best to provide a sanctuary for life." Valentina, her first obligation in life is to protect her child to provide sanctuary for a new life, and so she left me before I left her.

Episode 34

I'm walking around the yard, holding the hand of my son, and taking time to breathe and calm my soul. Going back inside, my mother is cooking, and my father is drinking coffee at the table with the newspaper now folded up.

I'm stuck on whether I should talk to them. My young son walked in with a fledgling bow-legged saunter, and went to his grandmother. She picked him up and held him tight with tears and a smile on her face. I'm sure she is happy and sad all in one with newer family blood in her arms, but her other grandson is in peril.

"You have to do the right thing," my father said without looking my way – instead, he looked at Valentina, who is wiping Tenor's hands with a damp cloth while my mom held him.

I knew what he meant. I now had two children, and I'm not married to either of the mothers. I want Valentina as my wife, and I am going to make it happen soon. However, my main focus right now is what I can do to help my son who is sick.

"Is anyone up at the hospital?" I asked.

"No, Kathy went home this morning. She spent the night with Baritone in the room with us. We figured you would want to be alone with Baritone, and we all left this morning."

My mother gave me a look, which is her way of asking a question.

"Yes, I am taking Valentina and Tenor up to see Baritone."

No one said anything. I knew mom and dad heard the story of how Valentina made it to our doorstep. Valentina told me that she told them of her travels to our doorstop with my son when she arrived. What they did not know is my younger son, Tenor, has something unique to believe in, and it is a one-time gift if he uses it. I contemplated knowing Tenor would no longer have what he is graced with if he heals his brother.

<hr/>

I drove along Lake Washington to the hospital. It is a clear day as the sun beamed off the water and often blinded. Seattle is a city cut in the middle of a forest with lakes and streams. I drove under the Interstate 90 floating bridge; a transcontinental Interstate highway runs and connects Seattle, Washington, to Boston, Massachusetts. It opened when I was away at war. The beauty of the outdoors of Seattle made Valentina turn her head quickly at each new view.

Views of snowcapped mountaintops are on the east and west sides of Seattle, but many miles away though it appears you can reach out and touch them. North and south of Seattle are immense elevations of two mountains a hundred miles away, but they are visually clear. I smiled at myself, seeing the days ahead, and hopefully taking both my boys fishing, hunting, and camping. I saw a future with a family and me.

Episode 35

Each time I entered the hospital, instantly, my stomach muscles tightened. This time I have my youngest son, my brand-new son, next to me, and he is tenderly holding my fingers as we walk down the hall. It feels as though he's leading me. I'm feeling encouraged. Neither my young son nor his mother knows the inside of a hospital. Valentina is no different than someone from the rural countryside's in America. She had shared the story of the birth of Tenor with a midwife and the delivery of my son. I realize I'm kind of naïve – although, I have a college education and experienced the birth of my first son. Baritone was born in a hospital, but for sure, a different experience than the one Valentina told me of, and it leaves me a bit astonished.

I walk into Baritone's room. I feel something different inside me as I look at the tubes hanging out of my son's mouth and nose. Another tube type bag hung low to his side to remove his body waste.

Valentina is behind me when we walk through the door. She grabs my arm, and I turn to her, and see fear etched deep on her face. Fear is not something I had seen in her before. She was tough and in control during war-bound times, but now she needed to be protected.

"Sirletto, I'm sure this hospital is a good place, but something feels unkind – something feels unfruitful of changes of sad to good. It feels cold in ways I have no words. They heal people here? How can someone feel better, there is no warmth of feelings?"

I know it's not about hot or cold. I put my arms around Valentina, and she held on tight. I understand she is a woman with softness and a resilient soul. She is a passionate lover with dimensions. I thought we were dreams at times, but here and now, and in this hospital, she feels a cold ache inside her being. It alerted me that I needed to step in directions to shield and protect her from two different worlds colliding in an extreme transformation for her life. She came across an ocean almost blind, in a sense, to a new world – for the love of me, and to have family love. I need to be committed to helping her understand the world is different over here. It will be a new world – a new understanding for the way things will be for the woman I love.

Ms. IV came around the corner, wheeling her cart. She stops to pour me some coffee. She asked Valentina would she like something, and Ms. IV made Valentina some tea. Ms. IV wore a smile of hope and squeezed Valentina's hand as she leaves the room. I sensed it made Valentina relax.

On the way to the hospital, we both talked of the anxiety in knowing one son might, or might not, be able to heal the other. I didn't exactly know what Tenor's spirited soul could do when on the same level of the doctors who said we could only wait it out for recovery if there is one. No change has come in Baritone's health. He is still lying there, and he does not look any better. He seems to be losing color and life.

My little son, he lets go of my finger and walks to the bed. His height won't let him see much. He grabs onto the side rails of the bed and tries to crawl up. Valentina rushes over and picks Tenor up so he can see, for the first time, his older brother. Sadly, for all of us, it is the first time of us all being together, and the moment is suffering in my soul seeing my son as he is. Tenor reaches out like he wants to be near his older brother. Valentina looks at me for approval, I nod. She puts Tenor on the bed next to his brother, and he stares into his sick brother's face. He touches his brother's sleeping coma face, and slowly over and over, he touches Baritone's face. Then Tenor lays down beside Baritone and appears to go to sleep.

Valentina turns to me, "Sirletto, let's leave the room."

"Why?"

"Please trust your young son."

I take Valentina's hand, and we walk down the hall to Ms. IV.

"Please follow me to the chapel, please?" Ms. IV coaxes us.

Valentina and I sit on a short pew. I see a painted picture of little Jesus who looked to be Shirley Temples brother talking to Biblical looking European men on the wall. On a small pedestal, there is a stone carving of a Virgin Mary. We sat in silence. Ms. IV stood behind us and placed the palms of her hands on our backs. I turned to look at her, and her eyes are closed with her head bowed. I prayed too. I squeezed my future wife's hand. Her life in European countries, with no formal religious affiliations...she still believed in God.

Twenty minutes later, we were back in the room with both of my sons. Tenor is still laying there next to his brother, but my son Baritone...his eyes are open. His eyes are open for the first time since I've been back. His eyes searched and showed fear as his eyes investigate his surroundings. I lean over the bed and kiss his forehead. His eyes connect to mine, and then a hand reaches out and touches my face. Tears run from the corners of his eyes as well as mine.

"Son, I'm here. I'm right here. You understand?"

He blinked – I assume he is saying yes. His lips part, but no words come. I'm sure his mouth is dry. I pour water from a pitcher, and then I put my hand behind his head and lift as he sips. I have concern about the tubes attached to him, but he seems not bothered by the tubes.

"Dad…"

"Yes."

"I love you."

"I love you more."

I wave my hand to Valentina, and she slowly walks over. There is apprehension in her walk. She knew one child healed another, and her son…our son, is a healer. She leans on me and takes Baritone's hand. At the same time, Tenor sat up. His eyes tired, but his face is changing to a smile. Twins born years apart, and by different mothers, smiled at each other.

"Baritone, this is Valentina. Do you remember I told you why I was going back to France? She is here, and a wonderful life is happening, and more is coming. Sitting next to you is your brother. His name is Tenor. You have to continue recovering your health so you can look after your little brother."

A smile showing all of Baritone's teeth made us all smile and chuckle. Tenor, when he saw us smiling, raised his arms, and I lifted him into my arms. I feel a weak, tired body, but my little guy is smiling.

Episode 36

By late afternoon, my mom, dad, and uncle were all in the room seeing a miracle. The doctor said the measures they put in place must have eased the infection in his brain, and I let it be the truth for the doctor. Who knows, it may be the truth. It is God's work one way or another, and it did not matter how it occurred. My son is well. I called Kathy and asked her to come to the hospital. I let her know our son is doing better.

Kathy walked into the room, and I'm feeling odd, but I did anticipate this happening. I see her eyes go straight to our son, who is sitting up and sitting next to his brother, but she wouldn't know, except maybe the fact the two looked like twins, just years apart. Her eyes captured Valentina, and then back over to the small child with aspects of a smaller version of her son. We were all joyous when she walked in, and our dispositions changed. An awkward moment arose.

"Kathy, let me talk to you, honey," my mom said.

"No, mom, let me," I said as I walked toward Kathy. "Let's talk out here." I point to the hallway."

Kathy pointed to her son. "My son?"

"Hi, Mom." Baritone waved at his mother.

I made eye contact with Kathy. "He is doing well as you can see, and in a day or two, he can leave from here."

She turned slowly to go with me out into the hall, and I knew her last vision was of Valentina.

Part of me felt guilt. Without her input or consent – she is the mother of Baritone – I made a choice concerning his well-being. I'll ask God to forgive me if I have done wrong. I'll keep telling myself God sent Tenor, and, he is a blessing, and he made a miracle happen.

"The little boy you see in there is my son. The woman is the woman whom I went back to look for in France. Although I did not find her, she found me."

"So now what...you have a perfect little family and all I have are some weekends with my son?"

"Her name is Valentina. She is as frightened as you are, and so am I. If I wanted to be an ass toward you in any way, my folks would never let me treat you badly, and you know me better than that. I believe you do. I will never deny withholding our son from you.

"A way to look at this is, you now have two sons — they are brothers. They need each other more than you, Valentina, or I will ever need. They are brothers, and it would be no different than when I found you and if you had another child."

"I lost a child, Sirletto. She was born at seven months and lived two hours. It is the reason the man I left Seattle with...why he eventually left me. He did not know if the child was yours or his. I didn't know either." One deep sob erupted from Kathy, but she gained control of herself quickly.

I wanted to hold her as the pain in Kathy's face cut into my emotions. Once again, my mom's words came clear. "A woman and her reasons for her choices when she has a child, it forces her to harmonize with her wants, and the life she has to lead."

"I'm sorry to hear this – it hurts me that you are feeling such pain as you are. Kathy, you now have two sons, and maybe between us, we can say we have two sons and a girl, only God knows."

She nodded and bit deep into her lip.

"Kathy, you don't have to be friends with her—Valentina, but you do have a choice to be happy our son is alive, and he should be pleased with the decisions of how his parents approach situations and how we treat people. Will it perfect...well, what is? I want you to feel empowered to speak up. We both should feel we can speak up and listen. It won't always mean you and me will always be right. We need to set our egos and wounds aside, for better understanding of what it takes for us to share our children."

"Brothers...Sirletto, I made some choices, I know, but I hope you respect how I may feel sometimes, and I will speak up when I feel I need to."

I wanted to say more, but Valentina touched me on my back and came beside me. She reached for Kathy's hand with both her hands. Kathy slowly let her have her hand.

"Ms. Kathy, I'm in a strange place. It is mystifying for me. I want to understand what it must be like for you seeing my son, and it might be trying for you as it is for me. I'm asking you to help me as we have two boys who are brothers, who look alike, and who seem to love each other already. Sirletto has told me of your divine beauty. I'm humbled and honored to meet the mother of the brother to my son."

Kathy covered her mouth and sucked air between her fingers. She released her hand from Valentina's and placed her thumb under Valentina's eyes to wipes tears at the same time tears ran off her cheeks.

"Please, may I meet your son?" Kathy asked.

Going back into the room, Kathy went to Baritone's bed to kiss him all over his face.

"Mom, I have a little brother."

"What is your brother's name?"

The smile on his face beamed with pride. We joked earlier with Baritone, letting him know the baritone saxophone is the big brother to the Tenor.

"Mom, this is Tenor."

"Hello, Tenor," Kathy caressed his head. Tenor loved to be picked up, and he lifted his arms to Kathy, and she lifted him into her arms.

I turned away to look out at the sunset of red skies and to hide my wet eyes. My mom wept from joy. Dad lowered himself to one knee to console her.

Later, mom and dad took Tenor home.

※ ※ ※

Valentina and I went to my motorcycle garage. I have a loft made into a cozy little bedroom. Reminiscent of our times in the mechanic tent back in France and our hideaway lovers' den, I laughed as I had dreamed of this time of Valentina being in this space. Also, waiting in the garage, my dog Jerri knew within one drop of the scent of Valentina when she walked in with me. Their friendship existed long before me. Valentina stooped down and held Jerri around the neck. My dog has aged, but still could hardly contain himself with prancing legs and tail wagging.

※ ※ ※

We are walking as we hold each other in the night rain. I don't think we are feeling a raindrop. Our lips are making love long before we make it back to the garage.

"Sir–Sir," Valentina loved to tease me with my nickname. She overheard it used by a few soldiers when they came to the tent while she hid out of sight. And I loved it when I heard her say my name with her slow, sultry voice.

"Sir–Sir, tell me one of your poems in my ear."

I looked up into the misting rain. We were under a streetlight, and my lover is in my arms. With my lips caressing her ear, I whispered.

"The thunder of battles...gone by

The windstorms of separation gone

Two shores now touch

Clouds of doubt - our hearts have erased

Love rains down on us

Growing a love to reach the heavens

I'm holding your hand and pulling you in close

Our noses nudge as the midnight mist kisses our faces

Let me kiss you deeply as we slow dance under the streetlight

Spin around and move your soul into mine

Stare up in the falling rain

Then

Lay your head on my shoulder

Let me hold you tight

Feel fear ease away

Feel the glow of love

Let me lead you away to dry off and be safe in the heart of our lover's world"

"Sirletto, take me to our home."

263

ABOUT THE AUTHOR

Alvin Lloyd Alexander Horn has lived, breathed the Northwest air, and floated in all the nearby rivers and streams leading to the Pacific Ocean. As in the stories of Hemingway, the poetry of Langston Hughes, and the novels of Walter Mosley, their writings – as well as Alvin's – are all byproducts of their childhood environments and their subsequent travels. Alvin's African-American experiences in his Emerald City background, shines through in his poetry, short stories, and novels.

Growing up in the "liberal on the surface" Seattle lifestyle, Alvin's childrearing was grounded by interactions with Black people who had jobs, who could go most places they desired, and who were not residents of stereotypical ghettos. He feels that his passion for writing was triggered by his mother sending him to the library when she placed him on restriction; often for daydreaming while in school. He also credits the little gray-haired white lady – the librarian for introducing him to the likes of Richard Wright and Zora Neale Hurston. Upon reading the work of Nikki Giovanni, Alvin knew he wanted to be a writer of love stories and poetry.

"Some of my erotic writing imagination came from my dad leaving Playboy magazines in a not-so-secret place. My friends were fixated on the pictures; but me, I just read the stories...most of the time."

Alvin also had a storied athletic career as an athlete, a coach, and as a musician; the skill, talent, and knowledge gained from those backgrounds often shows up in his writings. Alvin played sports at the University of New

Mexico in the mid-70s, and had a short sports career after college. Prior to launching his writing career, Alvin had a fifteen-year stint in the aerospace industry. For the last fifteen years, Alvin has worked in the field of education teaching life-skills, poetry and creative writing, and working with at-risk youth.

Alvin is a highly acclaimed spoken word artist The 2012 Billboard Award-Winner, of Best Spoken Word, which allows him to travel and promote his art of words. He has balanced his writing career alongside doing voice-overs for radio and TV, music, video, and movie productions, as well as acting. His writings have appeared in many periodicals ranging in genres from fiction to erotica. He can often be found all over the Northwest reciting poetry and playing stand-up bass at different venues, but he has a fond admiration for Houston, Hot-Atlanta, Vegas, Vancouver, B.C., and most parts of California and New York. Most of all, Alvin loves being on the back deck of his houseboat writing love poetry and stories.

Alvin L.A. Horn is the author of:

The World That fell into My Dresser Drawer; a book of poetry, 2001

BRUSH STROKES; a novel, 2005

PERFECT CIRCLE; a novel published by Zane and Simon and Schuster, 2012

ONE SAFE PLACE; a novel published by Zane and Simon and Schuster, 2014

BRUSH STROKES; the re-release, with an added short Story, 2016

BAD BEFORE GOOD& THOSE IN BETWEEN, a novel, 2017

HEART & HOME, a novel, 2019

All in available in paperback and e-book

✤✤✤

"Maybe he thought he could read her mind with her head next to his because he sure wanted her to know his thoughts. He wanted her to understand the world might be breaking apart; but no matter what, he knew in his heart and mind, she was his one safe place to lay his burdens down."

~ONE SAFE PLACE~

✤✤✤

"A woman is a King maker, a man is a Queen keeper; the sun rises, the moon never sets on their kingdom. The Queen is rich; the King protects her heart of gold. Her King leaves his legacy. His Queen is his authentication."

~PERFECT CIRCLE~

✤✤✤

"A man may admire what a woman does for a living; he may admire her education and social circle. He may be enamored with her physical beauty; but he only truly falls in love with the softest and warmest part of her – her soul."

~BRUSH STROKES~

✤✤✤

"I look at my ring and know every pawnshop has rings – wedding rings, promise rings, please-forgive-me rings, make-up-I'm-trying-to-kiss-your-ass rings, it's-too-late rings, and rings of the dead. I know there are millions of rings in pawnshop showcases; all shining back at potential buyers, wishing that they will be the ring of choice and will find a new home on the other side of the glass. I take a swill of my wine and wash my dry mouth that hasn't laughed for a long while. It's a sad thought, but every pawnshop has rings from a brokenhearted woman, and those rings are ready for another woman's finger. In time, a layaway plan of ninety days same as cash, some other accepting woman will smile, and her heart will flutter with joy and hope when she adorns the unknown memoir of agony. And as she stares at her finger, she may even pray that her ring will be a bridge to her man's heart upon which he will honor and cherish her.

Sadly, the tales of many women who walk into a pawnshop with the blues of a broken heart are waiting for the birth of brighter days as she is broke and in need of money. Too often, a woman rips a ring off her finger and attempts to throw it off a mental bridge. In her dreams, she sees a display piece for sale to the next dream come true.

One day, every ring sadly slides off a finger."

~BAD BEFORE GOOD & THOSE IN BETWEEN~

Alvin L.A. Horn is also a contributing author in the anthologies: Pillow Talk in the Heat of the Night, and The Soul of a Man 2, and a writer for the Inner City News, and a feature writer for Real Life Real Faith Magazine, as well as several other publications.

You may visit the author at:

www.alvinhorn.com

https://www.facebook.com/alvinhorn

https://twitter.com/alvinlahorn

Alvin L.A. Horn was also voted the 2012 Billboard Best Erotic Romantic Spoken Word Artist of the year. You can hear his voice audio art and leave feedback at https://soundcloud.com/alvinhorn.

Additional video art by Alvin L.A. Horn available at YouTube:

I AM THAT MAN

https://www.youtube.com/watch?v=UNTdcurtrHg

THE LONELY SUN

https://www.youtube.com/watch?v=Np8Qo4z9LUQ

MOUNTAIN TOP

https://www.youtube.com/watch?v=hCenJLmXyhc

ARMORIST FROM THE GALAXY

https://www.youtube.com/watch?v=dqA53TxlZbg&feature=plcp

HEART & HOME

Questions

#1: The scene, around the burn barrel, could you see the men from the different walks of the 1940s - Negro life? What are some of things the burn barrel represented?

#2: Sirletto had different kinds of blues in his life, what where they, and how many did you read throughout the story?

#3: Sirletto, had a limit to what he would take before he would do something severe. What in his in behavior did he show or it humbled him.

#4: Negro-Colored heroes were few to be seen in life with no TV and limited news, so the few were titanic in the community – name a few you are aware of before 1940s.

#5: For sure the soldiers had sex was on their minds. Do you conversations of sex was open or help in secrets and thoughts only. You read Sirletto's inner feeling and as in everyone, no one knows but you and what how you feel?

#6: Is there another of another race that you trust as much as you trust in your own race? Could be dangerous, and why because?

#7: What was the meaning of these passages?

"One must recognize who your friends are, and who can hurt you the most?"

"We all dread our families don't receive a knock on the door from a man wearing a uniform.

"Evil must ride shotgun to help summon up the backbone to kill other men. These men understand, when you make a deal with the devil, he then wants out of the bottle like a genie."

"But here, you and I, we can act like slaves trying to outdo the other, or we can take the freedom we have and live the best we can and help each other survive"

#8: Did Sirletto have a weakness(s), and what were his strengths?

#9: Lanky Slim is a tortured soul in more than one way. Why, and did Sirletto support him?

#10: In your family history was there ever talk of the supernatural, magic, spells etc.

#11 Sirletto hated to depend on others, why?

#12: Did the book make you think about the good you do for something or for someone, by maybe doing something not legal or immoral?

#13: Who (which actors) would play each part in a movie?

#14: Where did the character, Easy come from? Hint one of our best-well known writers of our times, stared "Easy" and his killer friend in a popular movie and in many of his novels.

"Notes:

Eulace Peacock was known to be faster than Jesse Owens. Peacock beat Jesse Owens many times, but pulled a hamstring before the Olympics, which we now know, Jesse Owens is the one who made Hitler look bad in the 1936 Olympics.

Executive Order 9981 was issued on July 26, 1948, by President Harry S. Truman. It abolished discrimination "on the basis of race, color, religion or national origin" in the United States Armed Forces ending segregation in the services.

The purple gas written about in this story is called Avgas; a high octane aviation fuel used high horsepower engines. The gas was originally used as primary fuel for, high boost-supercharged radial engines to propel aircraft and later for race vehicles.

The motorcycles that Sirletto might have found that he shipped back to the states, and they became extremely popular in the US until the 1970s: Ariel, BMW, BSA, Ducati, Indian, Lambretta, Norton, Triumph, Vincent, Zündapp

A line from the Heart & Home,

"I called her on the phone in the hallway of her apartment complex, and she never called me"

An apartment building in the 1940s, most apartments would not have a phone in each apartment, but maybe in the hall that all shared. It could even be a party line. If some called, anyone could answer and then go knock on your door to tell the person that they have a call.

Damel was the title of the ruler (or king) of the Wolof kingdom of Cayor in what is now northwest Senegal, West Africa. The most well-known Damel is probably Lat Dior Diop (1842–1886) who died in battle during the final French drive to capture his territory, which was one of the strongest areas of resistance.

The Germans developed a "courage drug" called Pervitin, and sometimes they called it D–1X. The drug it is a methamphetamine–based experimental performance enhancer tablet made with equal parts of cocaine and painkiller. It's the Nazi's dream of creating super soldier. An old drug turned into a newer version we know as Meth. The Americans soldiers also became addicted to amphetamines or speed.

The Night Clubs mentioned in the story were real in the 1940s

3 Deuces Jazz Club located on the south side of 52nd Street between 5th and 6th Avenue in New York

The Gatewood Blues Club, the west side of Chicago

The Black & Tan 12 and Jackson in Seattle

Malcom X – Quotes

"You can't separate peace from freedom because no one can be at peace unless he has his freedom."

"People don't realize how a man's whole life can be changed by one book."

"I believe in the brotherhood of all men, but I don't believe in wasting brotherhood on anyone who doesn't want to practice it with me. Brotherhood is a two-way street."

"There is no better than adversity. Every defeat, every heartbreak, every loss, contains its own seed, its own lesson on how to improve your performance next time."

"Education is the passport to the future, for tomorrow belongs to those who prepare for it today."

Made in USA - Kendallville, IN
1031071_9781701551220
12.06.2019 1050